The Chronicles of Dorian Christianson: Nephilim

AL HALSEY

COPYRIGHT

Copyright © 2015 Al Halsey

ISBN-13: 978-1542529884

ISBN-10: 1542529883

Publisher: Al Halsey

Literary Editor: Gypsy Heart Editing

Proof Reader: Kiri Thompson

Book Formatting: Josh Hilden

Cover Designer: Gypsy Heart Editing

The scanning, uploading, and distribution of this book via the Internet or via other means without the permission of the publisher is illegal and punishable by law. Please purchase only authorized electronic editions and do not participate or encourage electronic piracy of copyrighted materials.

This book is a work of fictions. Names, characters, establishments, organizations, and incidents are either products of the author's imagination or are used factiously to give a sense of authenticity. Any resemblance to actual persons, living or dead, event, or locals are entirely coincidental.

DEDICATION

For the men and women of the United States armed forces:

You are my heroes

Table of Contents

Chapter One	9
Chapter Two	61
Chapter Three	106
Chapter Four	175
Chapter Five	199
Chapter Six	294
Chapter Seven	381

Chapter One
—Enforcer—

Dorian Christianson stalked confidently down the wet sidewalk. A black, wool and cashmere Louis Vuitton double-faced jacket went over the top of a very expensive Brioni double-button suit. His black Brioni loafers contrasted the wet-gray of the Seattle concrete as he moved. The reflection that followed below him was like a vengeful, ebony angel, transmuted to a shimmer of a wraith in the water.

He stepped to the left to avoid a puddle. The city by the Sound was renowned for rain, and this spring had been no exception. Fortunately, in the upscale Ravenna section of the city, the sidewalks were level and smooth. They matched the perfectly manicured lawns, trees, and the few flowerbeds that the rich residents' gardeners maintained. The climate of the Sound was so damp most flowers were actually azalea and rhododendron bushes.

A large, three story house was his destination. The edifice was a pleasant tan color, with white trim and was surrounded by a six-foot high iron and brick fence. The windows were darkened, and reflected the humorless gray of the Seattle skyline. Dorian eyed the tiny dark dome near the front door—a closed circuit security camera. The occupant of the house knew he would be visited—even if he was not alerted by the security system, he knew this visit was in the works.

He brushed his hand across his short, black hair and checked the knot on his Italian-made Alexander McQueen, black silk tie. Then Dorian smoothed his Lois Vuitton jacket. He paused on the shoulder holster of his twin Heckler and Koch HK 45 pistols. The two buldges under the wool coat were concealed from prying eyes. If someone saw the guns in his hands, they were about to meet their end.

Dorian strode through the gate and up to the door. He stabbed the doorbell, and watched for movement through the door in the frosted, cut glass window. The chime echoed through the massive house as he waited patiently for a response.

Shapes coalesced and shifted through the glass. The fragmented kaleidoscope of colors formed into the shape of a man. Dorian watched as a hand slowly unlatched one, two, three locks. He listened as the bolts clunked and mechanisms turned before the door slowly opened. A whiskery face peered through the barely opened entrance.

"Mister Christenson. I wasn't expecting you," the voice of Edgar Ferguson rasped. "What a pleasant surprise."

"Is your housekeeper here?" Dorian said.

"No," Edgar said. "I don't have a housekeeper anymore."

"Is your wife home?" Dorian said.

Edgar hung his head. "She left me," he sniffled. "I'm kind of in a mess right now."

"That is an understatement. You home alone, Mister Ferguson?"

Edgar looked suspiciously at the man on the steps. "Yes," he said quietly.

Dorian planted one of his size twelve Brioni loafers on the door hard. The safety chain fractured, sending links of gold-colored chain through the air like shrapnel. The door smashed against Edgar's face and sent him stumbling backwards onto the imported Travertine tile. He hit the floor hard. The back of his head landing on the tile sounded like someone had dropped a melon.

Edgar looked up groggily as Dorian shut the door. He was dressed in a thick white terry cloth bathrobe and red silk boxer shorts. When he fell, his robe opened to show his underwear and a recently waxed chest. "Oh God Jesus, you're not going to kill me are you?" he cried.

"It's one of several options," Dorian said as he pulled his black Pineider leather gloves tight. "However, I have been given a bit of leeway to resolve this situation. If killing you was the only option, this conversation wouldn't be taking place—you'd already be dead. Close your robe."

"If this is about the money, tell Mister Giovanni that I am working on paying him. I'm having cash flow problems at the moment," Edgar protested. He reached up to the blood that trickled from his forehead where the impact with the door had split him open. "Please, don't kill me. I'm so sorry. Tell Leo I'm sorry."

"If you ask me not to kill you or apologize again, I will kill you," Dorian hissed. "I hate that. Don't whine. Besides, it is Mister Giovanni to you, not Leo."

Edgar started to say he was sorry, and then put his hand over his mouth. Dorian grabbed him by the back of the neck and pulled him up to his feet. Then he roughly escorted Edgar to a chair by a large, circular staircase and pushed him down. The chair creaked from the sudden weight.

Dorian leaned close to Edgar, grabbed him by his hair implants, and pulled his head back. He stared into his eyes. "You have been using. I can tell you are high right now."

Edgar sputtered, coughed, and crocodile tears began

to roll down his face. "Kendra left me. This economy is killing me. I can't keep up," he cried. "Then I had to let Adelita go. I'm drowning here. I miss my wife so much, but she isn't coming back and I'd just paid for implants for her birthday."

"So your answer is to start doing lines of our inventory?" Dorian growled. "That ought to clear your head straight away. Mistresses are expensive. Implants are expensive. Wives generally do not take too well to sharing. You are very indiscrete, on top of everything else. You are a clumsy oaf, both personally and professionally."

Edgar started to bawl. He sniffed and slurped, sucking a load of snot back up into his sinuses. It didn't work and he wiped his nose with his sleeve.

"I don't know what I'm going to do," Edgar gasped.

"I am going to tell you what we are going to do," Dorian said. "You are going to make things right with Mister Giovanni."

"Okay," Edgar whispered.

"Do you have any product left?" Dorian said.

"The cocaine is gone."

Dorian slapped Edgar's face. The report of the impact echoed against the Travertine and through the house.

"You do not say that. Sometimes the walls have ears. It's product. Inventory. So then, is it safe to assume you have the money to pay Mister Giovanni for the product advanced to you?"

"No," Edgar whined.

Dorian stood and smoothed his coat. "How much of the hundred thousand do you have?"

"None of it."

The report of another slap echoed through the house.

"Then we have reached the end of a productive and profitable business relationship. Ravenna was your territory to supply with product. Your personal sins are now intruding on what was a profitable operation," Dorian said. He scratched at a painting on the wall above Edgar's head and inspected the brushwork. "We had faith in you. Protected you. We kept out the Triads, the Samoans, and the Satanists. How do I explain to the boss we will take a loss on a hundred grand? That our man with exclusive rights to sell in this territory is pulling a Titanic on us? Do you assume we will be the ones to slowly sink into the frigid waters while you float away on the door? If you thought that was going to happen, you were wrong, Edgar."

Edgar tried to inch backwards to safety, to no avail. "I just need some time. Please. Tell Mister Giovanni that I can get him his money. If he advanced me another brick, I can make all this up."

"Time to squeal to the FBI? Snort another brick, or worse, run? No, we solve this today," Dorian said emotionlessly. "Is there anything you are really afraid of?"

"I don't wanna die," the drug dealer squealed. He pushed his hand under a cushion on a chair and then fumbled with a pistol.

Dorian leapt from where he inspected the art to

Edgar and kicked his hand. The Glock went tumbling across the tile.

"Death is probably the least of your problems right now," Dorian hissed.

Edgar shrieked again as a fist slamming against the side of his face sent him into blackness.

Cold water was forced up his nostrils and Edgar woke in a fit of sputters. Water sprayed from his mouth and nose as he tried to escape the sensation of being drowned. Dorian leaned over him with an empty lead-crystal glass. The dealer had been unconscious on the tile in his one-of-a-kind, custom built kitchen. He pushed himself up and put his back against his stainless steel refrigerator.

"What are you afraid of, Edgar? This is a serious question."

"Death," Edgar sniffled.

"You already said that. Everyone is. Anything else?" Dorian said as he pulled a small, scarlet drawstring pouch from the pocket of his Louis Vuitton. He held it near his face and shook the pouch gently.

"Insects, I guess. Spiders, maybe," Edgar gurgled. "Please don't kill me."

"Stay very still," Dorian instructed calmly. He laid the pouch on the dealer's chest. The pouch wiggled, and then expanded as the contents slowly stirred. Then a single, black shiny leg reached out of the sack. It was similar in shape to the leg of a Black Widow, with the same sick-wet shine, only fifteen times as big.

Edgar whimpered and began to shake. The leg waved as it savored the air, then slowly tapped, tapped, tapped at his chest as if its appendage could taste his flesh. As the leg waved he cried, then let out a whimper of despair as the tip of the ebony leg rested against his sternum.

Dorian reached over, opened the top of the refrigerator, and took out a Diet Coke. "Just stay calm. He will not bite, unless you provoke him. Sit still."

"Oh my God, I hate spiders!" Edgar sniveled. "Don't

let it bite me! That's the biggest fucking spider I have ever seen!"

Dorian pushed the Waterford crystal glass against the lever in the front of the refrigerator. Sparkling blocks of ice clinked into it. He wrinkled his face, dumped the ice into the sink, and then stabbed at the buttons on the machine. This time when he pressed the glass against the lever, crushed ice filled the glass and he was immensely satisfied.

"Just do not fidget. Lucky for you I found a Coke. Pepsi really pisses me off," Dorian said as he popped the top of can of Diet Coke. The can cracked and he poured the soda. He watched it foam, then leaned close to the vessel. The bubbles burst and tiny caramel colored drops shot into air above the glass. Laboratory-flavored starbursts that sparkled as the light hit the drops. "This will go faster."

"Please, make it stop," Edgar sobbed. "I hate spiders!"

"It will stop when he knows what he needs to know."

"How can a spider know anything?" Edgar shrieked.

"Appearances can be deceiving. Do not wiggle and it probably won't bite."

The spider leg waved in the air several times, then withdrew back into the pouch. Dorian took the pouch and then held it near his ear. He listened for several seconds, then put it back into his pocket.

"Thank God that is over." Edgar sighed, and then sobbed. "You're done, aren't you?"

Dorian took several gulps of the cool soda and then set it back on the marble countertop.

"We are done with you. Now, we collect on your outstanding debt and sever the organization's relationship with you."

"I have nothing to pay you with," Edgar said. "I need more time. You guys gave me more time after I missed the payment on the first brick. You fronted me a second brick."

"Giving you more time and product was already tried, and we just lost more money. I'm going to go downstairs and empty your safe. Help myself to the guns. I will have someone come by in a couple hours with papers to transfer the registration of the Catalina 315. That sail boat should square your tab with the company."

"Not my boat! Please! Take the house," Edgar begged. "Anything but the boat."

"You have no equity left on the house. Three mortgages will do that. You are so far underwater on this place there is no turning back. I am leaving you with the most valuable thing you have... your life" Dorian growled. "Lucky for you, your body parts are not worth a hundred thousand."

Edgar sobbed. "What am I supposed to do now? No money, no product, no distribution. No boat!"

"You cannot afford to pay the mooring fees anyway. My advice? Get Armando the fence to cut you a deal on the contents of the house. Load up your personal items, call the bank and let them repossess the house, then get in your Mercedes and drive. Do not look back. Go to somewhere you cannot easily find hard drugs and dry out. North Idaho. Western Montana. Utah. Yeah, Utah sounds good. Start over there."

"Dammit, Dorian! That's not fair," Edgar screeched. "This is my life!"

Dorian put a gloved hand around Edgar's throat. "This was your life. But you snorted and five hundred dollar-an-hour-hookered yourself out of it. If I see you again, this will end differently, understand? After our business is done, you are cut loose. Our protection ends. Have no illusions that if you weasel your way into some kind of witness protection, that I won't find you and put a bullet through your thick skull. I am giving you one chance to get the hell out of Seattle. Someday you might even realize this was a turning point for the better in your life."

The former drug dealer nodded. Dorian tipped back the Waterford and gulped the rest of the ice cold soda. He placed the glass in Edgar's hand.

"My people will be by this afternoon with some

papers. Do not run. I will find you. Thanks for the Coke."

***

Leo Giovanni sat behind a massive teak desk and fingered a Diamond Crown MAXIMUS #3. He held the cigar under his nose and drew in the rich smell of the Ecuadorian-grown tobacco. The old man meditated on the expensive smoke. He sucked the smell in several more times, hypnotized by the odor. His eyes focused on his cigar. After he was satiated by the smell, his eyes moved to Dorian.

"Quite a day," Leo said, a hint of Italian in his accent. Dorian had been in the office countless times, on this side of the huge desk. The dark wood paneling, the tacky yet expensive chandelier, the huge paintings that froze images of Italy in time. Vineyards, fields, a country church. Beside him a very angry, younger man sat in a chair. He was always angry. "Cigar?"

"No thank you, Mister Giovanni," Dorian said focusing on Leo. Even at seventy-four years old, his presence still filled the room. He was larger than life—

his accent, the way he talked with his hands. All of Italy, transplanted in America after migration across the Atlantic, was encapsulated in this man. A sense of the old country permeated his every word and action.

Rocco Giovanni, the thirty-five year old grandson of Leo had sat, jaw clamped and fists clenched silently since Dorian had arrived. He was like a teapot ready to boil over. It seemed like he was always ready to boil over.

"So this is the new business model? Flea market? What's next, used cars? Consignment clothing? How about Amway?" Rocco growled. "This is ridiculous."

Dorian stared straight ahead at Leo. The old man cut the end of the cigar, lit it, then took several gentle puffs until the expensive tobacco smoldered. He sucked in the vapors and blew them into the air.

"Rocco isn't happy with your efforts this afternoon, Dorian," Leo said. The smoke escaped from his mouth slowly as he spoke. "I am curious as to what your thoughts are on this matter. How do you justify your decision to let Edgar Ferguson live?"

"He owed us a substantial sum of money. I took the few liquid assets he had and other high-value assets that could be liquidated rapidly—the precious metals, guns, and the boat. My understanding was that I could make the decision to terminate him or not, on site," Dorian said emotionlessly. "To me, settling the debt was the priority."

"It makes us look like a bunch of pussies," Rocco said. He slammed his fist on the arm of the chair. "You should have taught him some respect. When I run this family there will be changes, I can tell you that."

Dorian's eyes slowly shifted to Rocco Giovanni. "You do not run it yet."

Leo smirked and Rocco shook with rage. "I put up with a lot, Dorian. The family needs an enforcer, and you are good at it. Never disrespect me. Never. A bullet will stop you just as quickly as anyone else," the younger man said.

"It is not as easy as you make it sound," Dorian said.

"Whoa, whoa, now that's enough of that, god

dammit!" Leo sputtered. He sat up in his plush office chair and sat the MAXIMUS in a gaudy gold-plated ashtray. "Grandson or not, I will not put up with that here. Dorian's loyalty to this family is unquestioned. Unquestioned! Apologize, Rocco. Now."

Leo's grandson shifted uncomfortably and stared out the window. "Sorry," he breathed sarcastically. "It's all bullshit, but I'm sorry. I get a little hot sometimes."

"There. All better," Leo announced, picked up his cigar and puffed on it. "Dorian, you of all people should understand the idea of respect. By not killing Edgar, do we risk looking weak?"

"We already look weak having a dealer using our own product. Business always carries risks. The primary goal was recovery of assets. Secondary, what to do with Edgar? He had been a decent dealer until his marriage collapsed and he started using. This business is about today, not what he did yesterday. Today, he was creating risk. However, killing him creates heat, which is potentially even more risk. Painting him into a corner with no way out means he could run to the Feds, which is a huge risk," Dorian said emotionlessly. "Besides, I would think once he missed payment on the first brick of product, fronting him a second was not the best business decision until we knew what he was doing-"

"Who are you to question how a capo runs his business?" Rocco interrupted. He poked a hammy finger in Dorian's direction. "I am the exclusive supplier to six raves in the next two weeks, just between here and Portland. Oxy and X. Got that big deal with the Satanists we inked last month. That's going to be an ongoing delivery of meth, far away from us, and the profits will roll in. They guarantee that they can move three bricks every two weeks. Plus the day to day stuff. Imports. Exports. Guns. Gambling. Prostitutes. The legit businesses that covers our other stuff. It is a full time job just helping manage the Asian Import and Work Specialists Corporation. To coordinate all of that, plus our interests from Portland to Seattle to Spokane. All you do is clean up when things don't go right. You're our enforcer. You're an overpaid janitor. Not even a made man, picciotto."

"He is the best at what he does," Leo said. "I think we are getting too deep into this drug thing, honestly. I was all right with a little X, a little weed, a little Oxy. We are going to make more in this state with the legal pot thing, anyway, than ever before. It's a license to steal. I worry we are supplying too much, now. The Feds really snoop into the drug trade. Rocco, you need to go cool off. It is still *our* business. Dorian is still my man. My enforcer. The Family's enforcer, until I drop dead, that is. You are also making big assumptions thinking you will run the family when I am gone."

Rocco exhaled loudly. "Sorry, Grandfather."

"A hot head isn't a good head for business," Leo murmured.

Dorian watched as Leo's grandson stomped out of his office and slammed the huge teak door behind him.

"I'm sorry he doesn't see how you fit into the big picture. There has always been a lot of jealousy in him, even as a young boy. I think you make him feel inferior," Leo said. He blew smoke into the air. "You have gifts, Dorian. He sees it and it makes him angry. Green with envy is an ugly color on anyone. Especially someone that angry. I've never understood where his rage comes from."

"I do not think I am special, in any sense of the imagination," Dorian said. "I have a lot of training and experience, courtesy of the United States government. A lot of time in the desert, I suppose."

Leo laughed. "Really? A couple tours in Afghanistan and Iraq are all it would take to duplicate you? Doesn't sound that special. In your humble opinion, of course. You minimize your skillset and your value to this organization."

"Probably," Dorian said, uncomfortable that the topic of conversation had turned to him.

"When your mother came to me she had nowhere else to go. The Church had recommended she terminate you. How often does the Catholic Church recommend abortion? You're so special," Leo said. "So special they would risk their very souls to see your existence snuffed out. I knew it from when you were in your mother's womb—you were destined for greatness. Not just the circumstances of your conception—I always had a feeling about you, Dorian."

"A series of events for which I will be eternally grateful, Mister Giovanni. Being a young, single mother abandoned by family and church is an impossibly tough place to be. My mother was an incredibly strong woman. Your support helped us through tough times. Helped me to be a man."

"The *Bible* refers to the Nephilim as giants. I always wondered why you are not taller," Leo said. "You are so fast. Focused. Strong. Heal so quickly. See things others cannot see. You could be such an excellent professional fighter. A boxer. Maybe one of those MMA guys. Could they have meant giant in more of a skills sense, or abilities, than just size? Their way of saying super human? It would have been amazing to know your father."

"The Nephilim were on the earth in those days—and also afterward—when the sons of God went to the daughters of humans and had children by them. They were the heroes of old, men of renown. Genesis 6:4," Dorian recited and shifted in his seat. "I will always wonder when my father fell from grace. Mister Giovanni, I could never be a professional fighter. I do not much care for the spotlight. I do not like crowds."

"So they gave out to the sons of Israel a bad report of the land which they had spied out, saying, 'The land through which we have gone, in spying it out, is a land that devours its inhabitants—and all the people whom we saw in it are men of great size.' There also we saw the Nephilim, the sons of Anak are part of the Nephilim, and we became like grasshoppers in our own sight, and so we were in their sight," Leo recited, and then puffed the MAXIMUS. "Numbers, 13:32 and 33. Dorian Christianson, the bastard son of a fallen angel. You are like a son to me, Dorian. You always will be. It's too bad

you don't have Italian blood in you. You could be a made man, capo, even my underboss or consigliore. We should consider the progeny of an angel Italian, in my humble opinion. The Church would have none of it and, at my age, passing to the other side is a concern. But I love tradition, and tradition is that a made man has to be at least half Italian blood. Not angel blood. I hope you don't hold this sentimental old man's clinging white-knuckled to tradition against him."

"We cannot all be Italian. I am the employee of a great man, Mister Leo Giovanni. I owe you for all you did for my mother. I am content to be an associate, as long as you're content to have me as an associate. I have done well for myself in your employ and hold nothing against anyone."

"Someday, I won't be the head of the family anymore. I doubt Rocco has the temperament to run the business, honestly. After I'm dead, I guess it doesn't matter who does what. Your skillset will guarantee you employment somewhere. I would hope my legacy carries on, but I will be gone," Leo said solemnly. "I wonder if the dead care what goes on in the material world after they die."

"Those days are a long way off, Leo," Dorian said and smiled at the old man. "We need to stay focused on the present."

Leo took a puff and put the cigar in the ashtray. He took a piece of folded paper from the desk and held it out. Dorian took the slip and looked at it.

"In the present, I need this problem taken care of. We never shit where we eat, as the saying goes. I would normally ask someone to come in from the outside for this business, but I have to make sure this job is done right," Leo said. "You recognize the tattoos in the picture?"

The mug shot was of a young man. He was dressed in a black shirt and had a smug look on his face. Dorian's eyes were drawn to the tattoos on his neck.

"The ink says he is a member of the South Side Sharks. Mixed race gang in Bellevue. He claims credit for five murders if the ink is not just bullshit," the enforcer said and stared at the five prison tat teardrops by his left eye. A name and address was written underneath. "Kerr Martinez. You need this cleaned up?"

"Yes, Dorian. This Martinez is a captain in their organization. One of our soldiers was killed by this punk while doing a drop to some of the South Side Locos over by North Beacon Hill. Our guy was caught in a drive by. I don't want to start a shooting war with the Sharks, but they need to know this crap doesn't fly. Did you know Alesio Conti? He worked for Tazio Bainchi's crew," Leo growled. "Accident or whatever, this Martinez is a dead man, he just doesn't know it yet. Alesio had a family. This guy and his crew need to pay. No one kills one of my men. That address is an apartment in Bellevue where this guy lives. I would like to see movement on this in the next couple of days. Sorry to send you to Bellevue. What a hell hole. Once this is taken care of, take a few weeks off. Get out of town, preferably. Lay low at least. There will be a lot of heat. Normally I prefer things quiet, under the radar, but this requires a message to be sent—loud and clear. The death of a made man requires the ultimate price."

"Yes sir, Mister Giovanni," Dorian said. "Consider this matter taken care of. Tonight."

***

The sun had warmed the dilapidated streets of Bellevue. The city was directly west of Seattle, across lake Washington. The potholes were filled with filthy rainwater, and steam rose from the asphalt where it would eventually condense into dirty clouds and rain again.

Dorian sat quietly in his Porsche Cayman GTS and watched a seedy apartment building. He adjusted his Oakley Flak Jacket sunglasses. The car was out of place in the run-down neighborhood—the spotless Porsche parked between a faded green Camaro and a beat-up Honda Civic.

The building he kept an eye on was a large, U-shaped edifice painted industrial gray. Several spots had been tagged with S³, the mark of the Sharks. Martinez lived in apartment number 106, in the middle of the complex. A steady flow of tattooed thugs came and went from the place.

On the west corner of the block in front of a scraggly bush, two thugs smoked blunts and laughed. Lookouts. When the wind shifted, Dorian could smell the sickeningly-sweet odor of the skunk bud the two puffed. Washington State had legalized marijuana, so no cop would waste his time shaking the two down. You would have to skin a hooker alive in public to get a Bellevue cop to drop his donut and work.

Dorian eyed the building across the street. There was a lot of cover and if Martinez left his apartment, there would be a clear field-of-fire to splatter his brains. This one would require his work to be close and personal, however. In Iraq and Afghanistan, killing was done at a distance. This job would be done the way he liked it— within arm's reach.

The bag in his pocket vibrated. He took it out and

held it in front of him. It stopped moving and a tiny red porcine hand reached from the bag and shook a clawed fist.

"So you are hungry again?" Dorian said.

The tiny grabber gave the thumbs up and disappeared back into the bag. The enforcer's eyes settled back on the thugs.

"See you later," he murmured as he watched his targets.

***

The Seattle First Baptist Church was a beautiful building situated downtown on Harvard Street. The church was three massive, interconnected buildings built from stone in the early 1900's. The well-kept red brick edifices were trimmed with white stone. A tower with white sconces looked over the church. The windows were immaculate stained glass, and the afternoon sun reflected on the blue and red panes.

Dorian sat in his Porsche and studied a newspaper. He read the obituary again, and then meditated on the photo of the deceased. She was a pleasant woman who smiled for the portrait. Clean, white hair spilled down to her shoulders. She had passed away in her sleep at seventy-six years old. Pauline Gray had been her name. Cancer had been her end.

The tiny bag vibrated again, and then jumped in his pocket.

"All right, all right, you are hungry. I get it," Dorian said. He locked his car and crossed the parking lot to the church. People slowly filed into a common room that was set up with cloth-covered tables and folding chairs. A chubby white-haired woman proudly handed out pamphlets and laminated bookmarks to commemorate the dead woman's life. This was to be an unconventional funeral.

An organist played on a portable keyboard. Dorian didn't recognize the tunes, but did recognize the somber tone of the music. On a table at the front end of the room, various refreshments were laid out. Vegetable trays, fruit trays, cold cuts with cheese, and cheesecakes were sharply arranged. Gray-haired church ladies dished up the cake and poured drinks.

Dorian took a single slice of cheesecake on a plate, and then sat in the back of the room. He watched the crowd—not a single attendee was under fifty-five years old, except him. The other tables filled up as mourners filed past the snacks.

The red bag in his pocket vibrated and jumped repeatedly. "All right, calm down," Dorian whispered. He took the sack and its agitated inhabitant and sat it in his lap. Gently, he cut a bite of cheesecake with his fork and speared the treat. He held the fork near the mouth of the sack. Two tiny red paws reached out, took the cheesecake off the fork and retreated into the bag. The sack quivered with joy.

A man stood up in the front of the room while Dorian cut another bite of cake. "Pauline's wishes were specific," the man announced. "No funeral. She called it folderal. So this is just a celebration of her life and her passing. Cheesecake was her favorite."

The bag jumped and Dorian lowered another bite of cake. Once again the scarlet fingers groped for the sweet and pulled it into the bag.

"Better than sex. Really?" Dorian whispered to the bag. He glanced around the room to make sure no one caught him. "Are you sure? I somehow doubt that."

"I'm Associate Pastor Alderink of Seattle First Baptist. We are here to honor her life, our friendship with her, and her faith and attendance. We are here to fellowship with one another, listen to music, enjoy our time, and think of her. It is what Pauline would want," the Pastor said. "Before we start, let us pray."

The bag jumped several times while Alderink prayed. Dorian glared at the bag and put a bigger bite of cheesecake on the fork. Every time the pastor ended a sentence, the sack twitched. The sacrilege was obvious.

"Shh," Dorian hissed quietly at the bag.

"Amen," the Pastor finished.

"Amen," the geriatric crowd said in unison.

"Amen," Dorian whispered.

"Is someone sitting here," a melodic female voice queried.

Dorian looked up. A sandy-blonde woman stood over him. She was dressed in a short, black skirt with a black and brown low-cut V-neck top. It didn't reveal enough to be immodest, but definitely enhanced her tan skin. The top was sheer lace over the subtle brown print, and over the top was a dark red knit sweater. Black and brown rectangular framed glasses enhanced her look, and she smiled with perfectly straight teeth behind scarlet lips. Someone close to his age. He was surprised.

"No one is sitting here," Dorian said.

"My name is Paige. Paige Gray. Pauline was my great aunt," she said. Her smile hinted at sadness, even as she tried to cover it. She could not maintain the illusion for long.

"Dorian Christianson. Sorry for your loss," Dorian said softly. "A wonderful woman."

"Is that a sugar glider?" Paige asked.

"A what?"

"Sugar glider. One of those flying squirrels. In the bag," she said and pointed.

A tiny, skin-pink paw with a bit of brown fuzz reached from the bag. The tips of the four fingers and thumb were tiny, curved tan claws. Several crumbs of cheesecake were stuck to the fur.

Dorian leaned close to Paige. "Rare breed, actually. Lousy temperament. They're nicknamed 'ass gliders' because there is nothing sweet about them. Can be biting vermin. Mutant breed of squirrels, actually. Illegal to important in most civilized countries, or should be."

"I've never heard of one of those," Paige said.

Dorian leaned back and the outer three fingers of the paw curled, leaving the middle finger and claw extended. Then it slowly retracted into the bag.

"Oh, my," she giggled. "It's almost like it knows we were talking about it and it flipped you off."

"Yeah. Almost," Dorian said, and then looked at her emotionlessly. He put the bag back in his coat pocket. "Almost like the little devil is flipping me off."

"What do you do?" she said.

"Freelancer. Imports and exports. A trouble shooter, if you want to think of it that way," he said. "Efficiency expert. What about you?"

"I'm a nurse practitioner," Paige said. "Harborview Medical Center. I work in the burn center."

"That sounds like it would be an extremely difficult job," Dorian said. "Incredibly sad, I would guess."

"It can be. But somebody's got to do it," she said. He watched as she lifted a bite of cheesecake to her perfect lips. "I make a difference in a lot of people's lives. They come in—burns over most of their body, but with therapy, medications, and grafts, they still can have nearly normal lives. How did you know Pauline?"

Dorian looked at the table of snacks. He thought about the answer. "I did not know her, personally. I knew of her."

Paige looked inquisitively at him. "You were not a friend? Were you an acquaintance?"

"No. I did not know Pauline Gray, other than what I

found out today from her obituary. She seemed to have a lot of friends, however," he said. "Says a lot about her. No one here seems particularly sad, in a bad way. A lot of joy, actually. You can feel the love. A celebration of a life well spent. We should all be so lucky."

"Did you know a relative?"

"No," he said quietly. "I saw the obituary in the paper and decided to attend."

"Are you serious?" she said angrily.

Dorian glanced around the room. Several eyes stared at Paige's outburst.

"Very serious," he said. Paige's raised voice had attracted attention.

"Are you some weirdo that attends funerals just trying to get a free meal? Some conman trying to prey on grieving relatives? You dress pretty expensive for a freeloader. Maybe that's how the rich stay rich," she growled. "She didn't leave much behind. Medicare has a lien on her estate for medical bills now. There's nothing to get."

He glanced around the room. More inquisitive eyes stared. Too much attention. This was ready to become a fiasco.

"I do not want anything. I am not here for money, just to share in the celebration of her life. I am truly sorry about your Aunt Pauline," he whispered and stood. Dorian walked out of the room, down stone steps and towards the doors. She followed closely behind him.

"I want to know how you can live with yourself, trying to pull whatever you are trying to pull by showing up to this. Do you do this at weddings too? Bar mitzvahs? This is one of the most offensive thing I have ever seen," she growled as he stepped out the door. "Mister Dorian Christianson, if that's your real name, big shot funeral crasher. Maybe this is some pervert thing. Do you pick up women at funerals?"

Dorian walked down the sidewalk and she followed. He stopped, turned, and glared. "When my mother died I was fourteen years old. A man in some respects maybe, but when the only person you have left in the world is gone, the world becomes a big, lonely place. We were excommunicated from the church due to the circumstances of my birth, and no one came to her funeral. In all those years, all she did was work and take care of me. Worked herself to death, actually. No friends. It was me and some drunken pawnbroker that worked as a minister on the side. I could smell the liquor on his breath at the funeral. No one else, other than the guy from Department of Social and Health Services, came. A drunk and a social worker. I swore that if I could help it, no one would ever feel as empty and lonely on a day like that like I did. So sometimes I go to these services so that someone, anyone is there," Dorian said. "So no one goes through what I did."

Paige stared. "Seriously? You would do that for a stranger?"

"I do not know who I do it for, other than I have yet to see a service that no one attends. Maybe I do it for me. My mother's service was the only one that I have ever seen where no one attended. So if we are done here, I need to move on with my day," he said. "I am sure you have someone else to accuse of something."

Dorian turned and walked away. She followed demurely again until he stopped at the Cayman.

"L-look, I'm really sorry," Paige stammered. "I really blew that. I flew off the handle. Truly, that was my mistake. I made an assumption that was totally unfair. Most people wouldn't worry much about the feelings of a total stranger. I feel horrible."

Dorian looked at her reflection in the tinted glass of the car. "Yes. Yes, you did make a mistake. You should feel horrible."

She fished in her sweater pocket and pulled out a business card, then wrote a number on the back.

"This is my cell phone. I would really like to make it up to you," she said. "Call me."

"It is a little hard to recover from the pervert thing, Ms. Gray," Dorian said. "You have anger control issues. I do not do relationships that require therapy. That is a road I have already been down and do not intend to go down again."

"Please, think about it. I would like to take you to lunch," Paige said. "I owe you. It's Miss, not Ms. I'm really sorry."

"I will think about it, I suppose," he said and pocketed the card. "Miss Gray."

***

Dorian was deep in thought as he drove away from Seattle First Baptist. Traffic in this town was always an unpleasant experience and today was no exception. He turned up the stereo in the car. Music to soothe him would have been a better choice. When angry, *The Offspring* was a good choice to keep the emotional embers hot.

The bag in his pocket vibrated and then jumped several times. He took the bag out and set it on the passenger seat. A pair of tiny, porcine hoof-hands reached out of the mouth of the sack and pushed it open. A miniscule humanoid figure crawled from the sack, stretched and yawned.

The red-skinned demon could have passed as the bastard progeny of the Michelin Man and a pot-bellied pig. It was virtually hairless except for a black ponytail tied behind its round head. A tiny pointed, prehensile tail twitched angrily. The feet of the miniature beast ended in black, cloven hooves. The body was fat, the distended belly hung down below a loud, pastel-printed silk Hawaiian-style shirt.

"Dat broad is fuckin' nuts," the demon said. The creature's New Jersey accent was always especially strong after it ate cheesecake. "Dames, I tell ya. Can't live with 'em, can't bury 'em in shallow graves. Stupid laws, anyhow. Once dey got da right ta vote, da republic went down da shitter."

Dorian sighed as the demon leapt onto the stick shift. "I hear you. You are quite the little misogynist today, Keith. It is not the nineties, anymore. Get with the times."

"Today? It's my goal every day ta be a misog...misam whatever dat word is ya used. And what's dis shit?" the demon demanded, pointing at the stereo. "Clangin', bangin', screamin' crap. You know what day dis is?"

"It is Thursday. *The Offspring* helps me put it all in perspective," Dorian said quietly as he pulled onto the freeway. "This music helps me keep my edge."

"And what's Tuesdays and Thursdays around here?" the demon said.

"Senior citizen discount night at the Sizzler? Half-off clearance sale at Sears? Buy one, get one free lap dances at Déjà Vu?"

The imp slid down the gearshift like a fireman's pole and pushed buttons on the stereo. "Tuesdays and Thursdays are my music days. Dat's da deal," it said. The tail of the demon snaked around and pointed into its mouth as it made a gagging motion. "So bring on some real music. *Da Offspring.* Blech."

"Could you give me a break, just this once? It has been a tough day and I have to work late," Dorian implored, irritated. "I am hitting the Sharks tonight. It helps me clear my thoughts."

"I don't give a shit who or what yer gonna kill tonight. Tuesdays and Thursdays are mine. Or I get to drive. Can we get ice cream after da job's done tonight?"

"Fine. Listen to that crap you call music," Dorian said. "You are not driving my car."

The demon pulled up his Katy Perry music file stored in the stereo. Her phony, auto-tuned voice filled the Cayman.

"Now, dat's music," the demon said as pretended to hump the gearshift. "Like a chorus of horny angels."

"Keith, get off the damn stick! That music is a lot of computer enhancement and silicone marketed to teen girls," Dorian growled as he turned down the volume. "It sucks. It is only music in the absolute loosest sense of the word. It is pabulum for morons."

"Dat dame's got balls. Better dan your middle-aged metal head bangers."

"Usually the balls of some dirt bag musician or lousy comedian are in her mouth. To say *The Offspring* is metal head bangers shows how much you know about music, anyway. Is that a new shirt?" Dorian asked.

"Way ta get your shots in, den change da subject. Very clever way ta try ta distract me from your losing argument. Careful what you say about my girl, Katy. I think she would marry me. We know dat she has low standards—she was married to Russel Brand and dated John Mayer. I have better hygiene dan either one of them. I have a shot," the demon said. "Dis is a new shirt, by da way. Missus Chang does all my tailoring. She custom makes these. Y'know her, dat broad down on 2nd Avenue who does alterations? Dis one was cut from one of dem Rush Limbaugh ties dat were so popular in da nineties. She uses a pattern for making clothes for a Ken doll. You know da ties. Wide. Loud. Designed to draw attention. Like him. I like da silk. Very decadent."

"You better not be using my eBay account to buy those ties," Dorian said. "I cannot believe the amount of money you pay for those gaudy old ties. I think it shows an unhealthy personality trait that you have all of your clothes made of out-of-print Rush Limbaugh ties. It is an obsession."

"I've read all of his books, too. And I buy his ties 'cause I can't buy real Rush Limbaugh skin on eBay. Besides, I don't use your account. Jesus, lighten up," the demon said. "I hack other people's accounts to buy all my stuff."

Chapter Two
—Payment—

Dorian sat across the street and the watched the building where Kerr Martinez's apartment was located. Clouds obscured the few stars that could have fought their way through the artificial lights of Bellevue. An occasional drop of rain kamikazied itself on the windshield of the Cayman.

"All right Keith. You reconnoiter the area. I am going to park the car behind the apartment. I will meet you there," Dorian said. "It is three-thirty in the morning. We get this done and get out of here."

"No problem, boss," the demon said. "Can we get some ice cream after you finish da job? It's a long ride home and I might get a bit peckish without ice cream."

"Did you open the package of Oreo Double Stuff cookies?"

"I ate all them already," the demon said demurely.

"The whole package?" Dorian exclaimed. "A whole package of cookies? There had better not be crumbs on the upholstery."

"I'm a demon of lust and gluttony. I could eat ten packages of cookies if I feel like it," Keith said. "And I'm amazingly tidy. No crumbs."

"Yes. We can get ice cream."

"With toppings!" The demon grinned with a tiny mouth of jagged teeth. "Let's get dis over with."

The imp peeled off his obnoxious shirt, then exhaled and clenched its tiny porcine fists. Slowly, the demon began to puff up, and then it collapsed. Its arms morphed into tiny wings and the cloven hooves became the feet of a bird. The neck compressed, and a needle-thin beak pushed out of its face. Keith shook and his transformation was finished. He was now a hellish-pink version of a hummingbird.

The demon took flight. Its wings hummed and Dorian cracked the window. The changed imp hovered and then threaded its way through the window. He flew toward the apartment building before he disappeared in the dark. As soon as the demon-bird had flown out of the car, Dorian turned off the stereo, took of his Louis Viton coat, and then pulled a bulletproof vest over his shirt.

The motor on the Cayman hummed to life. Dorian shifted the car into gear and pulled onto the street. He circled around the block, and then pulled into a small alley behind the apartment building. Cautiously he parked the Porsche between a pair of dumpsters.

Carefully, he screwed custom made suppressors on the barrels of the HK 45's, and then put them in the holsters. The weight of the pistols comforted him in an odd way against his chest. Dorian then placed magazines in the twin shoulder holster. They were filled with subsonic ammunition.

Subsonic ammunition had a smaller load of gunpowder in the cartridge. When he fired, the bullet would not reach the velocity to break the sound barrier. Consequently, the 'bang' of the sonic boom was eliminated. Subsonic ammunition was the quieter alternative for killers who didn't want to attract undo attention.

Every cartridge in the HK magazines had been loaded and double-checked. Nothing was left to chance. If one of his pistols misfired or jammed while he was outnumbered, the consequence for him would be death.

The HK 45 is one of the most reliable and accurate pistols in the world. The design uses a proprietary O-ring barrel for precise barrel-to-slide lockup. The barrels of the guns are constructed from cold-hammered forging. A unique internal mechanical recoil reduction system reduces the recoil and improves the accuracy. Ten round magazines required more frequent reloads, but Dorian was well practiced and could tell how many rounds were left in the gun by the weight. A .45 was a large round with a lot of stopping power.

Being outmanned and outgunned never bothered him. Firefights were won by stealth and speed. If your guys get a shot off first, you lose. If you can seize the initiative and down the enemy before they can react, you win. If this turned into a loud, stand up firefight in a crummy apartment building, even in Bellevue, it would draw way too much attention and escape would become impossible. Multiple gunshots, even in this city, would require a police response. SWAT teams, snipers, maybe even the Feds if it turned into something long and drawn out.

Dorian opened a messenger bag and double-checked the contents. Eight extra magazines of regular .45 ammunition, duct tape, gauze, nylon rope, knife, Israeli gas mask with cartridge, and a grenade.

The grenade was in case he ended up trapped with no hope of escape. It was a grim thought, but a possibility given his job.

Dorian pulled on a black Brooks Brothers overcoat. Not just an off the rack long coat, but one with Kevlar and ceramic shock plates sewn into the lining. It was heavy, but it would stop handgun bullets. Then he slung the bag over his shoulder. The buzz of hummingbird wings reached his ears. Keith landed on top of the car and transformed back into his demonic form.

"You gots one on lookout out front, one in da front of da apartment door. Both armed with pistols. Inside da apartment dere's five more, including your boy, Kerr," the demon announced. "Plus dree broads. Big fake tits on 'em."

"Dammit. That is a lot of guns," Dorian growled. "Are the women shooters?"

"Put a gun in any dame's hand and she'd pull da trigger," Keith said. "Especially if you off her meal ticket."

"Maybe," Dorian said. "They might panic when the first of the Sharks go down. Hopefully, they hit the floor and stay put. I would not trust any of them, though. In Afghanistan and Iraq you never knew who you would be facing when the door got kicked in—men, women, or children. They were all potential shooters."

"Or you might be dealin' with eight shooters at dat point instead of five," Keith said.

"Security system? Cameras?"

"Not in dis dive," the demon snickered. "Surprised it has cable."

"Keep the car running. I will be back in ten." He pulled his gloves on and then put on a pair of cheap, dark glasses.

"Den ice cream. Yay!" the demon said, and then tapped his little piggy hooves on the car in anticipation.

Dorian tied a black kerchief around his neck and stalked down the alley. He peered around the corner of the apartment. The single Sharks sentinel stood by the waist-high hedge and smoked a cigarette. The sweet smell of menthol carried through the turgid air and across the concrete sidewalk.

The streets were clear of traffic. Dorian walked down the sidewalk towards the lookout. As he approached, the lookout eyed him warily.

Dorian strode straight towards the lookout. He was bigger and more mature than a high school kid. The enforcer he guessed was twenty or twenty-one years old. Typical banger—pants that sagged, dark clothes, ball cap turned sideways, homemade tattoos. The bulge in his pants didn't mean he was happy to see Dorian—it meant a pistol was poorly concealed in his waistband. A walkie-talkie hung conspicuously from his belt.

The banger stood straight and took two steps towards Dorian. He flicked his cigarette onto the sidewalk, and then reached for his pistol. "This is Sharks territory, cracker. You'd better step off-"

The threat ended when Dorian's hand snapped and jammed his index finger into the Shark's eye. The strike was perfect, and the eyeball exploded in a splatter of bloody aqueous humor. The orb was crushed.

The banger's chest puffed as he pulled in the air to scream from the pain. Dorian's arm was already in motion. His bent arm, caught the banger in the throat. The point of the elbow was like a splitting wedge. The Shark's trachea and larynx were crushed instantly in a crunch of smashed cartilage.

Dorian grabbed his opponent by the collar and back of his arm, planted his foot behind the banger and took his weight on his hip. In a fluid sweep, he spun and delivered a text book Osoto Gari, a judo throw that hurled a person's opponent up and backwards. Dorian kicked his foot up, then back, and the Shark disappeared into the shrubs, concealed from prying eyes. The banger wheezed a couple times and then fell silent, as he died hidden in the hedge. His brothers wouldn't even know he had shuffled off the mortal coil until they joined him.

"Enjoy Hell," Dorian said.

The Giovanni Family Enforcer straightened his Brooks Brothers, checked the knot on his tie and crossed the parking lot of the apartment. The edifice had seen better days—the old paint had peeled and blistered in places, the result of too much rain. The white trim around the deck rails held up to time well, and contrasted the grim bleakness of the rest of the building.

Every third light bulb flickered or was burnt out. The complex's tiny swimming pool was covered and inoperable. Out of control, untrimmed bushes were spaced irregularly around the perimeter. Whoever was in charge of maintenance and upkeep of this place deserved to be fired.

Dorian walked between the cars in the lot till he could see the lookout stationed outside of Kerr Martinez's apartment. The lookout had his smart phone in his hand. His thumbs danced wildly over the screen. He didn't even see the other guard dumped in the hedge or his own impending death.

Dorian ducked and weaved through the cars, then crouched low behind a bush. The thump-thump-thump of bass vibrated the air. The music emanated from apartment number 106. Dorian moved quickly to where the sentinel could not see him, pulled the bandana over his mouth and nose, and then took a deep breath. He turned the corner.

Before the guard could react, the back of Dorian's fist hammered his jaw. Bones and teeth shattered from the strike. The enforcer spun backwards, lifted his elbow, and struck the gang member in the temple. He grunted, dropped his phone, and his eyes rolled back to show only the whites. He tottered forward and Dorian stopped his fall.

Dorian reached up, grabbed the Shark by the head, and spun his skull quickly. The neck of the banger gave way with a crack that sounded like a rotten cornstalk being twisted, and he fell to the concrete, dead.

He turned away from the corpse and put his thumb over the eyehole in the door. Then he smashed the single porch light with the suppressor of the pistol. The glass shattered and the light sputtered and went dark. Cautiously, he tested the doorknob. Locked. Dorian counted the deadbolts. Three bolts secured the door. He analyzed the structure of the jamb. He wasn't sure if he could kick it open.

If he shot it off its hinges, it would alert the crew on the other side that he was on his way through. If he kicked it in, and it didn't break, it would alert them and they would be ready. Decisions. He couldn't stand here exposed in the doorway all night with his thumb over the eyehole. His watch read 3:35 a.m.

Dorian turned, crouched down, and grabbed the banger's cell phone. He checked the contact list and looked at the K's until he found Kerr. Only one Kerr in the smart phone's contact list. The enforcer touched the button for text messages. He typed.

Kerr, I have to piss like a racehorse. Let me in for a second. Dorian pondered the message for a moment, and then hit send.

The enforcer grabbed the corpse, stood it up and held it close to the door. He ducked to conceal himself. The music thumped behind the door and he waited.

The lock on the door clicked. The gears in the first deadbolt ground and clunked. Then the second. Then the third. Then it opened.

"Lautaro, what the hell? You've only been out here-"

Dorian interrupted when he threw the corpse of Lautaro on the man who opened the door. The man was mid-twenties with dark hair. As the corpse toppled the surprised Shark, the enforcer drew his pistols and sent two slugs through the dead man. They passed through the corpse and struck the man who had opened the door—one in the throat and one in the chest. Scarlet sprayed from the entry and exit of the slugs as they tore through flesh. Even with the subsonic rounds and suppressors, the bullets made a noticeable crack as they left the gun.

Inside the smoke-filled apartment a woman screamed. The stale smell of tobacco mixed with pot assaulted his senses. The room was painted a dingy cream color. Several out of style lamps cast a low light. An eighties-era brown shag carpet covered the floor.

Stairs led upwards to the right near the entry. To the left were several couches set around a giant flat-panel television screen. An archway led into a kitchen beyond, and a hallway led to the back of the apartment. Between the living room and the kitchen was a breakfast bar. On the bar were several dozen bottles of beer and hard liquors. A coffee table was covered in ash trays, bongs, and beer bottles.

Four young men and three women were on the

couches. They all jumped up. The men were shirtless or wore loose-fitting basketball jerseys. The women were in skin-tight skirts. Kerr was recognizable, the farthest person from where Dorian had entered the apartment. The closest Shark was to Dorian's left—a shirtless man who pulled a pistol from his pants. Twin rounds barked through the suppressors. Two bloody holes were torn into the chest of the banger. Crimson splattered over his prison tats as he tumbled backwards over the coffee table. The women began to scream.

Kerr turned and lunged toward the hallway. A second gunman started to raise a Tech 9 that had been concealed in the cushions on the couch. Dorian fired two rounds into his chest. He stumbled and the machine pistol dropped to the floor. Bits of severed gold chain flew from the bullets impacts, mixed with the splatter of scarlet. As he fell, two of the women dove for cover and the third pulled a small pistol from her purse—a .380.

Dorian double-tapped again. The first bullet caught her in the hand, went through the handle of the gun, and tore a hole in the middle of her breastbone. The second caught her in the chest, popped her silicone breast implant and went out her back. Clear silicone gel mixed with blood splattered. The stray slug caught Kerr in the thigh and he stumbled into the hall. He screamed.

The last male Shark produced a 9mm from his pants and leveled it. Dorian lunged diagonally across the room, fired twice into the banger's chest, and ducked behind a couch. The bullets tore through his body and exited into the wall of the living room. Blood splattered over the bimbos who were prone on the floor. Their screaming increased in both quantity and quality when they were doused with blood.

One screamed and looked up. Her face was spotted with blood. Her dark eyes met Dorian's.

"Put your head down. If you try anything, you are next," he commanded and leapt over the couch as he jammed a new clip in the empty pistol.

She continued to scream and buried her head in her hands.

At the end of the hallway, Kerr had dragged himself over the obnoxious shag and into a back bathroom. A dark, slick trail left evidence of his injury. Dorian sprinted down the hall and kicked open the door to the bathroom. The knob mechanism shattered and splinters of wood scattered as the jamb broke apart.

Kerr fumbled with a sawed-off shotgun as he tried to level it at the door. Dorian kicked the gun, and it went wide and fired. The slug shattered the mirror and went through the medicine cabinet concealed behind it.

The enforcer spun and hammered Kerr in the middle of the chest with his heel. Ribs gave way from the impact and the Shark yelped. Dorian holstered one of the HK's, grabbed him by the several thick gold chains around his neck, pulled him up, and smashed his forehead into the banger's face.

Kerr's nose was crushed from the blow. He gasped and Dorian smashed him again. Blood spewed from his nostrils as the enforcer heaved him through the shower curtain and into the stall. The tile shattered as the back of his head hit it hard.

"The man you killed-"

"Fuck you," Kerr hissed. Dorian thumped his fist into Kerr's face, and slammed his head back against the shower stall. More tiles broke and clattered into the tub.

"The man you killed, Alesio Conti, had a family. Was part of the Giovanni Family. Mister Leo Giovanni wants you to know, an eye for an eye. What you did to Alesio, I have repaid seven times over with the death of your crew. When I kill you, it will be eight," Dorian said angrily. "All because of your sloppiness."

"Wait. I got money," Kerr said. "Please. Under the bed-"

Dorian leveled his .45 and shot Kerr in the face. Fluids and brain sprayed onto the green tile in the shower stall. The body jerked and twitched as remnants of the rapidly dying brain tried to communicate to his arms and legs. The corpse fell into the tub and seized.

The enforcer went into the back bedroom, looked under the bed, and found a shoebox. He grabbed it, opened it with the tip of a Brioni, and surveyed the contents. Stacks of cash held together with rubber bands were sealed in zip-lock bags. He grabbed the box and cautiously returned to the living room. The woman on the ground still screamed like a banshee. The other was slumped over the couch, her head blown open by the errant shotgun slug that Kerr had fired.

Dorian glanced at the hole in the wall. Perfect shot. Repaid nine times, not eight. His watch read 3:38 a.m. He checked his bandana and pulled it up, walked out the front door, then around the apartment and down the alley. Keith started the Cayman as he approached.

"Nine down. Eight by my hand. We are out of here," Dorian said as he threw his bag in the car and jumped in. He looked in the rearview mirror and shifted into reverse. "I think we sent the message Mister Giovanni was hoping for."

"I dought we were goin' out thattaway," Keith said and pointed with a tiny claw.

"Changed my mind. Kerr fired a sawed-off. That

crappy rap music will not drown that out," Dorian said. The Porsche purred as he punched the gas pedal. The car moved backwards down the alleyway. "Cops will be here quicker than I had hoped for. Keith, give them an image to conceal us. Something inconspicuous."

"Got it. Stomp on it, den!" the demon exclaimed. He raised his porky hands and conjured a mirage around the car to conceal the vehicle. "I got a good one picked out."

Dorian spun the car and then accelerated. The Porsche picked up speed and he turned onto a side street. Two blocks behind him he saw the strobe of red and blue lights as they cut across the intersection towards the apartment block. Two sets of lights shot by.

"That was close," Dorian said.

"Flatfoots were fast dat time," Keith said. "We need ta check next time ta see if dere is a Dunkin' close by and figure da response time from dere."

"We will hit a traffic camera at the next intersection. Keep us hidden," the enforcer said, "as long as we move. I will tell you when I plan on stopping."

"Got it. Illusion is in place." The demon kept his paws raised and looked up. "Any image in particular?"

"I do not care. Just keep them from seeing us!" Dorian ordered.

"Yer da boss," the imp said.

Dorian could see the light refract oddly through the windows of the Cayman. The imp altered the perception of the vehicle at the intersection to prevent someone seeing the car as it truly was.

"Dey can't see us, boss," Keith said. "A clean getaway. Let's hit a drive up window and get some dessert. All dis hard work makes me hungry."

"On the way out of town," Dorian said while he pulled a battery and a cellphone from an envelope. He put the battery in the phone and listened as the burner phone clicked. He dialed a number from memory and waited for the sound of someone on the other end.

"Is it done?" Leo Giovanni asked.

"It is done," Dorian said. He pulled the battery from the phone and threw it out the window. He watched it fragment into a hundred pieces on the street behind the car, and then wiped off a drop of Kerr's blood that had splattered on his forhead.

***

Dorian drove south on the I-5. The Porsche Cayman hummed as it hugged the road. It was early Friday morning and the roads were wet from rain that fell during the night. The drive was beautiful at night. The freeway cut through the hills and mountains of western Washington. The rain and pines filtered the air, and it was crisp and clean.

Keith had eaten half of a sheet cake, a quart of vanilla bean ice cream, and a container of chocolate chip cookie dough. The pair couldn't find a Baskin-Robbins that was open at four in the morning, so a compromise had to be reached. The demon had offered to forsake the sweets if he could have control of the music the rest of the day—Dorian had refused. He couldn't take any more Lady Gaga or Katy Perry. His head already throbbed from that phony crap.

Now the imp snored. He laid over the edge of the seat. His head was tipped backwards, jagged-toothed jaw open, a bit of frosting on the tip of his nose. Dorian watched closely to make sure the demon did not drool on the leather seat.

He took the exit near the small city of Longview, and parked the Cayman off a small street named Talley Way. Then he pulled the barrels from the pistols, walked across a train trestle that crossed the Cowlitz River, and dropped them in the middle of the water. He watched them reflect the light as they spun lazily and disappeared from sight. They splashed when they hit the water, and the enforcer was satisfied. Barrels left marks that could be traced—every time he fired a gun on a job, the barrels were changed after he was done and discarded somewhere they would never be found.

By the time he got back to the Porsche, Keith had finished off the other half of the sheet cake and had started on a newly purchased package of Double Stuffed Oreos.

"Jesus Christ, I dought you would never get back. I was afraid I might starve," the imp grumbled. He took another bite of an Oreo. "When are we gonna bed down for da night?"

Dorian reached over and grabbed a cookie. "I am going to stop in Woodland and get a hotel room. Tomorrow evening, I am getting together with Arashi Takahashi in Portland for a few drinks."

"Portland. Da borderline personality disorder Sodom and Gomorrah of the Northwest. Last time I saw Arashi he threatened ta chop me into a thousand pieces," Keith growled. "Maybe if he spoke better English he would understand I wasn't tryin' ta insult him. Stupid Jap has no sense of humor."

"*Mister Takahashi, Mister Takahashi, you rikey flied lice? I love you long time,*" Dorian mimicked the demon, and then smiled darkly. "I remember the conversation very well. You should probably find something else to do that night. He is a Yakuza enforcer. I doubt he gets talked back to much."

"I still dink he's a douche," the demon said. "Da Yakuza. Pfft. What have dey done for me lately? I would dink dat you could find better friends."

"I would rather you not start a war with the Yakuza because you cannot keep from running your cookie-filled mouth."

The demon stood up and saluted. "Here in 'dese United States, I got da Second Amendment freedom of speech. If dem foreigners don't like it, dey can go back to their own damn continent."

"Japan is an island." Dorian rolled his eyes and snorted. "Your knowledge of the Constitution is as suspect as your jingoism and geography."

Keith glared. "Dat's a lotta big words in dat sentence. You tryin' ta confuse me?"

Woodland is a small town of six thousand souls twenty miles north of Vancouver, Washington. Nestled amongst the hills and pines, it was a quiet place to stop for the night. Dorian checked-in to a hotel. He paid with cash, and the attendant asked for a credit card for a deposit and incidentals. He produced a photo ID with the name of Jerry Lundeberg, and a credit card to match.

The room was decent for a small town hotel. He pulled a suitcase of clothes and toiletries from the rear trunk of the Cayman. From the front trunk, he removed three large cases containing gunsmith and cleaning tools. It took him an hour to clean and replace the barrels of the pistols while he listened to the news.

Seattle news reported on the shooting deaths of eight yet to be identified alleged gang members in Bellevue. Dorian watched emotionlessly as cameras panned over the apartment he was at earlier in the morning. No suspects, but gangland revenge was suspected. He got away clean. That is what makes him a professional killer.

***

Seattle Detective Nicholas Paul walked across the asphalt. He ducked under the yellow police tape, strode towards several uniformed police officers, and held up his badge. The apartment building in Bellevue was overrun with police and forensics units. Yellow tape had blocked off the whole edifice, and crowds of gawkers had assembled just beyond the barriers. The uniformed officers kept them back. Several of the bystanders were hysterical. Their sons and brothers were Sharks, and they knew no one was left alive in the apartment except for one female brought out on a stretcher.

Markers were placed by every potential piece of evidence. Grids were established, neighbors were being interviewed, and security cameras from neighboring buildings were being scrutinized. So far, nothing was obvious as to whom the shooter was other than a trail of non-descript .45 casings.

One of the Bellevue detectives, Quinn Webb, waved to Detective Paul. "Hey Nick, good to see you," Webb said. He stood in front of shrubs by the parking lot.

"This looks like a doozy. What do we have?" Paul asked. "How many victims? Any suspects yet? Has the area been fully canvased?"

"Working on that. Uni's responded to the call. They

established the perimeter, surveyed the scene. They called in SWAT, but had established there was no active shooter by the time SWAT arrived. After they found a survivor, medical was called in. The EMTs said six were gone. They tried to save two more who died en route to Harborview. Eight dead. We are just marking grids and preparing to photograph now. It's possible one of the victims was killed by friendly fire. South Side Sharks. Local gang members and some of their bitches. Two women, six men. One survivor. Eleven .45 shell casings found. Considering the body count, not that many shots were fired," Webb said quietly. "Our survivor. She's hysterical. Has no description or information worth a shit yet. Total nutter. Tall white guy, dark jacket, dark hair, dark cloth over his face. That's all we can get from her. Whoever he was, he is an accurate shot, didn't just spray lead. Our perp is a trained killer, would be my guess."

"Hmm," Paul grumbled. "Let's run active and recently discharged military living in Seattle. Focus on any with gang affiliations, or criminal records for violent behavior. Have someone check with the Veterans Administration. See if anyone under treatment for PTSD might have gone ape-shit on some bangers. Marine. Special Forces maybe. Navy Seals. Delta."

"Transplanted Iraq Republican Guard migrated here after the war. Got it. Anything else?" Webb said.

"Make sure it's not one of yours. Check your SWAT team and Seattle Police Internal Affairs. Make sure no one is carrying out a grudge. Have you called the Feds yet?" Paul said.

"They are on their way. They called us. Saw it on the news."

"Let's get subpoenas from the cell providers. See if someone was sloppy enough to leave a phone on while they shot up these guys."

"Do you think if someone is capable of out-shooting an apartment full of bangers in a firefight, that they will be stupid enough to have an active cell phone?" Paul asked. He could hear a faint beeping noise.

"We might get lucky," Webb said.

"Do you hear that?" Paul said. "Listen."

The detectives froze and listened. A faint beep was carried to them.

"Sounds like a cell. Losing power maybe? Or a ringer set on low?" Webb said.

Paul listened, then turned and parted the shrubs. He could see a body concealed in the bushes. He moved quickly into the shrubs and felt for a pulse. The corpse was cold to the touch. "Your guys are doing a bang-up job canvasing this area. Looks like the body count is now nine. Let's check the other bushes and make sure no more bodies have been missed. Tell your people to be more thorough, detective Webb."

"Dammit. This makes us look bad," Webb groused. He signaled for one of the uniformed officers to mark off the shrubs and to get the coroner to check the body. "Let's check these other shrubs, ok? No more surprises. C'mon you guys, get it in gear."

A black SUV parked on the street. Two men in dark suits approached. One had short blond hair with a dark red tie, the other had short dark hair with a dark blue tie. They held up wallets with identification. FBI.

Paul recognized both of the agents, from the Seattle office. "Federal Agent Church, Federal Agent Reed, good to see you this morning. We could use your help."

Church and Reed shook hands with the detectives. "Quite a mess you boys have here," Agent Reed said. "What do you know?"

"Not much. The few casings found are .45s. Probably one shooter. A good one," Webb said. "Body count is up to nine now. All South Side Sharks. One survivor.

Agent Reed pulled a computer tablet from his coat. He turned it on, and then flipped through several folders on the screen. "We've had the Sharks under surveillance for the last six months. One of our confidential informants was close to the inside. They were into drugs, guns, theft, strong-arm robberies, and shakedowns. The usual for these ass-clowns. We set a concealed camera outside Kerr Martinez's apartment for a grand jury. We have video of your shooter. Just not very good video. It shows the moment that he killed the guard outside apartment number 106. The name of the dead man was Lautaro Rodriguez. Been with the Sharks for over three years."

The screen showed Lautaro as he tapped on a smart phone. From his left, a man in a long, dark coat appeared on the screen and punched him in the mouth. Then, the dark figure spun and caught the Shark with his elbow on the temple. The figure blurred and the gang-banger dropped into the arms of his attacker. He spun Lautaro's head to break his neck. Reed paused the video. Nothing was revealed about the attacker other than a black kerchief and short, dark hair.

"Attacker was light skinned. Hispanic or Caucasian," Webb said.

"So as you already know, Lautaro was out from two hits. First the punch, then a move called a spinning elbow strike. Pretty advanced martial arts move. Catches him as he falls, then breaks his neck. Your killer is so fast, the camera can't record all of the action. It's a blur. Few people can move that fast," Reed said. "They say Jet Li is so fast that he has to slow down when they film a movie so it can see him. Jet Li won fifteen gold medals and one silver when he was on the Beijing Wushu Team. Your guy is as fast. Champion athlete fast. Maybe faster."

"Batman is that fast," Paul said. "Shit."

"What's Wushu?" Webb asked.

"Amalgamation of all of the Chinese martial arts. Jet Li is a world class martial artist. This guy probably is as well. Or has the skills," Reed said emotionlessly. "Maybe a martial arts instructor. That would be worth looking into."

"Damn," Paul grumbled.

"So then he scopes out the door, looks like he realizes he can't get in, and breaks the light so no one else can see what's up. Then he texts Kerr Martinez that he has to piss. Kerr thinks it's Lautaro, sends this dope Jorge Perez to let him in. Your killer throws the body onto Jorge, and then shoots him through the corpse. Then he rampages through the apartment. Our camera doesn't catch all of that." Reed paused the video, and then rewound it. "Look at the guns. Suppressors."

The four watched the video of the figure inspecting the door, and then sending a text on Lautaro's phone.

"That text was sent at 3:35 a.m. We have a time marker. We already subpoenaed phone records," Reed said. "They didn't help anything other than to establish the time."

"Thanks for saving us the effort," Paul said.

The dark coated figure shoots through the body, and then disappears into the apartment.

"A shotgun goes off in the apartment at 3:37 a.m. Forensic ballistic acoustics in the Bellevue area indicate when the shot happened," Reed added.

"Where in Bellevue do you have microphones recording the city?" Webb said.

"That's classified," Church said. "NSA. Need to know."

"You'll also love this—NSA not only cannot identify the suspect with facial recognition software because not enough is visible, but they ran gesture and three dimensional skeletal recognition software on the video. That coat he wears conceals enough movement the software cannot pinpoint his joints with enough accuracy to narrow the search to less than ten million people in the NSA database. We cross-referenced it with archival footage from TSA, Interpol, and the CIA. Nothing."

"Do you know if our killer carried a cell phone? Did you subpoena triangulation for the signals?" Paul said.

"Yes. We had all the Sharks cell phones under surveillance. From this location in Bellevue, three towers pick up their signals. All of the Sharks phones were tagged, but no phone entered this location until EMS arrived. Our killer didn't have a phone that was turned on," Reed said. He switched his computer pad to another screen to show a map of the area. Red lights indicated the location of cell signals. "This image is a copy of last night, 3:35 when Lautaro's phone was used to text."

"In addition, our Stingray towers were tracking the

phones in this area. It's part of our warrantless wireless surveillance of Bellevue. It confirms the cell tower data," Church said.

"What is a Stingray tower?" Webb asked.

"A fake cell tower, set up by the Federal Government that pings cell phones. Tracks movement of the phones. Warrantless surveillance," Paul said emotionlessly. "How many of those are set up in this town?"

"That's classified," Church said. "NSA. Need to know."

"Then our killer leaves at 3:38," Reed said. "About three minutes total. So given the time he left, we tapped into the traffic cameras in a half mile radius. We got a picture of this car. It's an odd little car, license plate spells *FKOFF*. Obviously, not an official state personalized plate. The type of car is unidentifiable. Probably custom. We are... running clown cars in the database. Can't come up with a match."

Agent Reed pulled up a picture. The photo was clear, taken at an intersection. A white, VW bug, altered, with a painted clown face on the hood. A large key stuck out of the car that gave it the appearance of being wound-up. The silhouette of a driver was visible.

"Based on the location of this photo from four blocks away within a minute of our timeline, and the fact this car did not pass any other traffic cams, we believe this is the murderer," Reed said. He adjusted his tie, and then pulled up another picture.

"You're serious that the FBI thinks that our world-class killer made his getaway in a VW clown car?" Paul asked. "I just want to be clear on this. There has to be a mistake."

Reed held up the pad. "This is enhanced twenty times. Clearly shows the driver of the car."

Detectives Paul and Webb studied the picture. It was of a clown with a painted white face, dark frowny-face and a tiny beanie with a propeller over a wild mess of curly hair. His eyebrows were painted on and his nose was red. A gloved hand flipped off the traffic camera.

Webb stared incredulously. "This... looks nothing like

the killer in the surveillance video. He didn't have time to stop and put on clown makeup. There is no way. Are you guys serious?"

"As a heart attack," Agent Church grumbled. "Time frame combined with other traffic cameras, this has to be the getaway car and driver. Ninety-percent."

"Jesus Christ," Paul growled. "This can't be happening. It's like the Twilight Zone. Killer clown gun down eight, shoots up an apartment building. You can't make this crap up."

"You could if you were a really crappy writer," Agent Webb said.

"This clown is just wearing makeup. If you wash him with skin tones, you might get a good picture of his face. The bone structure is under that paint. A single color would also eliminate the cover up of the eyebrows and nose. We might see that face well enough to identify him," Paul said.

"We already thought of that. We're the FBI," Reed said. "Our IT people ran this image through hi-tech software to alter the skin tone to see behind the makeup."

"Microsoft Paint?" Webb said.

"That's classified," Church said. "NSA. Need to know."

Reed pulled up another picture. It was the driver of the clown car. The tone of the paint had been altered to clearly show the face.

"Wow," Webb said. "That's the getaway driver. Amazing. The likeness. Spot on. There is no way you can mistake that face for anyone else."

Paul squinted at the photo. The eyes, the ears, the goofy smile. All familiar. "The getaway driver was George W. Bush? Are you serious?"

Reed scowled. "Yeah. When you recolor the clown paint to skin tone, that's what you get."

"George W. Bush," Paul said. "Should I put out an APB on the former President, or should I just fly down to his ranch in Crawford, Texas and arrest him?"

Reed shook his head. "I can't explain it. The tech

guys are the best at what they do. All ex-hackers who work for us."

"There is some mistake," Paul said. "Someone is trying to make us look bad."

Agent Church shook his head. "Given that there was an undiscovered body in the shrubs, I doubt we can make you look any worse than you already do."

Chapter Three
—Portland—

Dorian packed the Cayman and stopped at a tiny convenience store in Woodland. Keith required Mountain Dew and candy bars for the road. It's not that the demon required food constantly—he was an imp of lust and gluttony. The continual consumption of sweets was the creature's nature. It was an expensive habit to feed at times.

Within metropolitan Portland, Oregon almost two and half million souls dwell. Near the confluence of the Willamette and Columbia rivers in Multnomah County, the city bustles day and night. Oregon is considered by many to be filled with odd people. Portland is the heartbeat of the oddness that is Oregon. The gravity of a black hole will not even allow light to escape—the culture of Portland does not allow the strange to escape. In fact, they are pulled towards it.

Portland is an odd contrast. Freeways run hither and yon across the city, crowded strips of concrete interspersed with vegetation fed by the Pacific rains. The Northwest rainforest grows trees and shrubs at accelerated rates, and anywhere earth is exposed plants take root.

The city is overrun by vagrants who beg and steal lounging in the downtown area. Clouds of marijuana and tobacco smoke mix above them. In the summer months, the smell of human waste is strong as the hobos relieve themselves wherever and whenever they want in public. Business owners are frequently weary from the urination in their doorways and roust the culprits, who return the next day to repeat relieving themselves.

Dorian followed the I-5 interstate into the heart of Portland. At 71 Southwest 2nd Avenue, there is a two story brick building that is the home of the Thirsty Lion Pub and Grill. He parked the Porsche on the street near the bar.

"Yer gonna leave da windows rolled down, right

boss?" Keith said. "It gets stuffy."

"You afraid it might get too hot for you?" The enforcer smirked.

Keith held up an unopened Snickers candy bar. "My candy bar will melt."

"You can listen to your crappy music, but it had better be turned off by the time I get back," Dorian said.

"Only if ya bring me a slider with extra pickles," the imp demanded.

"If you could behave, you could have gone in. It is your problem. Enjoy your music."

The Thirsty Lion was an exceptionally clean establishment, with seating both inside and outside on the sidewalk. The inside of the pub was covered in dark panels and earth tones. A huge, square bar made of granite sat on top of stained wood. Around it were centered flat panel televisions tuned to every sport imaginable. Dark brown wood stools upholstered in black pleather surrounded the bar. A stand in the middle of the granite island held liquor bottles and a cash register.

Dorian cautiously entered the building. Several small groups of people were scattered throughout the pub. They drank and talked as he walked past. The enforcer focused on a single figure who sat at the bar. Arashi Takahashi.

Arashi was a slightly built, average height, Japanese man. His black hair was cut short over his ears, and he was always clean shaven. He dressed in dark suits over a white shirt, and then put an expensive coat over the top. When he moved, a hint of a tattoo became visible on his right wrist.

Dorian pulled up a stool and sat down. "Arashi," he said and held out his hand.

"Dorian Christenson," Arashi said. "A pleasure to see you again. How have you been?"

"Good. Busy." Dorian laughed. "Never ends. You?"

"I just got back from Tokyo on business. You came from Seattle?" Arashi asked.

Dorian looked around as the bartender approached.

"Yes."

"What can I get for you gentlemen today?" the blonde bartender asked and smiled.

"Bourbon on the rocks," Dorian said.

"Make that two," Arashi said.

She retreated to the other side of the island to pour the drinks. Arashi watched her quietly until she set the drinks in front of the pair on the granite counter. He handed her a twenty and held up the glass. Dorian took his and they toasted.

"To health and good fortune," the Yakuza enforcer said.

"Health and good fortune," Dorian repeated. The glasses clacked together and they gulped the bourbon. It was a rich, full drink that burned. "So how is the old country?"

"Crowded. Irradiated," Arashi said. "China keeps pushing and pushing. War in our lifetime, I would guess. Global domination is their goal as the United States weakens. The Triads are a continual thorn in our operations. The Samoans are gaining ground. Now we are practically in open war with the Triads in Malaysia and Indonesia. Our foothold on the Asian continent is continually challenged. However, we did just reach a lucrative distribution deal with the Satanists. The one bright spot in the business last week. Drugs. Guns. They agreed to pay top dollar. I'm not sure how they can even begin to distribute all of it."

Dorian thought about the deal. "Hm. Our Capo just agreed to sell to them, also. I wonder what they are going to do with all of it, or even pay for all of it. Maybe they are mobilizing their contacts in the Wiccans to distribute the product."

Arashi shrugged. "Not my problem, unless it goes bad. Then I kill them."

"Keeps you busy, though," Dorian said. "Thankfully, things are slower here. We are pushed on all sides, however."

"I watch the news. Looks like you've been really busy in the last couple days. Kumichō Ito has an open invitation for your employment with us. He always reminds me that your recruitment would be very financially rewarding to me," Arashi said. "Mister Giovanni is lucky to have you in his employ. If you were to join us, Kumichō Ito guarantees you will be more than an associate."

"As long as Mister Giovanni runs the family, I will stay with him. He was very good to my mother when everyone else had abandoned her. If something were to happen to him, I would consider Kumichō Ito's offer. I doubt that there is anything that Arashi Takahashi cannot handle, however. I would just get in your way." Dorian laughed. He signaled the barkeep for another round of drinks.

"Kumichō Ito would pay for your services per job, if Mister Giovanni permitted duel employment," Arashi said. "The offer is most lucrative for you, also."

"Please tell him, with all respect, that I am satisfied with my current arrangements with the Giovanni Family, but if something changes I will happily negotiate with the most honorable Kumichō Ito for possible terms of employment."

"He will be most disappointed, but I will communicate your reply," Arashi said.

Dorian watched as the bartender sat two more bourbons on the bar. He finished the first with a gulp and she took the empty. Arashi's eyes never left the attractive woman.

"Still have a thing for blonds, my old friend?" Dorian laughed. "Old habits die hard."

Arashi laughed. When he lost concentration, his real features became apparent to the enforcer. His teeth looked sharper, and a hint of reptilian pupils overcame the mirage of human eyes. The half-dragon lineage from his father's side showed through the illusion he kept. Most people would not have noticed, but Dorian could see things that normal people couldn't.

"Always. A fascinating hair color. I can tell when it's artificial, out of the bottle. Japanese women are never blonde," Arashi said and smiled. He gulped the bourbon, and then his expression became serious. "Did you finally come to your senses and drop that evil little sprite in a mailbox addressed to Afghanistan? Sent him back to where you found him? Next time I see him I will cut him into a thousand pieces. He has a vile little mouth and he is filled with spite."

"That demon is immensely useful, at times. We have a relationship that is mutually beneficial. He can get into places unseen that I cannot, and then he eats me out of house and home. It is amazing something so tiny can pack away so much food," Dorian said.

"Mystical creatures don't follow the rules of our world. You can't trust that demon. Any demon. He may seem like your friend now, but without knowing his real name you can never truly trust him. Listen to me, my friend. Get rid of that thing now, before it brings you more grief than just cleaning out your refrigerator," Arashi said seriously. "It will bring you nothing but trouble. You will go to hell for consorting with a demon, even one as inconsequential and tiny as it is. It is a poor reflection on your true character and honor."

"Demons will never tell you their real names. Then you can bind and control them. I do not need that. Keith works with me. Anyway, technically, you're a mystical creature. According to the Priests of my mother's church, my conception damned me to hell, Arashi. Salvation is as foreign a concept to me as aliens from Mars. Besides, I have already walked near the fires of hell. I was almost married once, remember?"

The half-dragon nodded in agreement. "Half mystical. I remember, and I know. I was there too. For now, I'm hungry."

"My turn to buy," Dorian said. He signaled for the bartender. She arrived with a smile. "Beer Cheese Soup and Baja Fish Tacos for me."

"I'll have the same," Arashi said. "Beer Cheese Soup from Europe, Bourbon from Kentucky, and Baja Fish Tacos. Around the world in one meal."

The waitress laughed.

***

Detective Nicholas Paul sat at his desk in the Seattle Police Headquarters at 610 5th Avenue. He had picked the wrong time to try to give up smoking. The Seattle PD's IT guys down in the basement had taken several stabs at reinterpreting the image left on the traffic cam.

The original image was legit—it had not been altered. No matter what software they used, or how they altered the image, it came up as George W. Bush in clown makeup driving the getaway car. Worse, as best they could understand, the car was a custom chop-job. Parts of a VW Bug, a Honda Civic, and a Yugo appeared to be used to make the rig.

The Detective had guys from the motor pool try to get a handle on the picture of the vehicle. An expensive custom job and no part of it could be identified as anything other than random pieces. No rhyme or reason to its assembly. Those could have come from a thousand junk yards, or even ordered as parts from anywhere and assembled in to the car. Tracking them was impossible.

Nicolas opened another file—the spent shells were

all .45's, fired from two pistols. Scratch marks on the brass could not identify the type of gun in which they were used. The bullets were all recovered. Ballistics indicated two guns were used on the South Side Sharks. Splatter and drip patterns inside the apartment indicated one shooter had moved through the place. No fingerprints were found on bullets or shells—not even passive prints.

Webb had called twice. The coat the suspect wore was a common, black Brooks Brothers long coat. Only about a half million in existence, all over North America and Europe. The brass used in the guns were common shell casings. They had scratches that indicated the bullets had been pulled, the powder charges altered, and then reset. The charges had been lowered to make the bullets subsonic. Quiet.

The shells were common over the counter ammunition available to purchase in many states and by mail order. The ammo was cheap, solid-core brass. Impossible to trace. Not only was the shooter a world-class killer, he was also a smart gunsmith, or had access to one. The rifling on the bullets matched nothing in the FBI database. As far as they could tell, this was the only time these .45s had been fired. No other slugs had been recovered. This case was becoming more frustrating by the minute. The South Side Sharks had been shot up by a ghost.

Several things bothered the detective. First, there were the three AK-47s in the closet in Kerr's bedroom. They never had a chance to get to them. Also, why had someone brought in a professional hit man to kill a bunch of two-bit gang bangers in Bellevue? Gangs do drive-by shootings for revenge, for territory, to prove a point. They never hire professional hit men to settle scores. They do it themselves, for free. Maybe the gun deal with the Mexicans went bad, somehow.

The Bellevue Police Department seemed set on the theory that a professional hit man was hired to kill Kerr. Detective Paul wasn't buying it. It was too out of character for one gang to bring in a pro. There was something here he couldn't comprehend. Some hidden skein that could be pulled to reveal the answer. For now, that thread had yet to be discovered.

Nicholas began to pull the files on the Sharks one by one. He read every scrap of information on them contained in the database—from their earliest entry into the juvenile justice system to their untimely deaths at the hands of the mysterious gunman in Bellevue. If the detective could find that odd thread, that odd connection, he could start to unravel the mystery. It was what made him the best at this job—he could find the missing threads.

***

Dorian and Arashi talked late into the evening. The Thirsty Lion Pub was a popular place, and revelers came and went all night. The two of them were constant fixtures at the bar all evening. The half-fallen-angel metabolized alcohol quickly, and the half-dragon could get very little effect from the alcohol contained in non-rice based spirits. It took saké, Japanese rice wine, to buzz the son of the dragon.

The pair was most satisfied with the Beer Cheese Soup and the Baja Tacos. Arashi laughed while they drank their last bourbon of the evening. The bartender had cut them off even though neither one displayed the symptoms of being drunk. The perky blonde had no way of knowing the unusual physique or heritage of the pair.

Arashi settled the tab and left a sizeable tip. He loved blondes. She seemed receptive to him, and now he debated with Dorian if she was interested in him. The pair stepped out onto the concrete sidewalk, under the hum of electric lights.

"She is a bartender. She is interested in anyone who will leave her a tip," Dorian chortled. "You are wasting your money."

"I know blondes," Arashi said. "I was married to one, once. I can get into their heads."

"Get into something." Dorian snorted. "If your wallet is big enough, get into everything."

Arashi turned and smiled. His teeth glinted in the

lamplight, and the illusion failed faintly for just a second. His teeth were sharper and longer than they should have been.

"Dorian-san, just because you have a history of failed relationships and have given up, doesn't mean I have. I don't consider confirmed bachelorhood a badge of honor."

"Well, I do. Been there, done that. No more."

"Yet you will carry that demon around in your pocket. You are a misguided fool, Dorian Christianson." Arashi laughed. "I would rather carry that blonde bartender around in my pocket."

"Carry her around with your wallet. Or she carries your wallet around with her."

The pair laughed together as they walked to Arashi's car—a Black Mercedes CLS Coupe.

Dorian surveyed the car. "Damn. That is a nice car."

Arashi smiled. "You like it? The only thing I love more than blondes."

"Probably cheaper, in the long run," Dorian said.

"More reliable."

They looked at each other and laughed again. Something scraped on the blind side of the Mercedes, out of sight, and the pair separated instinctually. Arashi went to the front of the car and Dorian went to the back. They both stopped and listened. Both could smell the strong scent of stale sweat, rotten meat, urine, and stale alcohol.

Arashi pointed, and the two moved in unison around the CLS. A man in a tattered jacket was slumped against the side of the car. He held his head in his hands. Dorian took his hand off of the handle of his pistol.

"Hey, man. Are you all right?" Dorian said.

The vagrant looked up. His hair was wild, and he had patches of unkempt whiskers. Dirt was smeared on his face, and his clothes were filthy and frayed. He nibbled at a crust of pizza, using a battered, greasy box as a plate. That was not the most unusual thing about the hobo.

Around his neck a dark, snake-like tendril of dark

crimson and scales was coiled tightly. The reptilian appendage was attached to a black ball of wild hair and quills. The body of the creature had merged with the back of the vagrant's head. Through the forehead of the man, a face was visible. Slightly rodent, slightly demonic, the visage seemed fused with his skull. Red eyes glowed dully on the face of the demon, and it blinked in unison with its homeless host.

"You rich fella's have a dollar for a guy down and out on his luck?" the possessed hobo spit angrily. Dorian and Arashi could see the demon—normal people couldn't. Both had sight that extended beyond the material world and into the realm of the spiritual.

"Give a man a fish and you feed him for a day. Teach a man to fish and you feed him for a lifetime," Arashi said, and then scowled. "Ancient Chinese proverb. Please move—you're touching my car."

The human eyes of the hobo blinked with the red orbs of the demon. "Big fucking rich man, fancy fucking car. Maybe you sons of bitches want a bite of me. You know who the fuck I am?" the possessed vagrant hissed.

Dorian looked at Arashi and shrugged. "No. A bum? Is this a trick question? Should we know who you are?"

The hobo struggled to get up. He stood, obviously inebriated, and kicked the box across the sidewalk. "I'm Felix Peacock, that's who. I'm a celebrity. Local writer. I write the blog Vagrant Diaries and have over two hundred followers on Facebook. I'm raising money to make a documentary about overwieght homeless people oppressed by the government. Now do you know who I am?"

"Doesnt ring a bell," Dorian said flatly. "You need to move on so we can go."

Arashi cocked his head. "I don't know who you are. You smell. Just move away from my car. We are leaving."

Felix staggered towards Arashi, and then stabbed a finger in the air. "Let me tell you somethin', you fucking swells. You think you are better than me, don't you?"

"Actually, yes," the half-dragon said. "I am gainfully employed. Anyone with a job would technically be better than you. They contribute to the common good. I doubt writing would classify. Especially not a blog."

The possessed hobo glanced down at the sidewalk, then bent over and picked up a cigarette butt. He held it up to the light, picked at a bit of tobacco still attached to the filter and slipped it into his filthy jacket pocket.

"You fuckers," Felix growled. "I just wanted a dollar. Like you'd miss it."

"If you work a job, you could have hundreds of dollars. Even thousands," Arashi said. "Maybe you should take your medications regularly."

The vagrant began to shake in anger. "I don't like being told when to get up. Where to go. It's the Man, keeping me down. Fuck that shit. I hear the call of the streets!"

Felix lunged at Arashi. The Japanese enforcer deftly stepped to the side and caught the hobo in the temple with the ridge of his hand. He grunted when the half-dragon struck his head and dropped to the concrete.

"Nice move," Dorian said.

Arashi produced a tiny bottle of hand sanitizer and squirted the crystal liquid into his palm. He vigorously massaged the strong-smelling disinfectant on his hands. "Filthy hobo," he said. "I hate hobos."

Dorian kneeled down beside the vagrant. The red eyes of the demon rat-ferret stared back. "Well, you did not kill him. He is still breathing," he said.

Arashi continued to rub his hands together, then squirted another dollop of sanitizer. "He better not have scratched the Benz. I hate beggars."

The demon began to cackle. "You half breeds," the fiend snarled. Its tiny mouth, filled with yellowed teeth, chattered on Felix's head. "Both of you. Smug in your superiority on this mud ball."

"You managed to wiggle your way out of hell, and this is the best you could do?" Dorian laughed. "Possessed some hobo in smelly, downtown Portland? Have you heard of the good life in Hollywood? You should have higher goals than that. Smoking cigarette butts other people have thrown in the street. That sucks."

The demon laughed. Its snake-like tail coiled tighter around the neck of the vagrant and it cackled manically. *"Give to him that asketh thee—and from him that would borrow of thee, turn not thou away.* Matthew 5:42," the demon recited. "You half breeds are going to hell. Both of you."

"Not really. I'm Shinto, kami-no-michi. We don't really have hell as you would understand it," Arashi said. "Besides, that's my dollar that smelly hobo wanted, not Saint Matthew's. If I go to hell for not giving my money to some lazy bum, so be it. I'll take my chances."

Dorian shrugged and stood. "It is like the gospel. He does not give to bums. Especially not when they have touched his car. According to the Catholic Priests, I am going to hell anyway, whether your host Felix bought liquor with a dollar or not."

"The day of reckoning is coming. The end is coming. Armageddon is coming!" the demon shouted. Its scaled tail pulsed with anger, and its spines rippled like a wave.

"When we rule this mud ball, you will pay!"

"Kami-no-michi don't believe in Armageddon, either," Arashi said. "This conversation is pointless. This one is worse than yours."

Dorian reached out to shake Arashi's hand. "The good thing about a conversation like this is that at some point, it ends. Good to see you, old friend."

"Until next time, Dorian-san. Good health." They shook.

Arashi unlocked the Mercedes and drove off while Dorian watched. He looked down at the hobo. "No Armageddon without the antichrist, right? You have the inside scoop on where and when?"

"The unholy savior is alive and well, mortal," the demon snarled. The red eyes glowered unblinking. "You will have a special place when this place is turned upside down, given your lineage. Hell is coming, half-breed. We are coming."

"I have already been to hell. It is why I am single, now," Dorian said.

***

Nicholas Paul drove home in silence. Usually he would peruse the talk radio channels, or some easy-listening seventies music. Tonight, he just wanted to be left alone with his thoughts.

Seattle traffic was usually busy, but tonight there was a wreck on the I-5 so his drive home was incredibly slow. An hour and a half after he left Headquarters, he arrived home. The clock on the dash of his car read 9:55.

He parked his 2008 Nissan Sentra in the garage and quietly entered the house. His wife, Serenity, was in the living room on the sectional couch with a bowl of raspberry sherbet in her hand. She was in her pajamas watching television. He crossed through the dining room, and then stopped at the table.

"Long day?" she asked quietly. He put his briefcase on the dining room table and came up behind the couch. Nicolas leaned over and kissed her on the forehead as she leaned back. Serenity Paul laughed quietly and patted the couch beside her. He kicked off his shoes, then stepped over the back and flopped onto the seat.

He went limp and leaned into her lap. "You don't even know," he said. "Kid in bed? Did you watch the news?"

"Yeah, in bed under protest, I'm sure. That shoot-em-up in Bellevue. That's yours?" she asked as she rubbed his shoulders. "You're tense."

"I am on loan. Much like a library book, or a cup of sugar." He laughed quietly. "There is so much to go over. I arrived at the scene this morning. They hadn't even found one of the bodies. He was in the bushes. Glad I heard his cell phone or they wouldn't have discovered the body 'til it started to smell. Sometimes Bellevue is like the Keystone Cops."

"It's Bellevue," she said. "Probably bodies in a lot of bushes."

He didn't usually try to burden her with his work, but he ran the case down for her. Serenity was shocked by the amount of people dead. He talked about his theories of why it happened—revenge, robbery, turf dispute. He just couldn't quite work it out, and especially without more evidence.

"How was your day?" Nicholas asked.

"Busy. There was a lice scare in Mrs. Comrey's class and the secretary went home sick. The usual," Serenity said. "Grade school troubles."

"I wish I had grade school troubles. Not murder shooting-spree troubles."

"You might be able to get work as a substitute with an undergrad degree in criminal justice. What was your minor in?" She giggled. "Theatre?"

"Ok, dammit. It was communications." Nicholas laughed and bit her leg. She slugged his arm.

"Oh. My. God," Tessa Paul announced behind them. The seventeen year old was in her pajamas at the refrigerator. She brushed back her blonde hair and sighed. "At least give me a chance to get out of here before you do it."

Serenity and Nicholas looked at each other then started laughing. "Just a little biting among spouses, dear," he said. "Your mother and I are heading up to bed. When you get old enough, I will explain the birds, bees, and nibbling."

Tessa rolled her eyes. "Thank God I am adopted. Whatever is wrong with you two genetically ended with no biological children. The universe was saved from your special brand of depravity. Don't bother explaining any of your sickness. We take human sexuality in junior high. Don't act offended or surprised. You signed the note. If you wouldn't have, I would have had to go to the library with the Mormon kids."

"It's normal for people who love each other. Remember when you believed Grandpa when he said he found you in a cabbage patch?" Serenity said.

"I was like six," the teenager said and rolled her eyes. "Just keep it down. I have school tomorrow."

Nicolas laughed, and then rolled over. He used his wife's lap as a pillow, and within two minutes he was asleep.

***

Dorian walked back to the Cayman. He used the remote to unlock the door. Before he even got close, he could hear the repulsive auto-tune voice of Lady Gaga. The half-breed smirked, and then tapped the panic button on the remote. The lights flashed and the horn blared. He let it honk for almost a minute before he tapped the button again.

Keith sat on the passenger seat, arms crossed. He had a foul expression on his face as Dorian turned off his music.

"Dat... was dirty pool, old man," the imp bellowed. "No consideration fer others, I'm tellen' ya."

"So there was this vagrant back there," Dorian said. "It was an unusual situation. I can see them, but usually they don't talk to me like that."

The demon stuck out his stubby paw and read the enforcer's thoughts. "Um. Yeah. So da demon in dat guy's head is a demon of rage. Foul things. Dey exist and feed off anger and hate. Course, only a handful of folks can even see da darn dings unless they want to be seen.

You and dat cranky rice-nibbler you hang around wit just happen ta be people who can see 'em. Da fact dat it was imbedded into his head like dat means dat is a deep possession. If it was more of a passive possession, da demon would have been in an area away from his head. Like da stomach or arm maybe. As da possession goes on, da demon becomes more and more a part of da person dey possess," the imp said. "It exerts more and more control. At some level, da person allows it. As a general rule, dey are susceptible because of their issues to start with. Everyone can get angry, but when dey let their emotions control dem, dey are open to possession. It was a chatty one."

"What the hell is all the talk of Armageddon? What did that demon mean by bringing that up?"

Keith shrugged. "I'm kinda outta da loop on a lot of dat. Dose demons in hell have dis obsession with da Antichrist and all dat Armageddon crapola. Dey's always trying to bring it about. Once dey manage ta free themselves from hell, dey come here and obsess over dat, instead of enjoyin' da finer dings dis place has to offer. Stupid dicks."

Dorian looked skeptically at the imp. "So you are saying you are the one demon in the world that is not gunning for the Apocalypse? I find it hard to believe you're the standard bearer for common sense and good taste amongst the demon community. I have seen you eat five containers of cookie dough in one sitting. Then a bag of pork rinds while listening to Katy Perry. Yuck. They do all kind of go together, now that I think about it."

"Pfft," the demon scoffed. "Dat's why. So let's say dem idjits can bring about da birth of da Antichrist. Den what? I doubt as da world spirals inta da final war, dat cheesecakes will become more plentiful. Doubt Gaga will make more records. I'm livin' da good life on dis mud ball, Dorian. I hang with you's because it's easy livin'. I'm pretty far down da food chain, as demons go. Every day is a chocolate-covered vacation for me, here. If I was back in Hell, or if Hell took over dis rock, I would be low imp on the totem pole. Bein' a demon of lust and gluttony is pretty boring in a place where dere is nothing ta lust over or eat."

Dorian laughed. "I am so going to Hell."

"Been dere, done dat," Keith said and shrugged, then pointed. "Guess ya gotta live better, den. Hey, Taco Bell is open twenty-four hours. I could use a bag of tacos for the ride. Vivir más mis amigos gordos!"

***

Nicholas Paul woke early. He laid in bed beside his wife and listened to the distant sounds of sirens. Once the alarm went off she woke, then brought him coffee in bed. As the vice-principle of the Bryant Elementary School, she had to get ready to go. The early morning commute could be a killer in the Seattle area.

After she showered, Serenity sat at a bureau and applied a bit of makeup. She glanced at Nicholas in the mirror. "Any revelations come to you in the middle of the night? I hope you got some sleep."

"Just trying to work the connections in my brain.

There will be something that sews it all together. Some fact that leads me down the rabbit hole. I just have to get to that precipice to jump in.

Serenity opened a compact case, and then ran a brush across the foundation. "It will happen. It will come together. Always does. You are the best at this, Nicholas."

"I know. It's a tough one," he said. He set the coffee cup down on a nightstand. "Could take weeks to get DNA evidence back. Although, I am not holding my breath on that taking me anywhere useful."

"These cases take months, sometimes years. Eventually, something will click and you will get your man. You also have the intellectual firepower of the Bellevue Police Department on your side," she laughed.

Nicholas rolled his eyes. "Yeah. That's a huge help."

He showered, dressed, and grabbed two granola bars and a mug of coffee on the way out of the house. Traffic was heavy, but he eventually arrived at the Seattle Police Department Headquarters. Nicholas checked his email and phone messages. The data from every traffic camera in Puget Sound was screened and collated—nowhere else did the clown car appear. BPD circulated an image of the mutant mini-murder mobile, hoping a patrol officer might have remembered seeing it. Nothing. The killer clown was still on the loose.

Nicholas finished every file on each of the murder victims. Without a doubt, Kerr fired the slug that killed Naomi Hernandez, one of the women at the murder scene. She was dead instantly when a 12 gauge slug entered the side of her head near the right ear, then blew the left side of her skull out.

The one survivor of the massacre was named Jill Washington. Her jacket had a couple misdemeanor possessions of controlled substances and two arrests for solicitation. Currently, she was in Harborview Medical under heavy sedation. Detective Quinn Webb had tried to question her several times, but her psyche was pretty fragile after seeing the mass murder.

Webb had tried to get her to look at mug shots, but

she just screamed shrilly until he left. Nicholas would give her a couple days and try again. Maybe a different face might get somewhere with her.

***

Dorian had checked into a hotel room in the Portland suburb of Troutdale. He peeked through the curtains of his room to see a gray, rainy day. Then he watched the news and read the local paper. The Bellevue Police Department had no leads, but news reports said that a survivor was cooperating. That would have been the woman he left in hysterics on the dated carpet in Kerr's place. It would have been safer to finish her, but she wasn't a threat. Yet.

Keith insisted on an espresso, so Dorian hit the drive-up at the McDonalds by the freeway.

"Three espressos, please," Dorian said into the speaker.

"And six Egg McMuffins wit' hash browns," Keith shouted. He jumped up, using the passenger seat like a trampoline.

"Scratch that. Just the espressos, please," Dorian corrected. "No food, only drinks."

"So you don't want the Egg McMuffins?" a scratchy female voice said on the intercom.

"Yes, we do!" Keith bounced up again. "Extra cheese."

"Would you stay the hell down? Knock it off," Dorian growled. "Just the coffee."

"You wanted espressos, or coffees?" the voice asked.

"McMuffins!" the imp demanded.

"Dammit. Not in my car. Fried food stinks and I do not want it on the upholstery," Dorian said. "Just three espressos, please."

Keith dejectedly sat with his arms crossed. "Food Nazi. Upholstery Nazi. Clean car Nazi! American's have constipational rights, dammit. It's not fair. I am an oppressed minority. Dere are laws against dis."

"Constipation is totally different. At best, you are an illegal immigrant, and I think that is a stretch," Dorian said. "I do not think the Constitution was written with gluttony demons in mind."

"So you do want the Egg McMuffins, then?" the voice in the box said.

"Yes!" Keith shouted.

"No!" Dorian said, emphatically. "No McMuffins, just the espressos. I am sorry, ma'am. Kids. What do you do with them, nowadays?"

"I hear that," she said.

"I hear dat," Keith parroted mockingly. "Kids nowadays starve to death in violation of dere constipational rights here in America!"

"Six dollars at the second window," she said.

After the fracas at the window, the demon pouted as Dorian drove towards Portland. With time to himself, he decided to relax a few days before heading back to Seattle.

One of the largest bookstores in the Northwest was Powell's Books on West Burnside Street. Nestled in the heart of Portland, it was a four-story brick labyrinth of every new and used book imaginable. Dorian parked his car nearby and looked at the imp who had drunk all three espressos on the drive. He held the velvet bag in his hand.

"You think you can be good in the bookstore? I suppose now that you have drunk all of that coffee you will need to use the bathroom," Dorian said.

Keith shrugged and then crawled into the bag. "I don't follow da laws of nature. I only pee when I want too."

Dorian stared at the bag. "So all those times that we had to stop to use the bathroom, you really did not have to go? All the time you passed gas, you had control of it? You are such a miserable, disgusting, vile creature. Total vermin."

"I get bored easily," was the muffled response from the red bag. "Fartin' makes me happy. It's funny."

"Oh, my God," Dorian grumbled. He stuffed the bag in his jacket pocket and locked the car. He followed the sidewalk to the corner entrance to Powell's. Two homeless men sat on the street near the corner. Both held signs asking for money and they passed a cigarette back and forth.

One of the men wore a ratty, camouflaged military jacket with patched jeans. The second wore a dirty hoodie, pulled up over his head and black sweat pants. Both had scraggly beards and wild hair, and they leaned on large backpacks with attached bedrolls.

The hobo on the right blew smoke. Dorian could see some type of octopus-like demon attached to the back of his head. The thing's tendrils reached into the sides of the vagrant's skull, fused with the skin. When the bum blew out smoke, the demonic entity also breathed out the vapors.

The second had a demon fused and impaled through his chest. The entity was shaped similar to a shark, but the scales were black. Instead of fins, the creature had talons on the end of stumpy simian hands. It looked as if the demon had been hurled like a dart through his chest, where it melted into its host.

The pair turned to stare at Dorian. The octopus had

six eyes that glowed red, and the shark-thing had two. All eight demon eyes followed him as he walked.

"See, dat calamari lookin' one is a rage demon, just like dat one from last night. The other is a demon of compulsion. You would probably refer ta it as an addiction demon. Demons have a hierarchy. Like Amway. Da guys at the top, they're da heavy hitters, getting most of da goodies, controlling most of da mojo. Getting a percentage of da action, a cut, all da way down da food chain. Dese little guys we've seen da last couple of days, da one in da bum last night, dey're sixth-stringers, picked last at recess, bottom of da barrel. Like me, ta be honest. Da big guys, head demons, don't much concern demselves with us fooling around here on earth. Dey are more concerned with da whole enchilada, da big picture. You ever read da *Dictionnaire Infernal*?"

"I cannot say that I have," Dorian said as he walked cautiously closer to the pair. The imp had settled on his shoulder. "Why did you sneak out of the bag?"

"I wanna see what's going on. I ain't Superman. I

can't see drough clothing. I like ta be where da action is. Besides, no one can see me," Keith said.

"Can they see you?" Dorian asked. He pointed at the demons. They glowered at the attention.

"Dey can see me, just like we can see dem. Normal folks, dese idiots wanderin' around can't see dem. Even possessed people can't see demons. Only if the demon want to be seen, and dat's rare. Da *Dictionnaire Infernal* was originally printed in 1818. Da best, most used edition was printed in 1863. It was written by Jacques Albin Simon Collin de Plancy, a French occultist, and illustrated by Louis Le Breton. The book describes the hierarchy of Hell and who runs da show. Lucifer, Mammon, Moloch, da whole lot. Me and dese pussies here don't even come close to qualifyin'."

Something about the military jacket on the hobo bothered Dorian. The sign he held not only asked for money, it also said he was a veteran. Upon closer inspection, the insignia on the uniform was United States Army.

Dorian leaned close. The eyes of the demon, fused to the hobo's head stared. The orbs shifted from the enforcer to Keith, then back. "Money for a veteran, brother?" the tramp said. He wobbled the cardboard sign.

"Is that your uniform?" Dorian said. The demon pulsed in rage. It could tell he was more than just human.

"It is. Same one I mustered out of the Army in," the vagrant said. "Uncle Sam just ain't taking care of me very well. VA is a mess, y'know. Can't see a counselor, doctor, nothing. I could sure use some change."

"You have a United States Army insignia on a MARPAT jacket. MARine PATtern camouflage. Different branches of the service have different camouflage patterns on their uniforms," Dorian growled. "You are a fraud."

The hobo stood. "The fuck you say?" he spit. "I'm a veteran!"

"What do you call a 60mm anti-tank weapon?"

Dorian said calmly. "Every infantryman would know that. Everyone trains on them in basic. Just tell me the name and I will give you a twenty. For a fellow veteran."

"Um," the hobo said, and then stuck up his middle finger. "I don't remember, you asshole. What's it to you, anyway? It's just money. You look like you got plenty. Fucking one-percenter bitch."

The shark-demon grinned from the chest of the other man. "You want a scene here in front of the bookstore, half-breed? I might eat you and your little pink poodle-demon pet for lunch," it hissed from a mouth of razor-sharp teeth. "Lust demons taste like chicken."

"Hey, fuck you, dickhead!" Keith shouted and waved his little piggy fist. "You want a piece of dis, hotshot? I'll stick my foot up yer ass, tuna-noodle style. You'll never swim da same again!"

"I bet you taste delicious," the shark hissed. "Come closer, little imp."

"Bet yer mom's ass tastes delicious," Keith shouted.

He lunged for the shark demon and Dorian caught him mid-jump.

The enforcer shook his head as the imp struggled in his hand. "Take the patch off the jacket, and quit lying about the being a veteran. Understand? Next time I see this charade it will end up badly for you. I am not afraid to kick some homeless junkie's ass in broad daylight."

The octopus puffed in anger. The two hobos muttered curse words under their breath, slung their packs and left. Dorian held Keith by the scruff of his neck. "Dey're lucky you stopped me. I woulda pulled both dem demons outta deir hosts by da giblets and beat dem ta death."

"Do demons have mothers to threaten? Does that really work?" Dorian snorted as he put the imp back on his shoulder.

"Works for me," Keith said. "You shouldn't get so hot under the collar when dose bums pretend ta be vets. Dey're just scammin' for cash. Besides, I can cause trouble 'cause no one sees me."

"Pisses me off," the enforcer said as he walked to the entrance to the bookstore. "Fucking hobos always have some scam they're working. Veterans earned that title. Possessed or not, they were lucky I did not want to make a scene in public."

Dorian entered the store, and then wandered for several hours in the huge building. Powell's was like the Labyrinth at Crete, and the enforcer felt like the Minotaur that wandered forever. The difference is that he enjoyed it. Minutes turned to hours, and as it approached lunchtime he had found seven used books he wanted to buy. At the end, he always stopped at the section on military history.

Keith had retired back to his velvet bag for a nap. All of the excitement drained the little fellow, so now he napped, waiting for a promised lunch at Olive Garden. All you can eat bread sticks made gluttony demons happy.

Dorian sat his books on a shelf. Now he held a book on the assassination of Arch Duke Ferdinand and the days before World War One. He flipped through the large volume, and then noticed two men with beards and dark complexions slowly walking towards him.

He tensed. Dorian's heart began to pound in his chest as he watched them walk. One of the men wore a black t-shirt that said *Free Palestine from the Zionist Invaders.* They glanced at him, then turned and began to peruse a bookshelf. One of the men spoke. While his Arabic was never great, he understood that the man had found what he was looking for.

The bookstore seemed suddenly warm. Dorian tried to calm himself, but felt the sweat start to bead on his forehead. It was the look in their eyes. The same look of anger in the Iraqis and Afghanis. He tried to focus on the book, but his hands began to shake. The two talked in a language he recognized as Dari—common in Afghanistan and Iraq. One of the pair pulled a book off the shelf. It was about guerilla warfare and improvised explosive devices. They flipped pages and pointed at diagrams.

He winced as he recalled the overpressure of the IED

as it blew up the Humvee in front of him. It was like it happened yesterday. Fragments of the shattered vehicle pattered against his ride like rain. The windshield snapped as pieces of metal hammered into it. Cracks grew outward on the windshield, cobwebs of broken glass. Flaming debris scorched his Humvee's paint. Ammunition overheated, then discharged randomly and fired out from the wreckage.

Concealed Jihadists opened fire. Dorian started to shake as the image in his brain replayed. He dismounted with his M-4 rifle raised. Bullets whistled, then punched into the vehicle and he lunged for cover. His gun spit brass to the right and fire to the front. An RPG rocket whistled, and an explosion threw him through the air. He lost consciousness against a stone wall in Tikrit.

He realized in the here and now the two men stared at him. Dorian's heart pounded like artillery—the pressure in his chest tightened and he struggled to breathe. The book he held hit the floor. The two men looked at him, mumbled something in Dari, and he retreated out of the bookstore. The stack of books he picked out was left on the shelf.

Dorian tried to compose himself. He rhythmically breathed in through his nose, then out through his mouth. Slowly, the pressure in his chest started to subside. He wiped the sweat from his forehead. This wasn't his first panic attack, but it had been awhile.

He leaned against the car and listened to music. This moment of weakness would pass, and then Dorian would be angry at himself. He never had a panic attack while overseas—they started once he got back. Sand, heat, and sun didn't trigger the attacks—people did. Eyes that reminded him of the war zone did. The eyes of the men in the bookstore he had seen a thousand times before.

If they looked like Iraqis or Afghanis, it took him back. Then, his heart would pound and his chest would tighten. He didn't think he was possessed, but he certainly had demons of his own he couldn't overcome. Not every time, but enough.

Dorian drove to the 405 south, and then took the off ramp to the right on the Sunset Highway. The Oregon Zoo was a well maintained, peaceful place that helped him put his thoughts back together again. The panic attack was extremely troubling—it was his first in over three months. It seemed like they were in the past, but apparently not.

He had left Keith in the Porsche. Dorian just wanted to be alone right now. The last time he brought him into the zoo the imp provoked the primates and caused total monkey anarchy. Animals could sense demonic entities, and did not respond well to their presence.

The possessed hobo was right about one thing—the VA was a mess. Veterans couldn't always get help they needed, and Dorian sure as hell hadn't. Maybe he should try to schedule an appointment. Then again, why bother? Have some career, impossible to fire government asshole make him fill out paperwork and make excuses for no results. It'd be a waste of time.

He sat on a bench near the monkey enclosure. The

chimps cavorted, chased each other, and groomed incessantly. The panic attack in Powell's now seemed a distant memory. Dorian closed his eyes and listened. The sound of birds, animals, and people echoed through the trees. It soothed him, and he breathed deep.

"Do you mind if I sit?" a man asked. He was in his mid-thirties, with short brown hair parted on the left. He had an impeccably trimmed beard. A black suit jacket was fitted perfectly over a white shirt. A dark crimson tie with a gold-tack holding it down completed the outfit. The tack was an upside down star. An inverted pentacle.

"Sure," Dorian said. He looked at the tie tack. It seemed like an odd choice.

The two quietly watched the chimps for several minutes. "It's amazing," the man with the evil tie tack said. "It used to be thought that chimps and humans shared 99% of their DNA. Of course, recent studies show us that Genome-wide, only around 70% of chimpanzee DNA is similar to humans. That is under optimal sequence-slice conditions. It calls into question the theory that chimps and humans have a common ancestor. Some anti-evolutionists use the comparison of a watermelon's water content at around ninety percent to the content of a human, at about sixty-five percent. An odd argument, considering with just a difference of twenty five percent, but what a difference. A lot of science books are outdated the second they are printed, in this modern age. Knowledge is evolving so fast. Next week, someone will prove the DNA between man and ape is closer. You just have to wait long enough. Wild times."

Dorian looked askance at the stranger. "That is interesting. Regardless of similarities, I did not evolve from some ape."

"Oh ho! A religious man. No evolution for you," the stranger chortled. "It's funny how many humans, who think they are above such things, yet they act like primates."

Dorian shook his head. "No. I am not descended from an ape. That is all. Somebody might be, it is just not me. Religion is irrelevant to me. I am already going to hell. Do I know you?"

"Do I look familiar?" the stranger said. He stuck out his hand. "My name is Lou."

"Vaguely," Dorian said and cautiously offered his hand. "I am not sure where I know you from. My name is Dorian."

"That's what I thought. Dorian. It's hard to see someone from somewhere else, out of context, out of uniform and remember them sometimes. Iraq," Lou said. "Green zone. Bagdad. CIA headquarters."

Dorian stared. "I was in CIA headquarters for about five minutes. Long enough to drool over the ladies in bikinis by the pool. They gave me a Diet Coke and sent me on my way. I did not talk to anyone other than to say yes to the Coke. They gave me two."

"We didn't talk. I saw you across the pool. I also saw you in Afghanistan."

"Really. Again, I do not remember you. Are you CIA?" Dorian said suspiciously.

"I was with the UN when I was in Afghanistan," Lou said. "I get around. The UN is more my kind of people. Heartless dictators and bumbling bureaucrats on somebody else's dime. I truly love the UN. Any organization that would put Iran in the Commission on Status of Women Committee is more than laughable. The irony."

"So, is it safe to say this meeting is less than coincidence? Are you following me?" Dorian said. He looked around for someone out of place, or the glint of a scope lens. His hand snaked to his holster.

"You are not going to need a gun. No one is in the bushes. No snipers. No bullshit. You can't hurt me with one, anyhow."

"It all sounds like bullshit right now, Lou," Dorian said. "You see me in the Sandbox, recognize me, and now you just happen to run across me at the monkey cage in Portland. I do not believe in that kind of providence, Lou."

"Providence. Interesting choice of words. You saw

through me, Dorian. Interesting you would use that term, providence. No such thing. It's all about choices. Soon you will have to make a choice. You will have to choose what side to be on. Light or darkness. You said you are already going to hell. Then a choice would be easy. You have nothing to gain by choosing light," Lou said. "Join us."

Dorian stared. "Are you going to tell me Lou is short for Lucifer? Oh, please," he scoffed. "Did Mister Giovanni put you up to this?"

"Leo Giovanni. No, he did not," Lou said. "Yes, Lou is short for Lucifer."

"Lucifer. As in *the* Lucifer. The Devil."

"Yes," Lucifer said. "The Devil."

Dorian stared. Then he started to laugh. "Oh, my God. That is so funny. Do you take medications?"

"Is it so hard to believe? That I am The Devil?"

"You do not look anything like Al Pacino," Dorian said. "You are killing me. I hope this is not one of those hidden camera shows."

Lucifer stared. "I hate that so much," he said. "I wish that Jim Carrey would have tried out for that role. Do you know what it is like to be compared continually to Pacino? It pisses me off more than you can imagine. To have to take a backseat to an actor. Admittedly, one of the greatest actors ever, but still... you would think being the first among the fallen angels would trump that. I was flattered at first, but it has become rather tedious."

"I am surprised you do not have a red suit," Dorian said.

"Tiny little horns. Cloven hooves. A pitchfork. Spitting image of that little devil on the can of ham. It gets old. There is a certain dignity and respect one such as myself should be afforded."

Dorian stood, and then glanced at the primate enclosure. Oddly, the chimps now all sat quietly and stared intensely at the pair. Their eyes never left Lou. "Well, this has been enlightening. I would like to say that this has been useful time. You have made me laugh, Lou. Lucifer. Satan. Scratch. See you around."

The sounds of the park suddenly squelched. Inside the enclosure, the chimps froze in place. One started to jump from a tree, and floated mid-jump above the other primates. In the eerie silence, Dorian could hear his heartbeat. Time had stopped, and he was frozen in it. He drew his pistol and pointed the HK at Lou.

The Devil smirked, and then took a package of gum from his jacket. Spearmint. He pulled a stick from the packet, unwrapped it, and then popped it into his mouth. Lou held the package out. "Gum?"

"What the hell did you do?" Dorian growled. "Make it stop. I have had enough of this. Whatever you are doing, it is not funny anymore. I am not afraid to kill you. If you know me like you claim, you know I am not afraid to pull the trigger."

"You think a gun will kill me?" Lucifer said. "I survived a fall from heaven, as much as your tiny brain can understand it, and as grotesque as the physics that can be compared to that ultimate spiritual event. You are an ant waving a grain of sand at a giant. A monkey wannabe waving a fist full of feces. I'll cut through it, Dorian. The end is coming. I was hoping, given your lineage, that you would consider allying with us. This is a chance to get in on the ground floor, if you will. Better to rule in hell, than serve in heaven. You know how that saying goes. All that Book of Revelations crap was written by the side that thinks they can win. Don't be so sure."

"I am on the side of Mister Leo Giovanni. Always. He is the one who showed my mother kindness. My loyalty to him is unquestioned. The family comes first, no matter whoever or whatever you are, or what powers you possess. I have my own gifts and am not afraid to use them."

"You need to start thinking bigger than playing the Sopranos. It's going to be passé, pretty soon," Lucifer said. "You've seen the demons. The ones in the know about coming events sometimes have big mouths. They sense your unusual nature so they blab. Blab, blab, blab. Stupid demons. It's why I don't tell them too much.

Operational security, to use a military term you would understand. Besides, you're not religious—you've already said that. You have nothing to lose by joining us. The free-for-all that's going to ensue will be... magnificent. Chaos beyond belief. I thought the war in Iraq, the Taliban, ISIS, was some of my best work. Nothing compared to what's coming. It will be bloody marvelous."

"I have a moral code. I will not work for you, Lucifer. In any capacity. Even if I believe that is who you are," Dorian growled. "I have standards—honor."

The Devil laughed loudly and then stared. The echo of the inhuman laughter rebounded in this frozen slice of time. "How many people did you kill in Iraq and Afghanistan? Dozens? Hundreds? How many have you murdered since you went to work for Leo?" Lucifer said, and then grinned evilly. "You don't even know how many lives you have snuffed out. Funny thing is, I do. I keep track of stuff like that. The tally has grown mightily in the last few days."

"I do not know," Dorian said quietly. "Quite a few I would guess. I do not enjoy it. It is business. It was war. It is a job."

"Oh, is this one of those Julia Roberts moments? When we realized she is the sensitive, misunderstood, cum-guzzling whore with the heart of gold? You're responsible for the deaths of three hundred and thirteen people worldwide. Like I said, I keep count of such things. You're not a soldier. Not a mob enforcer. You're a serial killer, and not the nice Dexter kind. Dorian Christianson, you can try to have your heart of gold moment, but we both know better. You already work for me, whether you can admit it or not." Lucifer chortled mockingly. "You guzzle the lives of strangers. So shoot if you must—waste your ammunition. Call in an air strike, if it makes you feel better. You can't kill Hell—you can't kill me."

The chimp who hung midair suddenly was in motion again. The sounds of the zoo and its patrons returned. The enforcer holstered his pistol, straightened the knot on his Alexander McQueen and smoothed his Louis Vuitton coat. He stared angrily. The primates lined up again to stare.

"The hard sell turns me off, Lucifer," Dorian said. "You have nothing I want. I especially do not want to be part of Armageddon, even if I believed in it. Not on your side. Not on any side other than side of the Giovanni Family."

Lucifer snorted. "The other side has already made it clear they don't want you on their side. Going to be no room for water boys in the big game. You'll have to pick a side. Besides, I have one thing I think you might be interested in. Three hundred thirteen. I didn't count the airstrike you called in. That makes it three hundred twenty two. I daresay you are a sociopath, Dorian."

"What is that, Lucifer?" Dorian said. "What do you think I am interested in?"

"I know who your father is."

Dorian stepped back. The pressure on his chest from earlier in the day ratcheted down again. "That is not possible."

"Why? Why is it not possible? What makes you think that you are the one unique oddity in this corner of the world? A universe of miracles and wonders, not all of them holy. What makes you think that your interpretation of reality is the only one? He lives, and if we come to terms, you could have a family reunion with old pops. Maybe ask the question why he loved and left your dear, departed mother all those years ago."

"Fuck off, Lucifer. If that is who you really are," Dorian hissed. He slowly retreated from The Devil. Once he gained enough distance to be comfortable, he turned and skulked away. How much space would one need to get a safe distance away from the Father of Lies?

"Good talking to you," Lucifer shouted at his back. "I'll have my people get a hold of your people. Let's do lunch sometime and catch up. I have this great Chinese place in the Dalles, Oregon. I love it. Best barbequed pork and egg rolls in the world. Great lunch specials. Big portions. The things that make humans happy."

Chapter Four
—Overcharge—

"Agent Nabil Al-Kanani, Department of Alcohol, Tobacco and Firearms," the dark-skinned man in the black suit introduced himself. He was huge, easily six-foot-six and thickly built. The agent held out a strong hand, and Detective Nicholas Paul stood and shook his hand.

"Nicholas Paul," the detective said.

"I just wanted to touch base with you before I head out to Bellevue. I have been assigned to assist in the investigation of the gangland shooting of the South Side Sharks. I understand there was a witness. I heard she was in the hospital, under heavy medication. Do you have any leads so far?"

Nicholas shook his head and grabbed a copy of Jill Washington's chart. "Nothing concrete. Still waiting for DNA. Of course, it was like Grand Central Station in that apartment. Looks like we have full sets of prints for all the Sharks all over the place, plus partials for at least fifty more. Video shows our suspect wearing gloves, anyway. Of course, the shell casings and bullets are clean. He wore gloves when he reworked and reloaded the cartridges. He never dropped an empty magazine during the shooting, so nothing there. Our witness is filled with 200 milligrams of Clozapine, twice a day. An anti-psychotic. 150 milligrams of Burpropion HCL XL twice a day. An anti-depressant. Trazadone, 150 milligrams at bedtime for sleep. Xanex, .5 milligrams three times a day for anxiety. Lamotrigine, 100 milligrams daily as an anticonvulsant. It helps to counter the side effects of the antipsychotics. Haloperidol Lactate, 5 milligrams, for when she starts screaming uncontrollably."

"This is personal now, for us. One of the Sharks killed was on our payroll. He was feeding the Feds information about a Mexican connection. Two of those three AK's found in the closet were from our failed Fast and Furious gun running operations. I'm sure you watch the news. Some guns kind of got away from us."

"Creates a hell of a mess for us on the front lines, agent," Nicholas grumbled.

"The Federal Government runs its own playbook, Detective. We aren't all that concerned with how it affects local jurisdictions unless it makes our job harder. We are the big picture people, Detective," Agent Al-Kanani held out a file and a portable disc drive. "Metadata NSA files. Data from all the Stingray towers in the Puget Sound area. Every wireless tap and transcript of every call made by any of your victims in the last week. You must understand, this is for your eyes only. When you are done, I need these files back. No copies. Understand? I'm violating several dozen laws to show you this, but the people above me want to know who killed our man. I do have one question—this traffic camera photograph, have you seen it?"

Nicholas shifted nervously. "Yeah."

Al-Kanani pulled the picture of the clown car from

the folder. "Is Bellevue PD serious about this? I know this came from my people, but still-"

"As a heart attack," the Detective said.

The agent stared at the photo. "Interesting."

"What can I do with this? Do you have any recommendations for me?" Nicholas asked. "We have nothing to go on right now. I don't even have any suspects."

Al-Kanani shrugged. "Look for patterns. Outside the box. They say you are good at investigations. The ATF would have this solved in three days, if we had the manpower to dedicate to it. Let's see if you can do as well."

"Really? Three days? I would like to see how that would work." Nicholas laughed.

The agent stared at him. "I was serious."

Nicholas grimaced. "I thought you were joking. Maybe you guys should do it."

"I wasn't joking," Al-Kanani said. "Pardon me, but I need to go. Detective Webb is meeting me at the scene.

A pleasure meeting you, Detective Paul."

"Likewise, I'm sure."

***

Dorian cautiously walked to the Cayman. Even with the windows closed, he could hear the auto-tune shrieking of Katy Perry. He remotely unlocked the door and opened it. For a few seconds he sat, stared at the stereo, and watched the lights.

Keith sat on the floor of the passenger side. He had manufactured a hammock from espresso cups and a Dunkin' Donuts bag. Dorian stared at him as he raised his porcine hand to the enforcer and pointed.

"You... saw him," Keith whispered. He jumped onto the console and pushed the off button on the stereo. "Lucifer. I see it in yer mind. I can sense him. Amazing. What did he say? Da Dark Lord here, schmoozing with you at da Portland Zoo."

"I saw a man who claimed to be The Devil," Dorian said. "He was just some crazy. This has been the day for crazies."

Keith shook his head. "No. It was him. I've seen him in hell. Before dat crazy Arab summoned, den bound me in Afghanistan. I can't believe he is here at da zoo. Dey should do a commercial with him. Da Devil's favorite zoo is in Portland. Attendance would go through da roof."

Dorian could feel the pressure in his chest. He tried to slow his breathing. Control the panic. "He said Armageddon was coming. That I had to make a choice. That he knew my father."

"Dat would all make sense. Remember, he's called da Father of Lies for a reason. He cherry picks information ta tempt you with. Speaks in half-truths. Uses yer feelin's against you. Takes a little bit of fact, pretzels it up wit whatever is most convenient for him, and den works you like a ten-dollar hooker at a Republican Presidential Convention. It's ugly," the demon said.

Dorian looked at the imp. "I still do not get why you seem so eager to turn on your former employer, if you will. Understand, at this moment, my faith in everything is at an all-time low," the enforcer mumbled. "I have seen demons before. Seen possessions before. Seen the evil men inflict on each other before. Hell, I am as much if not more of that evil than about anybody, I suppose. It just seems up in my face all of a sudden."

"Part of it could be Portland," Keith said. The demon began to morph into a tiny carnival barker with a top hat. "Fuckin' freak show. It's like da center of da oddball universe. Step right up! See da freaks. Cannibals. Blood drinkers. Possessed. Hobos dat shit in public. Welcome to Portland!"

"Get out," Dorian said. He hit the switch and the passenger window rolled down. "You and me. We are done."

The demon returned to his red, piggy form. He straightened his Rush Limbaugh tailored shirt, pointed a porcine hoof at the door. "Are you's serious? You want *me* ta go?"

"Yes. I am afraid I am. We have had some good times, but it ends. I cannot trust you, anymore. At the end of the day, you are a demon of lust and gluttony.

We are not friends. This relationship is about how much you can cram in your pie-hole," Dorian said. "Sorry. I need to move forward from here. I seriously doubt that you will pick me over Lucifer if the time comes."

"C'mon man, don't be like dis," Keith whined. "Yer a bit emotional. It was dat panic attack earlier. You always get P-M-S-ie afterwards. Take a deep breath."

"Out!" Dorian commanded. "I hate that worse than anything. Take a deep breath my ass. That's how you calm children down!"

"You remember when you found me in da big litter box over there? Afghanistan? Bound in ta a brass lamp like some stupid genie? Some dirty old Mullah hoverin' over me like Anna Nicole Smith over some billionaire about ta drop dead. Ordering me around, tryin' ta get me ta grant wishes, like I could fucking grant wishes if I wanted. If I could grant wishes, I woulda wished myself out of da fuckin' lamp. He was a lot better with magic dan common sense, I can tell you dat. I was ripped from da depths of Hell, which, on a good day, sucks salty shriveled balls compared ta this place. Dat's why it's hell," the demon said. "C'mon Dorian, we're buddies. All for one, one for all. Don't let it end dis way."

"Out. Get out of my car."

"Dorian. Man. We got it good together. A team, me and you. I have been nothing but loyal ta you and Mister Giovanni. Have helped every time you asked. Never refused."

"You are a demon. You are not going to side with me against Lucifer. Honestly, I do not even know why I am so stirred up over all this. Nothing that has happened in my life would indicate Armageddon is coming. I will never get married," Dorian growled. "Arashi is right. I can never be sure about you. Never trust you."

"My real name is Kseryth Nysreff. My secret name dat a demon never reveals. Now you have total control over me," the imp said. "Try it. Use it ta see."

The enforcer glared. "Kseryth Nysreff, get out of my car."

"Shit," the demon said. "I never saw dat coming.

Dirty pool, old man. Do you dink Batman ever kicked Robin out of da Batmobile? Dat da Skipper kicked Gilligan off da Minnow? Dat Snookie ever kicked any scumbag guy out of bed?"

He clamored up the side of the door, stood on the latch, then jumped out. Tiny hooves clicked on the sidewalk. Dorian fumed for a few minutes and listened to the pathetic cries of the demon. He could hear Keith sniffle and blow his nose. The enforcer leaned over, unlatched the door, and stared at the imp who was sprawled dejectedly on the concrete.

"Kseryth Nysreff, get in the car," Dorian ordered. The demon stood, blew his nose on his shirt and jumped onto the passenger seat.

"I knew you'd come around," Kseryth said.

Dorian stared. "How do I know that you are not just playing me? That you are just doing what I say to pretend that the name you gave me is your real name. What could I come up with that would be so repulsive, so horrific, that I can know one hundred percent you are on my side?"

The imp shrugged. "I have low standards. I doubt you could come up with anything dat would be beneath me."

"Say that Hillary Clinton has great gams."

"Dat's just stupid," the demon hissed. "And gross. You've found one ding, I guess, dat creeps me out."

"Kseryth Nysreff, I order you to say Hillary Clinton has great gams," Dorian ordered.

The imp shuddered, gagged, and then struggled as he formed the words. "Hillary Clinton... has great gams. It's repulsive, but dere, you sick fuck. Dat should prove you have my real name. You can't get me ta sink any lower."

"Say you want to nibble on her toes."

"Fuck man! Really?" the imp shrieked. "Have you no shame? Dis is worse than Hell!"

"Kseryth Nysreff, I command you to say you want to nibble Hillary Clinton's toes," Dorian said.

The demon fought it. "I want... ta nibble... Hillary Clinton's toes," he shrieked. "Sick!"

"Erase your music from the stereo. Gaga, Perry, all that mindless crap has got to go."

"N-no way," the demon stuttered. "You can only push me so far before I open a can of whoop-ass, understand? I ain't touchin' my music."

"Kseryth Nysreff, erase your music files from the stereo. Right now."

The demon staggered to the console, then began to punch buttons. "Dis is a buncha bullshit right here, Dorian. You've made your point. I demand an iPod. I ain't gonna listen ta your music all da time, I can tell ya dat. Stupid metal crap," Kseryth said. "Call me Keith, by the way. I don't want everyone knowin' my real name. And I need a couple of boxes of Twinkies ta make up for dis debacle. You owe me if you want me ta be your sidekick."

"If you think about turning on me, I will shoot a hundred holes in you. Understand?" Dorian said.

"Pfft. You're sure in a pissy mood. Just one chat with The Devil and now you're all stressed out. You take dings way too seriously," Keith chortled. "Let's get some Twinkies. Three boxes should be good."

"I am serious when I don't understand what is happening around me," Dorian said.

* * *

ATF Agent Nabil Al-Kanani surveyed the run-down apartment in Bellevue. The yellow police tape had sectioned off the shrubs near the parking lot entrance, and the entry to Kerr Martinez's apartment. Several uniformed officers were loitering near the entrance with a watchful eye on the place.

The agent had surveyed the scene. He walked through the apartment, escorted by Bellevue Detective Quinn Webb. Al-Kanani had reviewed the hidden camera footage of the shooter several times. It revealed nothing, and now the walk through of the shot-up apartment had yielded the same results. Forensics had come up with a big goose egg so far.

He sensed something... unusual. Something that did not belong. A normal person would not have felt it, but he could. Oddly, he detected mixed impressions. Something vaguely demonic, something vaguely angelic. To the door of the apartment he could feel both but, upon entry, only the angelic side reached him. It made him uncomfortable. Either the shooter was an angel, or he had an angel closely following him. Not a guardian angel, but something else. Darker.

The demonic entity was also troublesome. Could it have been following the angel? It would be impossible that both entities would possess one human. Maybe the demon preceded the angel. Then the other question became, was the shooter a third person? He had hoped his extra sensory abilities would have helped to ferret out the culprit—instead it served to only muddy the waters.

He stopped in the bathroom. The final confrontation had happened there—he could sense it. Al-Kanani looked at the shattered tile of the shower, splattered with blood. He could almost taste the moment a slug tore through Kerr Martinez's brain. It was delicious.

Al-Kanani looked at the blood splattered mirror in the bathroom. Webb chattered non-stop about the physical evidence that had been collected. While the agent looked in the mirror, he could see a hint of his true self. Webb couldn't see the hint of the horns, sharp teeth or forked tongue magically cloaked to obscure his true identity, but the agent could.

The agent finished the walk through with Webb. The two chatted about mundane possibilities for a few minutes, exchanged cards, and then parted ways. He crossed the street and unlocked his black Chrysler SUV remotely.

Al-Kanani watched the police from his SUV. It was parked across the street from the apartment building. He never fed the meter—he didn't need to. He was an employee of the Federal Government. It was the equivalent of an endless free lunch, with no responsibility.

A run-down 1987 Honda Civic with faded red paint pulled from traffic and parked in front of his vehicle.

Before the driver of the car had turned off the motor, the agent was out of his Chrysler and at the driver-side window. A little old white-haired woman, easily eighty, slowly rolled down the window. Al-Kanani pulled his wallet out and showed his credentials.

"Federal business, ma'am. I need you to park somewhere else."

The woman looked at him. "I pay my taxes. I'm gonna park where I want," she grumbled.

The agent opened up his coat to show the handle of his pistol. "You will move this car, or I will shoot you in the face. Understand?" His hand grasped the handle of the gun.

Her lower lip quivered. "You'd shoot an old woman in the face over a parking spot?" she gasped.

"I've shot them for less than that. Get out of here," Al-Kanani ordered. "Putting a bullet in an old bag like you is doing this world of rotting-meat bags a service."

The gears ground as she jammed on the stick-shift. "Bunch of bullshit!" the old gal shouted, and then stuck up her middle finger. The Civic lurched into gear and belched a cloud of oily smoke. She pulled back out onto the road and drove away.

The agent shook his head and sat back in his SUV. Shortly, a matching vehicle pulled up and parked in the spot hastily vacated by the senior citizen. A man in a dark blue pinstriped suit exited the vehicle. Al-Kanani climbed out of his Chrysler.

"FBI Agent Ibrahim Al-Faqih, welcome to Bellevue," Al-Kanani said.

"Agent Nabil Al-Kanani, this had better be important to get me on a plane from Washington, D.C," Al-Faqih grumbled.

"It is," Al-Kanani said. "Government business always is. This is bigger than anything you know."

***

"I thought we had agreed that you would take some time away after you took care of the Martinez situation. At this hour, it must be important for you to get me out of bed," Leo Giovanni said. "Just lay low until the smoke clears. My sources inside the department tell me that their investigation is at an absolute dead end. They have an APB out on some clown car and George Bush impersonator. Served a subpoena at a local clown college. Carted away boxes of balloons, big red shoes, and jugs of white makeup. Brutalized a bunch of fellows in a balloon animal class. Absolutely insane. I don't know how you do it, Dorian."

"Maybe it is magic," Dorian said emotionlessly. "Kumichō Ito has offered me employment. Maybe that would be for the best for a while."

"You work for me. Magic. That's funny," Leo said. He took a MAXIMUS from the humidor, and then clipped the end off. "Cigar?"

"No, thank you," Dorian said. "Something happened. Something odd, when I was in Portland-"

"That's all that goes on in Portland, my friend. It's why it's Portland," Leo interrupted. He laughed, and then lit the MAXIMUS. The smell of the tobacco as it burned made Dorian more comfortable. Without the smoke, the office did not seem normal. "It doesn't surprise me you saw something unusual in that town. Some guy in studded leather with a dame on a leash. Chicks with dicks. Everyone has a tattoo on their ass. Earrings in their eyebrows. Holes in their cheeks. I'm having a hard time adjusting to this brave new world, Dorian. I don't get it, I guess."

"This man. Knew all about me. Knew about places I had been in Iraq. Said he saw me in Afghanistan. He had powers... abilities that were beyond belief. He demonstrated them to me. Claimed that he was Lucifer. The Devil."

Leo meditated on Dorian's words, and then crossed himself. "Are you sure it wasn't a Fed trying to shake you up, maybe? Playing one of their weird little mind games with you?"

"Mister Giovanni, this guy stopped time. I could sense a power. I honestly believe he was who he said he was," Dorian said. "To say I was scared would be an understatement."

Leo puffed several times at the MAXIMUS, and then blew smoke. "It would make sense, given your lineage—the possibility exists of other supernatural beings showing themselves to you. I'll be honest, Dorian, I struggled with your mother, believing that you were the bastard son of a fallen angel. Honestly, it seemed so far fetched. Until I saw you at that first Karate tournament, that is. You were undefeatable. I knew then that you were more than human. When you moved, it was a blur. You must be part of a greater plan, if The Devil tried to recruit you. It says something about free will. Sounds like you have a choice. I know you have a lot of hard feelings towards the Church, but maybe it's time to consider the reality of the world. You represent something fantastic. It may seem humorous to you, but you have bolstered my faith. If there are angels, there has to be a God, no matter how far removed from us he is."

"That was my last tournament. I do not like being the center of attention. Mister Giovanni- Leo, what if all the odd things I have seen in the last few days are signs of the end?" Dorian asked. "Armageddon."

Leo puffed the cigar, then snorted. "I can only speak from the standpoint as the head of this family. Armageddon will be bad for business. People will lose jobs—have less money to spend on gambling. Drugs. Prostitutes. As the head of this family, our official position is that the Apocalypse and ensuing chaos of Armageddon is extremely bad for the bottom line. Don't let it happen, young man."

Dorian stared. The old man started to smile, and the Giovanni family enforcer started to laugh. "Then I have no choice but to oppose the final battle against good and evil. If I am not going crazy."

"Well, a little evil is all right. Helps keep us in business." Leo laughed. "Too much might be overwhelming. Like overcharging a battery."

"Maybe a little bit," Dorian said.

Chapter Five
—Fire—

The Kushibar Japanese Restaurant in downtown Seattle was unique. Some people called it Oriental kitsch, but it was one of Dorian's favorite restaurants. It was nestled on the southwest side of Second Avenue, near the intersection with Bell Street.

The long, thin restaurant was finished in stained wood that covered the floor. The paneling also covered partway up the concrete wall, and was used for a long, bar-like table that ran half the length of the place. The counter on the other side of the diner was made from the same wood. Plaques lined the wall, painted with Japanese writing. Dorian liked the food and it was always clean.

With all the odd events of the last few days, he decided a break was needed. He ordered his favorite—Yaki Soba noodles with chicken and saké. Dorian sat in the far corner of the restaurant and waited for his food. Always with his back against the wall. Keith had accompanied him for lunch, with the promise of good behavior.

He took the velvet bag from his pocket and the imp climbed out of the sack. Dorian laid a *Bible* down on the table. The demon yawned, stretched and sat by the book.

"So, explain what you know about this antichrist thing to me," Dorian said. "I was not welcomed to church as a child, as you can imagine. I do not really know much other than what I have picked up from movies and such."

"It's like dis. Traditional Christian theology holds dat Jesus will return ta Earth ta face off against da antichrist, who is da greatest false messiah in history. In Islam it is believed dat da *Al-Masih Ad-Dajjal* will appear ta deceive da world. Da actual word antichrist is made of two words—αντί and Χριστός which translates from Greek. It means *against da messiah*. Da antichrist is referred ta dat many times in da New Testament. Some think it's a group of people rather dan one person. Some Protestants, after da reformation, thought dat da Papacy was da antichrist. Mormons think dat it's anyone who fakes da gospel, whether da Devil or his agents," the imp said.

"Mormons," Dorian snorted. "Can't drink coffee."

"Yeah. Anyhows, da Jews didn't have a figure equivalent ta da antichrist. Johnny Rotten, lead singer of da Sex Pistols said he was da man. Seems like he has lost interest in da title, now dat he is older. At his age he's probably just happy ta eat solid food and have a warm glass of milk before his eight o'clock bedtime," Keith laughed. "So I'm not so sure he is da antichrist now. More like da gerontology-christ. A rocking chair and a cup of warm, not too hot Ovaltine, and he is happy."

"Did you learn all about the antichrist when you were in hell?" Dorian asked. "Are demons schooled in such knowledge, or are you just born with it? Collective consciousness? Racial memory?"

"Fuck, no. Wikipedia," the demon said. "You should read sometime. It's good for you."

"I left my books in the bookstore," the enforcer grumbled. "I like books with lots of pictures."

"I wasn't high enough in rank ta know anythin' about da master Armageddon plan. Dis may come as a shock, but I don't know everything. I know what Wikipedia and Bill O' Reilly tell me I need ta know. Fair and balanced, y'know what I mean?"

"I assumed with the Jersey accent, knowing everything came with it," Dorian said. "Show me what I need to know."

Keith flipped through the book. He stopped at 1 John 2:18. The imp cleared his throat dramatically, and then read, *"Little children, it is the last time—and as ye have heard that antichrist shall come, even now are there many antichrists—whereby we know that it is the last time."*

"That is not much help," Dorian said. "Do you have anything more substantial?"

The demon flipped more pages, and then read again, *"And I beheld another beast coming up out of the earth—and he had two horns like a lamb, and he spake as a dragon. And he exerciseth all the power of the first beast before him, and causeth the earth and them which dwell therein to worship the first beast, whose deadly wound was healed. And he doeth great wonders, so that he maketh fire come down from heaven on the earth in the sight of men, and deceiveth them that dwell on the earth by the means of those miracles which he had power to do in the sight of the beast—saying to them that dwell on the earth, that they should make an image to the beast, which had the wound by a sword, and did live. And he had power to give life unto the image of the beast, that the image of the beast should both speak, and cause that as many as would not worship the image of the beast should be killed. And he causeth all, both small and great, rich and poor, free and bond, to receive a mark in their right hand, or in their foreheads—and that no man might buy or sell, save he that had the mark, or the name of the beast, or the number of his name. Here is wisdom. Let him that hath understanding count the number of the beast—for it is the number of a man—and his number is six hundred threescore and six.* Book of Revelations, 13:11 through 18."

"So that is where the number six-six-six comes from? This beast like the lamb is the antichrist? No offense, but it is all pretty cloudy to me," Dorian said.

Keith held his head in hands. "Yer so dense, sometimes. Yeah, da antichrist. His birth on da Earth brings about Armageddon, da end of it all. Some believe he may already exist. I'd read more passages, but without pictures I doubt ya would get it. Trust me on dis. Maybe I could draw a diagram on a cocktail napkin."

"Why would anybody want to bring about the end? It seems kind of like you are throwing the baby out with the bathwater on that one."

"Pfft, Satanists are douche bags, dat's why," the imp said. "When you're in a religion dat gets its power from fatties dancing naked in the woods and smearing yourself with goat's blood, you are pretty far down da food chain. More pathetic dan Unitarians, in my humble opinion."

"Ick. Unitarians. So what now?" Dorian said, exasperatedly.

"Now, da fun begins," the demon said, then crawled back into the velvet bag. "Good luck."

"What?" Dorian asked. "What fun? Huh?"

"Borderline psycho bimbo at dree o'clock," Keith laughed. "Enjoy yer lunch. A side of Prozac would probably help."

Dorian looked up to see Paige Gray as she walked toward him. "Oh, damn," he grumbled. "A whole huge town and she can find me here? What the hell?"

Paige was dressed in a dark blue shirt and short, black skirt. She had on black flats and carried a black purse that matched. Dorian tried to avert his eyes. She made eye contact, smiled and sauntered towards him. He sighed—it was too late. Caught without an avenue of escape.

"Well, what a coincidence," she said. "Mister Dorian Christianson. How are you today? Here for lunch?"

"I am all right, I suppose," he said. "How are you, Miss Gray? Are you a regular here?"

"Good. No, this is my first time," Paige said, then smirked. "I was wondering why you hadn't called me so I could smooth things over from the other day. Are you meeting someone for lunch? I don't mean to interrupt if you are."

"No," Dorian said and forced a smile. "Just me. Kind of a lone wolf thing. Basking in my solitude."

She pointed at the *Bible*. "Are you a religious person? Spiritual? Do you go to church?"

"No," he said and shook his head. "Not really. A little research. I read a lot."

"Interesting," Paige said. "For your job?"

"Not really. Personal edification. Just trying to understand the Good Book. Might even try to be a better person, but it sure seems like a lot of work."

"I think you are a fine person. Well, let me buy you

lunch. I hope you don't think I am too forward," she laughed. "Did you already order? I have never eaten here before."

"I did. Try the Yaki Soba noodles with chicken. I ordered saké. If you do not drink, or if you are in recovery, I will hold off on that," he said. The waiter set a bottle and two small ceramic cups on the table. "Another order of noodles for my friend, please."

"No. I'm not in recovery, but thanks for considering that, I guess. I can't get sloppy drunk in the middle of the day, but I will try some saké if you promise to take it easy on me. I am such a light-weight. A couple beers will put me under," she said and pulled out a chair, unslung her purse, and put it on the table. Paige looked at the velvet bag. "Is that hygienic to put your rodent on the table? Your ass-glider you called it?"

Dorian shook his head, then took the bag and put it in his coat pocket. "Surely not. Especially not that one. Filthy little beast. Always licking themselves. Ick."

"How come you didn't call me?" she asked. "I really

thought you would."

"The 'perverted funeral crasher' thing really took the wind out of my sails, Miss Gray. I did not plan on calling you, actually," he said. "No offense. I do not want to sound too sensitive, but criticism that harsh is never a good way to start a friendship."

Paige shifted nervously on her chair, and then pulled one of the cups to her side of the table. "Yeah. I feel pretty bad about that. I loved my great aunt a lot. It was a tough day and I took it out on you. Honestly, it was more about the funeral than you. Truly, I am sorry. It's amazing you care for people you don't even know. You're a true humanitarian."

"Humanitarian is a pretty strong word," Dorian said and nodded. "I appreciate and accept your heartfelt apology. It is not easy to admit mistakes."

She smiled. "Did you wonder how I found you?" she said.

"Not really. More surprised than anything."

"I was shopping with my friend, across the street,

and I saw you park your car," Paige said, then brushed her blonde hair away from her face. "It probably seems a little stalkerish, but I really wanted to talk to you and to tell you how truly sorry I was for what happened at the funeral."

"It is just a bit stalkerish," Dorian mumbled. He poured the saké in the cups. "Have you had rice wine before?"

"No," she said. "But I am eager to try it."

"This is Seishu, also called clear saké. Some people drink it at room temperature, but I prefer it chilled," he said. "I also prefer mine sweeter, closer to wine. The sweetness is measured by the Nihonshu-do, or the Saké Meter Value. About a minus one is good for me. That means it is a sweet saké."

Paige held the cup close to her nose, sniffed it, and then took a sip. She pursed her perfect lips and smiled. "I bet that's an easy to acquire taste," she laughed. "You sound like a connoisseur."

"I acquired the taste, for sure." Dorian laughed. "I am

glad you like it, since you are buying lunch."

"I saw something in you I liked. Thank you for giving me a chance," Paige said.

Dorian shook his head. "Miss Gray. Please do not read anything into this. I have no interest, other than lunch. I appreciate the peace offering, and the company, but I do not want to seem rude. I am single and plan on staying that way."

She seemed wounded. Her head tilted to the side and her brow furrowed. "Oh, my God. I am so sorry," she whispered. "I didn't even think. Well, I have come off as a hussy. Do you know how hard it is to find a decent man in this town? It's filled with deadbeats, disability frauds, pot-heads, momma's boys, wimps. Of course *you* do. I feel about two inches tall. Of course *you're* not interested in me," she said. "I have been so naïve."

He looked at her inquisitively and his eyebrow arched. "Why are you naïve?" he said. "I don't understand. You lost me in this conversation."

"I am such a fool sometimes. The perfect car. The

perfect clothes. The perfect hair. This is so uncomfortable. I should have seen it." She started to blush. "I thought I was a little more observant. Maybe it's desperation. My biological clock is ticking, and I'm not seeing the forest through the trees. How embarrassing. I sure do know how to pick them."

"I still do not understand," Dorian said.

"You're gay."

The velvet bag in his pocket began to vibrate like a coin-operated bed stuck on the honeymoon setting in a pay-by-the-hour hotel. A hysterical, muffled laugh emanated from his pocket. The enforcer stared indifferently at Paige.

"Is that your phone?" she asked.

Dorian started to talk, nodded his head, and then angrily tapped his pocket hard several times. "Cell phone. I downloaded the *'asshole laughing hysterically'* ringtone. Ignore it."

"Well, I hope we can be friends," Paige said, then laughed nervously. She fanned her face with her hand. "I can pick them. It sure got hot in here all of a sudden. Oh, my God, not the first time—probably not the last time."

"I am not gay," Dorian grumbled after a long pause. "It's the in thing right now, I understand. Not for me, however. I can't say I'm flattered."

Paige squinted. "Are you sure?" she said quietly. "It's totally ok. I won't judge."

"I think I would know," he said flatly. "I like women. For sure. Thanks for assuming I don't."

She took another sip of saké. "Maybe I am getting too old to be single. I'm not used to chasing men. It has been a long time since I have been in a relationship. There is just something about you I like, Dorian. I think the fact that you worry about how a stranger might feel after the death of a family member shows an amazing sensitivity for others. You have an odd magnetism about you."

He took a deep breath, leaned back and gulped a swallow of saké for bravery. "I would like to lay it all out on the table, so to speak, but I'm not sure you can handle it," he said.

"I'm pretty tough, Dorian. Lay it out. I'm an adult," she said with a smirk.

"Ok then. So my second tour in Iraq ended badly. It was after two tours in Afghanistan, so I was pretty weary of all of it. It is so hot over there. Most of the people there are just numb. Life means nothing to them—it is a culture of death. Long before we invaded, long before anyone heard of Saddam Hussein, George Bush or Kuwait, death was the ultimate currency. A hundred and five, maybe ten or fifteen degrees every day in the shade in the summer. No rain for months. Sand in everything. No grass. There comes a point, that the mission just seems pointless. It is not just the endless brown-gray-tan of the terrain, and the homes, or if you are in an area that has hills. It just seems pointless after a time. You are just fighting for the guy beside you. Fighting for your team, for everyone to get home alive, fighting to get back to grass again. I had no one left since my mom died—those guys were the closest thing to family I had.

So, then my team is blown up in an IED attack on a little road on the north side of town. After several weeks in the hospital in Germany, I came home. The doctors were amazed at how fast I healed. Miraculously, they said. That is a story for another day. So my body put itself back together from wounds that should have killed me, but not my mind. My mind was not healed. It was shattered to bits. Not broken, but shattered in a million depressed pieces. I always thought I was strong enough to withstand whatever the world threw at me. I wasn't."

"I'm sorry about your friends," Paige said. "What a horrible experience in such a horrible place. There's a reason that they say war is hell."

Dorian shook his head and continued, "Not just friends. Those guys had become my family. So I came home to her. We had been together on and off through my time in the military. I carried a lot of pain with me. Not just physical—emotional. Then I came home to a woman so distant, so cruel, that I decided to end the pain that my four tours had left me with. There was no support, no light at the end of the tunnel. I was the only survivor from the explosion under that Humvee that killed my military family, and it hurt inside. I should have died with them. The night I finally worked up the courage to kill myself, I held the pistol in my hand and stared at it for the longest while. She always had time for everyone else. Always had time to text her ex-boyfriends, run into them at the mall, send them emails about how much she still thought of them, message them on Facebook, be so proud that they were still friends. She was in her usual place in the living room, in front of the television, ignoring me. It was a Wednesday night. I had held the gun to my head for several minutes. With the last bit of self-preservation I could muster, I put the gun on the corner of the bed and asked her to hide it. A moment of self-serving cowardice that, to a certain extent, I still regret. She was busy watching American Idol, and could not be bothered with my petty concerns about life, death, or wanting to die. I fought with every ounce of strength I had to just grab the pistol and fire it into my head. I fought it until I fell asleep. I woke up in the morning, and that pistol was still on the corner of the bed. She did not want to miss any of her show to hide the gun. She fell asleep in front of the television, like she always did. She was too busy. In the end, I was worth less to her than American Idol. There is a little bit of me that is ashamed I did not blow a hole in my head that day. Just to prove a point to her. In a way, it is a secret shame that I live with every day. I never thought of myself as a coward until I survived that night. Truth is, I am a horrible coward for being trapped like that, and for not being willing to pull the trigger when the time came. I had no problem pulling the trigger on other people. That determination did not surface when it came to firing a gun at myself."

"I'm glad you didn't kill yourself," she said quietly. "She doesn't sound like she cared that much. Not every woman is like that."

"So you can imagine, Paige Gray, as nice as you seem, as immensely attractive as I think you are, as intelligent as you are, and as flattered that I am that you stalked me here today when you saw my car, I am just not interested. I have wasted about as much time in my life with women who spend all their time with me sulking about Jim, Chad, and all the other guys who spent their college years polishing their nobs. I am done hearing about the ex-boyfriends who made you who you are today, and how wonderful they were. I am done, Miss Gray. Relationships are for suckers. I have no desire to repeat the same mistakes with you, or anyone for that matter. Thank you for lunch. I hope I did not come off as insensitive or disengaged. Any flirting or small talk that you think might lead down the relationship road is a waste of time. For you and for me. I have already had one too many things explode under me—it may be a clumsy comparison of an IED and relationships, but I think it is accurate. I am worth more than American Idol and will never risk being less important to anyone than a moronic television show again."

Paige shook her head, and stood. "I just wanted to

say I was sorry. I'm not her. The war is over, Dorian. All of them, if you and her have separated," she said. With a shaky hand she wiped an eye, picked up her purse and stalked out of the Kushibar. The enforcer watched her leave in silence.

The waiter brought two bowls of Yaki Soba noodles with chicken. Dorian watched the steam rise from the bowls. He watched her exit the restaurant. She did have great legs. A sudden pang of guilt tightened his stomach. That was way too harsh.

"Dammit," Dorian said. "I laid it on a little thick."

"Sir, can I get you anything else?" the waiter asked.

Dorian shook his head. "No. Just the check.

The waiter brought the check, and then Keith climbed out of the enforcer's pocket. He picked up a chopstick and used it to stab at a piece of chicken in one of the bowls. "Dames are crazy. Ya know what I'm sayin', brother? But, bipolar donut or not, it would be a worse shame if 'dese here Yaki Soba noodles went to waste."

"She was just trying to apologize. I was way too rude.

I think I just fucked up."

The imp slurped a long noodle from the bowl. "Dis is how dis shit starts. I suppose you're gonna track her down to apologize," he said while he sucked another long noodle down. "Dames. It's about da hot legs and sweet ass. Creates weakness and it just ends up being trouble."

***

Tessa Paul was up late struggling with algebra at the kitchen table. Logarithms were not her thing. She reworked the problem, looked at the book, and then put it together again. The goal was to look as studious as possible. Her mom, Serenity, had found her E-cig and she was going to be in trouble when Nicholas got home.

She listened as the garage door opener whined. The clock on the microwave read 9:35 p.m. Tessa could hear the steps of her father as he came up the stairs from the garage into the mud room adjacent to the kitchen. For courage, she downed two swallows of ice-cold Dr. Pepper from the glass in front of her.

"So," Nicholas said, "how was your day?"

She looked up from her textbook. "I've probably had better. How was yours?"

The detective kicked off his shoes and headed for the refrigerator. "So, I get this call from your mom. Says she found an E-cig in your backpack. Are you using one?"

"I could lie and say I was holding for someone else, but it's mine."

He pawed in the icebox until he found a nectarine and then closed the door. "Needless to say, your mother was in full freak-out mode. You know they are illegal in King County for minors, right? That you could get a ticket if you get caught with one of those."

"Yeah."

Nicholas bit into the fruit, then wiped the corner of his mouth with his finger. "Is there anything else I should know about?"

Tessa rolled her eyes. "Oh. My. God. Just the orgies, Dad. Just the orgies. Oh yeah, and I should mention I am a prostitute. Sounded like a better career choice than college. No student loans to pay. Dave Ramsey likes that—it's an all cash industry. Do you wanna see the glass table I just bought? At least it's a business expense. I saved the receipt. Seems like this is a good time to tell you about it. My pimp is coming over later for tea and crumpets."

"Funny. Barrel of monkeys funny. Super glued to the toilet seat in a Home Depot funny. Donner Party cannibalism funny." The Detective took another bite, then retreated to the cupboard and found a granola bar. He opened it, devoured it in three bites, and returned to the fridge for another nectarine. "I really don't need this right now. This case that I have been loaned to Bellevue on is a dead end, and now I have the feds up my ass. You wouldn't believe how many conference calls a day they require. I don't have time for these little things, Tessa. I rely on you just to get along without me having to micromanage your every move. I thought I was clear on drugs, drinking, and smoking. No fly territory."

"Are E-cigs smoking?" she said. "It's just water vapor.

With flavors."

"No, and I would rather have you using an E-cig than real cigarettes. There better not be any more surprises. Pot. Alcohol. You hear me?" he grumbled. "I will let this go and smooth it over with Mom. It ends at E-cigs. I don't want to be the dad who buys home drug tests because we have run out of trust. I trust you. Don't blow it."

"There is nothing else," Tessa said. "I just want to fit in, but I don't want to smoke. Don't like the taste. Don't like the smell on my clothes."

"What kind of friends require you to smoke to fit in? If you have to jump off a bridge to fit in, they are not the right kind of friends," Nicholas said. "I know it's hard at your age, but when you get older you will realize those kind of friends are fair-weather. They won't last very long. Lifelong friends are precious commodities and you don't have to ruin your health to have them."

"You know them, Angela and Marisol. They don't pressure me... much," she said. "Plus they help me with algebra, during study hall."

"Those two sisters have been wickedly weird since the fifth grade when they moved here," Nicholas snorted. "Now it's black clothes, black hair, little pentagram earrings, spider-web tattoos. I don't get the whole Goth thing anyway. Your friends are yours so I stay out of it, but it doesn't surprise me that they smoke. Their parents are weird, too. They might all be vampires."

"They go out in the sun and survive. They think it's weird you're a cop, Dad." Tessa laughed.

"Maybe they just think they are vampires," he said and trudged towards the stairs, caught himself and quickly doubled back to kiss her on the cheek. "Long day. No more trouble, you hear me? Love you."

"I hear you," she said. "Love you, too!"

***

Leo Giovanni leaned back in his overstuffed office chair and puffed thoughtfully on a MAXIMUS cigar. Rocco shifted uncomfortably in the same chair he was in when he tried so hard to provoke Dorian.

"So if they end up not paying, how deep are they into us now?" Leo asked.

"Three shipments. Three bricks each. Feels like we have become more of a savings and loan business. Does anyone pay upfront anymore?" Rocco grumbled. "It's the economy. In the toilet. These dealers think they can move this stuff and they can't. The Satanists said they could move this stuff through their brothers, the Wiccans. Lighter side of the same coin."

"It's your job to vet these assholes, Rocco," Leo grumbled. "We aren't the March of Dimes. I have misgivings about all this drug business anyway, and these endless problems with these two-bit hoods pound the nails deeper into the coffin. Dealing with devil worshippers gives me the creeps."

"Their money spends the same as any other business we're in. Protection, prostitution, gambling, guns. This drug thing makes a lot of money. I like the lifestyle," Rocco said. "With higher risks come higher rewards.

Balloon payments on the Mercedes. Cruises in the Caribbean."

"I can't even tell you when my last vacation was," Leo grumbled. "All this drama. Squeeze those devil worshippers and let's see some cash. If they don't pay, what's your plan B, Rocco?"

"Send your enforcer to collect. It's his job," the younger mobster said. "I hope if we do, he doesn't come back with a bunch of bric-a-brac or Green Stamps. It's ridiculous what he does sometimes."

Leo puffed the MAXIMUS. He blew several rings into the air, and leaned back. "You get us into bed with these deadbeats, and then he collects? I have my doubts about your business model," he muttered. "Lean on those assholes and get our money out of them. You hear me? Get my investment back."

"We need to put some fear into people," Rocco said. "Dorian needs to do his job."

"His last job was high profile. He needs to lay low a bit. Cops have no idea about it. My sources in the BPD are clueless. They're looking for a clown car. Literally," Leo said. "My one question is, if your devil worshipping clients are moving three bricks every two weeks, they are at least six weeks behind, if my calculations are correct. Seems like this got out of hand pretty quickly."

Rocco shifted nervously again. "It takes money to make money. I was trying to give them the grace period to get capitol moving," he said. "Once they see profits, they will settle up."

"They had better," Leo grumbled.

***

ATF Agent Nabil Al-Kanani and FBI Agent Ibrahim Al-Faqih were on speakerphone on a conference call with Detective Nicholas Paul. On another line was Detective Quinn Webb. The discussion had been heated. No forward motion in the investigation had the feds stirred up.

"We have a lot of irons in the fire here, Detective Paul," Al-Kanani said. "We cannot devote any more resources to this than we already have. You've made no noticeable progress on this case."

"I'm open to suggestions," Paul said.

"Have you hard pressed your only surviving witness, Jill Washington yet?" Al-Faqih said.

"The psychiatrist at Harborview and the team working with her say she is so deep into her Post Traumatic Stress Disorder she is unresponsive to questions about the shooting. The woman is on enough meds to tranquilize an elephant," Webb said. "We have tried to speak with her every day, but she just melts down on us. We have done a bit more research on her. Group homes, foster care, several inpatient stays in psych hospitals. She had quite a history of trauma before witnessing the events of the other day. I would not count on anything from her in the near future."

"I will give it a couple days, then go talk to her if there is no forward motion," the ATF Agent said. "I can be very persuasive."

"No offense, but Washington is our witness," Paul said matter-of-fact. "I see an overstep of jurisdictional boundaries."

"Those AK's put the ball in our court," Al-Kanani said. "We were hoping the locals could put something together here, but Attorney General Holder's people have been less than impressed by the lack of progress in this case. We apologize for the appearance of crossing boundaries, but we are going to move ahead on our end. I will interview this Washington woman and see what can be learned."

"For the record, I think this may end badly," Detective Paul said.

"I concur," Detective Webb said.

"You let us worry about that," Al-Faqih said. "What is in the record is what we in the Federal Government say, ends up in the record. For the record, Detective."

***

Late in the evening, two days after Dorian had the altercation with Paige in the Kushibar, he backed the Cayman into a space in the parking garage of Harborview Medical. He found a space near the exit on the ground floor.

The giant hospital complex covered several city blocks of Seattle. It was located a quarter of the way toward the center of the city. Eight blocks to the west were the ferries that carried traffic over Elliott Bay. To the east, forty city blocks away, was Lake Washington. All told, the giant complex of buildings, parking lots, and sky bridges sprawled easily over eleven blocks. The burn unit was located on 9th Avenue, near the corner of Alder, in a large building named the East Clinic.

UW Medicine Regional Burn Center at Harborview opened in 1974, and had seen well over twenty thousand burn patients in those decades. World class burn treatment was provided to all manner of burns. The center was a pioneer in the field of skin grafts and the removal of burned tissue. The survival rate of a burn victim treated there was ninty-seven percent, and a third of its patients were children.

"I just want ta go on record dat dis plan sucks," Keith spat. "Women are trouble. How do ya even know she is workin' today, anyhows?"

Dorian looked down at the imp. "I called and asked if I could deliver something to Nurse-Practitioner Paige Gray. Sounded very official. They would not tell me the hours she worked. I asked when the latest delivery would get to her and they said eight—therfore she is here now. So I'm going to try to time this right and catch her at work. The only other way to figure out when she works is to hover around the parking lots. That seems kind of stalkerish."

"Da whole ding seems stalkerish. She's rubbed off on you. So how do ya know how ta find her? Dey ain't gonna let you wander around dis ten-story hospital aimlessly askin' for some dame," the demon complained. "Fancy places got security. Why ya would waste good chocolate on some bimbo is beyond me. We should eat it. Maybe we'll get lucky and dis broad is allergic. She gets a whiff of da goodies and she puffs up like a Ball Park Frank. Dat would make my day."

"Nurses would probably be at a nurse's station,

right? It is not that complicated of a plan. She is somewhere in the East Building. Anyway, it is not your problem. You stay with the car."

"At least crack da window so I don't suffocate while you are *whining* and dining dis broad. If I promise to be good can I go in?" Keith begged.

Dorian glared at the imp. "Apologizing is not whining and dining. It is wining, not whining."

The demon stuck up his tiny porcine paw. "You will be whining. Whatever. Talk ta da hand. Use my real name ta make me behave den, if you have dat little trust in our relationship. Yer startin' to sound like dis dame ya got da hots for. Wanna play doctor with her?"

"Hardly. And I do not think that will be necessary to compel you to stay out of trouble," Dorian said. "Just behave. Maybe you would be useful to black out the cameras. Ferret out Paige's location so that I do not have to wander aimlessly. We will be in and out a lot quicker if you cooperate."

"Fine. I'll do it. Besides, humans can't see me anyway

unless I want dem to, so really, dey don't know when I misbehave. Just you," Keith said. "Dey think its wind, or coincidence, or whatever. Superstitious lot, humans are."

"That is comforting," Dorian grumbled as the demon leapt to his shoulder, then climbed into the bag in his pocket. The enforcer grabbed a package off of the passenger seat of the Cayman and tucked it under his arm.

"On my best behavior," the muffled voice of the imp called out.

***

ATF Agent Nabil Al-Kanani watched as the psych techs wrestled with Jill Washington. One of the Seattle Medical Center nurses drew up a syringe filled with Haloperidol Lactate and a massive dose of Benadryl to quiet her screaming. Enough chemicals might give her some solace. It was doubtful, but they tried.

Her mind was already fractured—he could see that when he touched her mind. The pervert uncle, the handsy PE teacher in grade school, years in sub-standard foster homes. The life of drugs and prostitution that started at age sixteen, the heavy hand of a merciless pimp. At best, Jill's emotional tank was on empty.

So when Al-Kanani entered her mind, it couldn't handle the stress of such an *unnatural* presence. Couldn't handle as Nabil psychically gnawed her fragile ego to the core. Mined her soul for information, eating what he wanted and regurgitating the rest back into her brain. Fragments of memory arrived in a shattered, vomitus form with no regard to her recollections. To call it rape would be a step backwards in how he treated her fragile mind.

Now she was shattered beyond repair.

Her mind didn't possess much more information than what the hidden video revealed outside of Kerr Martinez's apartment. There was that sense of distant divinity, however, as he looked through her eyes at the shooter. Long black coat, twin pistols, dark scarf pulled up over his face. Whatever made the murderer divine was not readily apparent, but Nabil knew that there was something unusual.

Al-Kanani walked down the sterile corridor. His shoes clicked on the linoleum floor, and he stopped at the elevator. A thick finger stabbed the down button and he impatiently tapped his foot. Something caught his attention.

At first the distance clouded his perceptions, but Al-Kanani sensed a presence. He discounted it at first, and then cocked his head from the left to the right. A faint... divinity danced at the edges of his inhuman awareness. How could that be? Somehow, the very being that shot up the apartment in Bellevue, the ghost that had vanished without so much as a trace was nearby. As unbelievable as it was, the gunman so sought after was about to fall into his lap.

Al-Kanani pulled his pistol from its holster, double-checked the magazine, then the safety mechanism. He doubted the man he sought would listen to reason. The ATF Agent needed to find this mysterious being and understand his unique state.

Then crush him to a pulp.

***

Dorian walked into the 8th Avenue Entrance of Harborview Medical Center. Through the entrance, a hallway would go through the massive building and turn to the right. That is where the Burn Center was located. He looked up, pushed his glasses squarely on his face, and straightened his tie. Then he surveyed the ten floors that pointed into the cloudy sky and entered the glass doors.

"Keith, make sure there are no security cameras leaving evidence of our visit today," the enforcer ordered.

"You got it, boss," the imp said and climbed out of his pocket. He sprouted wings and took flight towards the hospital.

"Should I ask what image you're projecting into the cameras?" the enforcer said.

"Just leave dat to me," Keith laughed. "Mostly static,

but I got some good ones. I'm a professional at dis."

"That is what worries me."

Once through a double glass door airlock, Dorian looked around. The inside was spotless and smelled of hospital disinfectant that had been recirculated by ducts. Flat dark-blue carpet dominated the reception area. To his left were several large waiting areas furnished with industrial furniture and a water cooler. Many of the chairs and love seats had people sitting in them, no doubt waiting for appointments or for loved ones to reemerge from doctor's visits.

A small art gallery was in the large lobby area. Diverse artworks, many abstract, focused on healing and medicine were displayed. The theme of comfort and restoration dominated the images, and in some small way they soothed Dorian. Corridors led to the left and right past an information desk. Behind a large laminated-topped desk sat an old woman. A flat-panel monitor and a keyboard sat on top of the reception desk. A sign on the desk said *information*, and the woman quietly read a

National Geographic Magazine. She wore a name tag that said *Barbie-Volunteer*. Dorian sauntered up to the desk and the demon landed on his shoulder, and then climbed down his arm onto the laminate desktop.

Invisible to the old gal, the imp pressed a tiny hand against her time-ravaged tit and concentrated. He turned as he pawed the fabric of her blouse, grinned devilishly at the enforcer who just sighed and shook his head. Keith tweaked her breast before he climbed back up Dorian's arm. The woman absentmindedly scratched where the demon had ruffled her feathers.

She looked up. "Can I help you?" she asked.

"She's on da fifth floor." Keith giggled. "Straight drough dis long corridor past dis old bag. Den, after a decent walk, we turn ta da right. Another long corridor will lead ta da East Clinic, den ta da elevators. On da fifth floor, da nursing station is back toward da heart of da building, to da left. Dat's probably yer best bet ta find your bimbo."

"No, thank you," Dorian said to the woman, and

walked down a hallway toward the elevator. "A new low. You molested a senior citizen."

"Pfft. Barbie was into threesomes when she was younger. Ah, da eighties. What a decade of decadence," the imp snickered. "Those aren't real, anyway. Holdin' up well, considerin' da age of da implants. Silicone is an amazing substance. We live in an age of miracles and wonders, dat a gal on social security can have such perky titties. Besides, she ain't da first senior citizen I've groped. I love dis mud ball!"

Dorian walked through the building, then to the right. After a fair walk, he found the elevator and stabbed at the *up* button with his finger. He waited quietly and looked around, first to the right and then to the stairway doors to the left. The elevator buzzed and the doors opened. The enforcer waited for the passengers to leave the lift, and then he entered and rode to the fifth floor of the East Building.

The doors slid open. He peered out of the elevator, looked to the stairwell now on his right, then long corridor on the left. The sound of someone in pain reached his ears. A moan echoed down a distant hallway. Dorian sauntered down the long corridor until it split. Hallways went to the left and forward. He went to the left, then followed the corridor into the heart of the fifth floor until he found the nurse's station.

The station was a half-counter that enclosed a workspace. Computer monitors and files were on a laminated desktop attached to the inner side of the counter. A candy dish sat near the corner of the station. Two attendants, a man and a woman, looked at files. The woman glanced up and smiled.

"May I help you?" she said.

Dorian's mouth went dry suddenly. "Nurse Practitioner Page Gray, please. I have something for her," he blurted out.

The woman looked at the male attendant who smiled a toothy smile. The enforcer could see a nametag on the female that said *Mae-Nurse*. "Just a minute," she purred. "Let me see if she is available."

"I do not want to interrupt her if she is busy," Dorian stammered. "She is not expecting me."

"No problem," Mae said. "Who can I tell her is here to see her?"

"Dorian Christianson," he said, and then tried to swallow.

"Dorian Christianson, young and in love," the demon chirped, and then he made slurping-smooching noises.

"Knock it off," Dorian whispered.

"I'm sorry, I missed that," Mae said.

"I said thanks for your help," Dorian retorted unconvincingly.

She stood and moved with purpose through the nurse's station into a doorway in the back of the workspace.

The imp cackled on the enforcer's shoulder. "I've seen enough movies ta know how dis is gonna end. In da broom closet. Oh Dorian, it's so... average. Take me with yer forgettable mediocrity. It will be like porn, just really boring. Quick, too, I bet."

"The kind of movies you watch always end up with sex in the broom closet, you little pervert," Dorian hissed. The male attendant looked up at him suspiciously. Dorian nodded and forced a smile.

"You ok?" the male nurse asked. His nametag read *Rex*.

"Yeah. Just a little nervous," the enforcer said.

"Paige is a great woman. I can see why," Rex said, and then smirked. "Great catch. A lot of guys will be jealous."

"I am not catching anyone," Dorian said emotionlessly. "Just here to apologize a little bit."

"Do a little horizontal mambo action. Play a little doctor with Doctor Gray," Keith snorted. He morphed into a demonic version of Miley Cyrus, and then began to twerk crudely. He opened his mouth and a long, pink tongue unrolled down Dorian's shoulder. "Spank me, Daddy."

The enforcer swatted the demonic Miley from his shoulder. The imp tumbled through the air until he/she sprouted wings and recovered. He/she glided slowly in a circle, and then landed in the candy dish. Hershey's miniatures scattered as Keith turned back into his tiny, piggy self and wriggled under the sweets. Only his spiked red tail stuck up through the confections. It writhed as the demon gorged.

The drama with the imp unfolded invisibly to Rex. "Well, good luck with that, my friend," the nurse laughed.

Dorian shifted nervously at the counter. The sound of shoes echoed down a corridor slowly, and then he saw her as she turned the corner to his right. Paige was dressed in a white lab coat over a red blouse and black skirt. A name tag was over her heart—*Paige G.-NP*. Her flats quietly made contact as she padded down the hallway toward him.

Her face was expressionless. Neither joy nor anger as she approached him. Paige stopped, and then leaned up against a wall. The enforcer ambled towards her, then stopped in front of her. Dorian hung his head slightly, almost demurely.

"I do not mean to disturb you at work like this," he said. "What you do is very important."

"But you have," she said through perfect, taut lips. She tensed. "I hope it is important."

"It is important to me. Seems like we have become a ping-pong game of apologies. I want to stop and start over. I brought you this," Dorian said quietly. He held up a gift wrapped in paper.

Paige slowly unwrapped the paper and held up a box. It was small carton of candy bound with a pink ribbon. Tucked inside the ribbon was a single purple iris and a card. Her flat expression hinted at a smile and she opened the tiny envelope and relaxed. It was a gift card to the Kushibar Japanese Restaurant.

"It is a great place to eat. You can take anyone you want, now. Ask for the Yaki Soba noodles with chicken. Order Seishu, the clear saké, and you want it-"

"Chilled," Paige interrupted. "Minus one on the Nihonshu-do. Sweet like wine. I've been reading about it. What's in the box?"

"Chocolates. From a little candy shop downtown called Fran's Chocolates. They make everything there. You might have heard of it. Best salted caramels and dark chocolate truffles in the world. You eat candy, right?" Dorian said.

"I will manage to choke them down," she said, then lifted the iris to her nose and inhaled the sweet bouquet of the flower. "Best in the world. I love Fran's."

Dorian held out his hand. "Can we start over? Forget what went on before. Part ways as friends?"

Paige smiled, then reached up and took off his sunglasses and folded them. She gently pushed them into his jacket pocket. She took his hand in hers. "Yeah. But, now I have this card to the Kushibar. I don't want to use it by myself. We don't have to part ways."

"You can take anyone you want. It is a gift card," Dorian said.

"Then I want to take you," she said and smiled. "Mister Dorian Christianson. Nice to meet you."

"The pleasure is all mine, Miss Paige Gray," he said. "It is nice to meet you. I am sorry about being so rude the other day."

Paige patted his shoulder. "We're starting over, remember? You're forgiven."

"Thanks."

"So, Mister Christianson, I know you already think I am a stalker. How come no matter how hard I search for you on the internet, I can't find you? No Facebook, no Twitter, nothing. I even tried to spell your name different ways. No electronic imprint at all, that I can find," Paige said. "It's like you don't exist."

"I like my privacy," he said quietly. "Business stuff. I have a lot of nurses stalking me. It's a tough life."

Dorian looked past her down the corridor at movement. A large figure in a dark suit strode confidently towards the pair.

"This might be trouble," he said quietly. "Paige. You need to leave. Now."

She stared at him. "I work here. I will not leave, no

matter what."

As the figure got closer, Dorian could see him as he was. Six-foot-six, thick arms, muscles like coiled steel. This guy could have been a linebacker. It had no eyes as humans could understand them. Just eye sockets, black and empty holes, as if someone had torn the orbs out. Small horns jutted out from either side of the creature's head. His teeth were sharp and set like that of a piranha. Its skin was rough and dark with a bluish tint, its crimson tongue forked like a snake. He had seen a creature like this before. His mind returned to Iraq.

Azizz Al-Sudiari had been a colonel in Saddam Hussein's feared Iraqi Intelligence Service, the Jihaz Al-Mukhabarat Al-Amma. The IIS were cold men, feared for their brutality by the Iraqi population. The IIS used violence to keep the Arab Socialist Ba'ath Party in power. The colonel worked in Directorate 9, Secret Operations, the group that worked mostly outside Iraq. They specialized in murder and sabotage. The April 1993 attempted assassination of former President George

H.W. Bush had been a Directorate 9 operation. They were good—the only thing that kept the assassination from being successful was that the CIA was better.

During the Iraq war, the colonel had escaped coalition forces and was commanding a unit of resistance fighters near Fallujah. In the days following the initial invasion, large numbers of military and intelligence slunk into the shadows to conduct covert operations against the Americans and their allies. Al-Sudiari led one of those groups.

During Dorian's first tour in Iraq, Al-Sudiari was targeted by the CIA. After a two hour running firefight through the edge of Fallujah and several artillery rounds, the colonel was the last man left standing in his group of insurgents. Bleeding from shrapnel and bullet wounds that would have killed a normal man, he was apprehended. It wasn't until he escaped from coalition imprisonment without a trace that the enforcer realized what exactly he had captured. He could see Al-Sudiari for what he was—the rest of his unit couldn't see anything but the Iraqi captive.

"Seriously. You need to get out of here," Dorian said.

"What do you mean?" Paige said angrily, and then looked over her shoulder at the approaching man. "My shift isn't over for another hour. Friend of yours?"

"Doubtful," he said quietly. "He does not look like he wants friends."

The giant pulled a wallet from his pocket and held it up. Dorian looked into the empty sockets that should have been eyes. The case opened in his hand to show federal credentials.

"Agent Nabil Al-Kanani, Department of Alcohol, Tobacco, and Firearms. We need to speak," Al-Kanani growled. "I've been looking for you. It is fortuitous for me that our paths have crossed. Probably not so much for you, however."

"For me?"

"Yeah. For you," the monster breathed.

"Dorian, what is going on?" Paige asked.

The eyeless fiend smirked and glanced at her

nametag. "More than you know, Paige. The best thing you could do now would be to walk away."

"I certainly will not. This is my floor. I work here, Mister Al-Kanani. This is a hospital. Whatever issues you have, you need to take them outside," Paige ordered. "There are patients resting."

The agent leaned towards Dorian. "She doesn't see me as you see me, I can tell," he hissed, then reached up and laid his strong, meaty right hand on the enforcer's shoulder. Long talons dug into the Louis Vuitton. He wiggled his finger, and then traced the strap of the shoulder holster under the jacket. "Leave the normal human out of this. Let's go outside and talk."

"Am I being detained?" Dorian asked quietly. "Arrested?"

The monster grinned. The jagged teeth glinted menacingly in the glow of the fluorescent tube lights above their heads. "We will call it an arrest, but you know that is the last thing this is. At the very least. I am curious about your nature, your spark of divinity. Yet it is tainted somehow. You are a marvelous riddle to solve. "

"What the hell is he talking about?" Paige questioned. "Normal human? Divinity? Like the candy?"

"Oh. She's marvelously naïve. How quaint she doesn't know what you are."

Dorian reached over the agent's right arm, then under and slid his arm into the notch by Al-Kanani's elbow. He pushed up a little, locked the joint out, then smashed his head against the jaw of the fed. The empty eye sockets opened wide in surprise as black blood splattered from the impact.

Al-Kanani staggered back a bit, but his outstretched arm kept him from retreating. Dorian rammed his head against the agent's face twice more, then punched him in the nose. The monster then caught an attempted third punch and stared with nothing but the hollow sockets.

"So, that is the way it is, eh?" Al-Kanani said. He lifted Dorian up by the locked out arm and flung him across the hallway like a rag doll.

Paige screamed and dropped the box of chocolates.

Dorian slammed against the wall, and then dropped into a crouch on the industrial linoleum floor. The agent reached over and popped his right arm back into socket. The joint crunched wetly and he winced ever so slightly. Al-Kanani strode toward the enforcer and they both drew pistols.

The pair leveled their guns at each other. Dorian was just a split-second faster and his Heckler and Koch HK 45 barked. The two hundred thirty grain bullet travelled at one thousand feet per second, and struck its target with five hundred and ten foot pounds of energy. The target was the agent's gun. His pistol, a Sig P228 shattered as the .45 bullet penetrated the slide of the gun.

The force knocked the Sig out of Al-Kanani's hand, and pieces of the firearm clattered across the linoleum floor. Paige screamed again and ducked for cover in the nurse's station.

Dorian was in motion before the fragments of the agent's pistol had come to a stop. He lunged forward, and then slid feet first between the legs of the dark-suited monster. As he slid, he drew his second pistol and crossed his arms. When he passed between Al-Kanani's legs, he fired a round into the side of each knee of the monster.

Al-Kanani grunted and fell forward onto his face. Dorian then proceeded to put two rounds into the back of the prone agent. He holstered one of his pistols and went into the nurse's station. Paige was crouched behind the counter. The enforcer reached down, grabbed her by the wrist and yanked her up to her feet.

"We have to get out of here. Now!" Dorian ordered.

"Oh, my God, you killed that man!" she shrieked.

"No, I did not," he answered as he pulled her down the hall. "He is not a man as you understand it."

Al-Kanani looked up at the pair. He stood, and for a split second the mirage that kept him concealed from the world weakened and his real visage was visible. Paige's feet stumbled as she stared at him.

"What was that? He doesn't have any eyes!" she shouted. "Where are they?"

"His eyes are not as you understand them, either," Dorian said. "But he sees us, just fine."

Al-Kanani stood, and then extended his right hand. His legs wobbled as black blood poured from his knees and the wounds in his back. Sparks emerged from his palm, like a welder as it cut metal. Silver liquid swirled and flowed into the air. Slowly it ran, as if contained in an invisible mold. The molten metal began to take form, contained by unseen forces.

Dorian stabbed at the elevator button. The down arrow above the door lit. He could feel Paige shake uncontrollably and took her hand in his. "We need to get away from here. Understand? We are going to get in the elevator and get the hell out of here," he said angrily. "He is dangerous."

The metal began to coalesce and harden in a long shaft that emanated from Al-Kanani's hand. Sparks from the molten steel scattered and danced. Slowly, it rolled and formed a huge, curved sword as tall as Paige.

"Dorian! What is happening?" Paige shrieked. "What

is he? Why does he look like that?"

He stared as the molten metal found its final form. Al-Kanani tightened his meaty hand around the handle of the scimitar, and then swung it several times in a circle. His lips pulled back and bared those jagged teeth, and he advanced toward the pair. Dorian leveled his pistol and the giant swung the sword in front of him. The enforcer fired the pistol and emptied the magazine at the ATF Agent. Most of the bullets ricocheted off the thick, sharp blade. One bullet found its mark and dark blood erupted from Al-Kanani's suit. He seemed to realize his illusion or normality had dropped, and it shimmered back into place. The demonic look vanished and his human concealment returned.

Dorian could still see his true form though. He holstered his pistol and drew the other one. Keith ran across the floor towards the elevator door in his humanoid form. His tiny black feet skidded across the linoleum and he slammed to a stop against the closed elevator door.

"Jesus Christ on a crutch, boss, do you see dat thing? Holy hell!" The imp looked up and squealed, visible only to the enforcer. "I ain't seen one of dem since Afghanistan! How da hell did dat ding get a government job? Don't dey do backgrounds checks?"

"ATF has low standards," Dorian growled as the elevator bell chimed. The doors slid opened and the enforcer pushed Paige into the car. He reached into his jacket pocket and put on his gloves.

Al-Kanani charged the doors and the hydraulics slid the elevator entry shut. The car lurched downwards, and then stopped. The sound of metal shrieked, and then drowned out the hum of the elevator. A deafening clunk echoed in the enclosed space, the lights flickered, and the huge blade of the scimitar pierced the metal door of the elevator. Sparks flew as the steel of the sword scraped against the door. Paige screamed and fell backwards against the wall. Dorian stepped back as the blade vanished through the gash it had cut in the plate aluminum door. He stood back as the blade once again jutted through the door.

"He's a fuckin' psycho!" Keith shouted.

"I had not noticed!" Dorian retorted. He braced his back against the wall, and then pushed his feet against the giant blade that protruded into the car. With all his strength he pressed against the giant cleaver where it was impaled through the door. The force kept the cleaver from moving. He could feel the giant tug at the blade, but it was pinned in the door from the pressure the enforcer applied. The motor of the elevator ground loudly as it tried to move the car. Somewhere an alarm sounded in the hospital.

Dorian tried to keep the blade in place. The weight of the car suspended against the sword, combined with the tugs from Al-Kanani on the other side, made it impossible to keep it trapped. The car dropped and the scimitar cut upwards. The scream of the tortured metal drowned out Paige's shrieks. Slowly as the car dropped, the blade cut up through the door until Dorian dropped to his feet. The scimitar withdrew and the car lurched and moved downwards towards the first floor.

Tears streamed down Paige's face. Her mascara ran, and she wiped her cheeks. "What the hell is happening? Where are that man's eyes? Why did they reappear? How many times did you shoot him and why he is still alive? Where did that giant sword come from?" she shouted. "It appeared out of thin air!"

A bell dinged as the car passed the fourth floor.

Dorian drew his empty pistol, ejected the magazine and slid a full one into the HK. "He is not a man. He is a jinn. The word is الجن. Immortal beings made of fire that existed long before the *Quran* was written. The *Quran* says that the jinn are one of three creatures created by God that are blessed with wisdom. Angels, humans, and jinn. Of the three, only humans and jinn have free will. To be more specific, this is a Shayṭān Jinn. Think of it in terms of an Arabic demon, if that makes it easier. The world is not what you think it is. Sorry you have to learn of it this way—the hard way. Sometimes it is better to be ignorant."

"I don't believe in any of that!" Paige shouted. "That doesn't make it any easier at all. There is no such thing as demons. I don't even go to church!"

"Seems like this fiend believes in us, and now that he has seen us together your life is in danger," Dorian said and looked at the roof of the elevator car. The sound of metal ground again and the car dinged while it passed the third floor. "Get down!"

Once again the giant blade emerged, but this time from the ceiling of the car. Al-Kanani was on top of the elevator. The sword cut through the ceiling of the car, and then thrust down. Dorian pushed Paige down into the corner of the car. The agent pulled the blade back up, and then jammed it back down into the car.

The third slice caught the back of Dorian's coat—the scimitar cut the Louis Vuitton cleanly. When the blade slid back out of the car, the enforcer pressed the barrel of his HK into the gash in the roof of the elevator and fired the gun until it was empty. Brass shells clattered against the wall of the elevator. Al-Kanani screamed, and the car rocked as his body landed with a thump against the ceiling.

The bell indicated the second floor passed. Black blood dripped down from the ceiling where the agent lay bleeding on top of the car. The bullets the enforcer had fired found their mark. Dorian reloaded his pistols and the door slid open. He grabbed Paige by the wrist, jerked her to her feet, then led her out the door into the hallway of the ground floor.

Panicked people ran chaotically for the exits. A security guard waited just outside of the elevator. With a shaky hand, he pointed his revolver at the enforcer.

"Freeze!" he shouted. Dorian looked at his nametag. "Don't move. Drop your gun. The police are on their way!"

"Brent, there is this *thing* in the elevator shaft. It's on top of the elevator!" Paige shrieked. "It's trying to kill us!"

"This man has a gun!" the security guard said. "Miss Gray, are you ok?"

"I-I'm not sure," she stammered.

"Just stay calm, Brent," Dorian said to the guard. "No one is going to get hurt. Just point that gun away from-"

"I said drop it!" the guard interrupted. The sound of metal being bent echoed from the shaft. "Don't make me shoot you!"

Dorian held his hands up in the air and let his HK swing on his finger. "Brent. Just stay calm. No reason for anyone to get hurt. Unless that gun you have goes off."

The security guard's quivering hand reached for the .45 as it settled on Dorian's finger. Brent glanced at the elevator door. A panel fell from the ceiling, and then Al-Kanani dropped into the car.

"What the hell-"

The security guard's thought was interrupted as the enforcer caught him in the temple with the back of his hand. Brent grunted, dropped his revolver and fell forward onto the floor. Dorian scooped up the pistol, shoved it in the guard's holster and pulled Paige toward the door. Al-Kanani had cut his way through the elevator ceiling with the scimitar, and now he stood in the car with the blade in his hand. He pointed at the pair.

"There is nowhere on this earth you can hide from me, now," Al-Kanani said ominously.

Keith scrambled, leapt onto Dorian's back, and climbed up his jacket to cling to his shoulder.

"Dat freak is pissed and I don't dink a few bullets is gonna stop him, boss," the imp said.

"Then tell me how to stop it!" Dorian said as they ran down the hallway. An alarm sounded, not unlike a fire alarm, as they moved. "I hope you are making sure none of this ends up being recorded by the security cameras!"

"Who are you talking to?" Paige shouted.

"That is another layer of the onion you do not want to know about," he said, then watched Al-Kanani step through the elevator door.

The agent bent down and grabbed the security guard's pistol. The guard groggily reached for his gun. Al-Kanani rapped him on the noggin with the handle of the revolver. Brent grunted and lay still again. He pointed the pistol at Dorian and emptied the cylinder. The shots shattered plaster and sheetrock, but none of six bullets were on target. The Jinn looked angrily at the pistol, and then threw it at the unconscious security guard before he delivered a swift kick.

"High and to the left, rent-a-cop," he growled. "Get your pistol sighted in."

Dorian halted and returned fire. Every bullet he fired tore into the agent's chest. Ebony liquid erupted and he dropped to his knees. His mirage wavered for a few seconds, and his eye-sockets and serrated fangs became apparent. Then like a veil, he became human again, except for the flow of black blood. The giant scimitar clattered across the floor. He leaned forward, then backwards, and then lifted himself up.

"Why doesn't he die?" Paige cried.

"Because you cannot kill something like that with bullets. Only slow him down," Dorian said. "He is immortal—like the evil twin of the genie in Disney's Aladdin movie."

"Like, Jessie Ventura, evil!" Keith said, even though Paige could not see him. "Here he comes again!"

The jinn retrieve his sword and turned. "Keep running, little man. You're not quite human, not a demon, but not quite an angel. You'll run out of bullets eventually. When I eat your flesh, I will know exactly what you are," the agent hissed. He stormed down the hallway toward them. The scimitar sliced through the air with a diabolical whistle.

The pair ran down the long hallway from the elevators, then turned right and proceeded through the center of the first floor of Harborview Medical Center. People ran for the exits in panic. They cowered from the agent, who stormed down the corridor after them. The pair ran past the information desk. Dorian could see Barbie as she cowered under the table. Through the art gallery the two ran as a crowd was bottlenecked at the exit. The agent was not far behind them. He picked up a sculpture that vaguely resembled an elephant wearing a stove-pipe hat. Al-Kanani hurled the sculpture toward

Dorian who shoved Paige through the doors. The hydraulics opened slowly as she moved, but not quite fast enough. She bumped her head against them and fell to the ground with a thud. The atrocious sculpture slammed against the back of a man in a lab coat. The man grunted and crumpled to the floor.

"Paige! Get up!" Dorian shouted.

She mumbled something unintelligibly.

"She's down. Now's our chance ta get away from dat broad and cut our losses on dis adventure!" the imp squealed. "Tell dat jinn ta take da woman and let us go!"

Dorian turned, and then sprinted toward Al-Kanani. He ducked as the sword passed over his head, then stepped to the side as the agent circled the blade above his head and brought it down. The scimitar cut deep into the floor.

The jinn tugged once at the blade, but it was stuck. He reached up and tried to grab Dorian by the throat, but missed and grabbed his jacket instead. Al-Kanani pulled him close and opened his mouth. His jaw opened freakishly large, and he tried to bite the enforcer on the shoulder.

Dorian pressed the muzzles of the HKs against Al-Kanani's crotch and blasted away. The empty brass shells clattered across the linoleum as the agent's crotch erupted in blood. He roared, a blood-curdling scream, and dropped to the floor. The giant clutched at the remnants of his privates.

"Well, that answers the question if jinn have testicles," Dorian said as he landed on his feet. He pointed one of the pistols at Al-Kanani's head and executed him. After he had emptied the magazines of both pistols, he stepped back and tapped the monstrous sword with a foot. The massive blade was lodged solidly into the floor. The blood from the head wound slowed, and the agent moaned. The enforcer could see the bullet holes closing. "Had testicles. Dammit. Even his head wounds heal."

Dorian put his last two full magazines in the pistols and backed away. He kept his eye on the jinn as he moved. The creature shook and clawed at the remnants of its nuts as they regenerated. The enforcer pushed his way through the glass doors. Paige was sitting up, and held her head in her hands. A trickle of blood ran down her forehead from where she had knocked her head against the doorway. The imp was on her shoulder, unseen to the nurse but visible to Dorian. The demon jumped up and down on her in a vain attempt to revive her.

"Dis broad is pretty groggy. She's just gonna slow us down, boss," Keith said. "Leave her!"

Dorian holstered his guns and hefted Paige up. "I am not leaving her."

The demon clung to her shoulder and jumped to the enforcer. Dorian loaded her on his back, and the imp was squished between Paige and Dorian. The demon moaned and gasped for air as the enforcer exited the front doors of the medical center.

"Ask dis broad her weight. If she says anything under one-forty, she's lyin'!" the imp shrieked. "I can't breathe.

It's like being pinned under a horny, drunk, Chris Christie on sex night. Don't touch me dere, Governor. It's my special place! I can't take it!"

"One hundred forty-two," she mumbled. "Had a heavy breakfast."

"You do not need to breathe, you idiot," Dorian grumbled at the demon as he sprinted across the parking lot. He looked back as Al-Kanani who smashed through the glass doors and stumbled onto the sidewalk. The jinn had not quite recovered from the disintegration of his nuts. His rapid healing didn't seem to repair his berries as rapidly as most men would hope—he limped agonizingly slow. "You do not follow the laws of nature, remember?"

"Oh, yeah," Keith said. "I don't need ta breathe. Sorry. Lost myself in da moment for a second."

"I'm not an idiot and I need to breathe," Paige muttered. "Who are you talking too?"

"No one important," Dorian said.

"Da only one here not thinking with his pathetically

average dick, sweetheart," Keith said.

"I keep hearing voices," Paige said. "I think I am hearing things. Could you put me down?"

Dorian turned to see the agent crossing the parking lot towards him. Gently, he stood Paige on her feet. She wobbled and he kept her from falling.

"We have to move to the parking garage. Now," Dorian said. In the distance he could see flashing lights approaching quickly. Cop cars were converging on the hospital. He helped Paige towards the multi-level elevated parking lot. People were still running from the hospital. As he passed a row of cars, he saw movement close, moving against the tide of humanity. A Seattle Police Department officer had a Glock drawn and pointed it at the enforcer. They were close to the entrance.

"Stop. Is she injured?" the cop said.

"Took a bump to the head. There is some nut back there swinging a sword around," Dorian said and pointed back at Al-Kanani. "I think he fired some shots in the hospital."

The cop looked closely at Paige, then at Dorian. He glanced back at the agent who shuffled painfully. The cop stared at the back of the enforcer's coat. "You're wearing a shoulder holster."

"Yeah."

"Hands up! Show me your identification," the cop ordered. "Now."

"See that big guy with the sword? He is coming our way," Dorian said.

"I said, show me your identification. Concealed carry permit. Now. No sudden moves," the officer ordered.

"Keith, I need him to forget this," Dorian said quietly. Through the parking lot, Al-Kanani approached. He was enraged. The giant scimitar was in one hand and his crotch in the other.

The enforcer reached slowly for the breast pocket of his ruined coat and stepped closer to the cop. "I have a permit right here. When that big guy gets here, he will kill us all with that sword."

"Stay where you are," the officer said. Dorian took another step forward. "I will kill you."

"I do not want any problems. Here is my ID," the enforcer said. He held out his wallet.

The cop slowly reached out with his left hand, and kept the gun leveled. Dorian grabbed the slide of the Glock and slid it back. To no avail, the officer tried to fire the pistol as the enforcer hammered his fist into the side of his head. He grunted and dropped to the concrete. The imp immediately jumped onto him and touched his piggy paws against the cop's forehead. He cleansed the memories from the last several minutes out of his mind.

"You attacked a cop!" Paige shouted. "I'm not going anywhere with you!"

Al-Kanani moved towards them. He was within thirty feet of the pair.

"We'd better get movin', boss," Keith shouted. "He was pissed before, but I dink shootin' his nuts off has driven him totally crazy!"

"Do you think he cares when he gets here?" Dorian

said to Paige. "You feel safer with someone who I have shot several dozen times and has not died?"

"No," she muttered and he grabbed her hand. The two ran into the garage as Al-Kanani picked up his pace. He stopped long enough to recover the Glock from the unconscious cop and squeezed off several rounds. The bullets whizzed by the pair as they ducked behind parked cars. The reports of the shots echoed through the chamber of the parking garage. Two of the shots broke out windows, and the sound of alarms rang out.

Several people had made their way to vehicles and, in a panic, were leaving the garage. One of the drivers in a green Honda swerved and smashed into a parked blue Mazda. Metal screamed and glass shattered as it rained down on the concrete. A second car, a black Ford, rear-ended the Honda. People ran from the sounds of the gunfire in a mindless panic.

The pair worked their way through a maze of parked cars, and then cut across the rest of the garage. Dorian lay down on the concrete and looked under the surrounding vehicles. He could see the agent's feet as he looked for the pair. He leaned close to Paige and held out the keys to his Porsche.

"My car is near the exit of the garage. You get in it and take cover. Lock the doors. They are lined with Kevlar," he said loudly over the echoes of the alarms. Dorian watched Al-Kanani's feet shuffle between the cars as he prowled. He drew his pistol, lined the sight up on the agent's ankle and put several bullets into his foot. "That has got to hurt. Now run!"

Paige stood, took two steps, then reversed her course and ran towards the exit of the garage. Dorian could feel his pistol was light—the magazine was half full. His other HK had a full mag. This situation was beyond out of control, and he was almost out of ammo.

"I surrender!" Keith squealed, and then ran under one of the parked cars. "Don't hurt me, my dark lord. Kill da kaffirs!"

"You coward!" Dorian shouted.

Somewhere above him he could hear the whir of

chopper blades. A news or police helicopter. This was getting worse by the second. The only saving grace he had was that the jinn was lost in a blood lust, and had dropped any semblance of decorum in his hunt. Dorian had pissed the demon off in a royal fashion, and the monster would not stop until one of them was dead.

Dorian took several steps, and then turned to see the agent stand. His jaw unhinged, and he let out an inhuman roar that chilled the enforcer. He could feel goose bumps rise on the back of his neck. This was going to end badly, one way or another.

"Tiny angel-man. Come to me!" Al-Kanani screamed. He drew back his scimitar, and then cut through the hood of a Ford. The blade sliced the steel engine block cleanly and sparked as it penetrated the floor.

A red Toyota pickup sped past Dorian, the driver trying to escape from the hospital. The driver screeched on his brakes as the agent lumbered between the parked vehicles. He stood in front of the pickup, smashed his fist through the window, and grabbed the driver by the collar. The shards of the window clattered. Al-Kanani pulled the screaming driver out and threw him. He flew over several cars and landed with a sick thud on top of a Mercedes. His limp form smashed the front window and the roof. The alarm sounded and lights flashed.

Dorian ran down the line of cars. He could hear the agent rev the truck's engine behind him and jumped between two vehicles that were parked on his right. The Toyota crashed against the cars. Metal buckled and pieces of all three vehicles scattered as they were torn away. He drew his pistol and fired a bullet through the passenger-side window of the truck.

The round struck Al-Kanani squarely in the left temple and blew out the right side of his head. Black blood splattered as the jinn clawed at the side of his head before he slumped over the steering wheel.

"Killing him won't be that easy," Dorian mumbled. He jumped onto the car beside him, and then leapt onto the next car.

He looked back to see the side of the agent's head as

it knit itself back together. The rough edges of the open skull grew together. The skin crawled over the slick pink bone like a thing with its own insidious mind. The shreds of flesh groped at each other as they moved, then pulled against the newly reincarnated skull.

Keith peeked out from under one of the cars. "Is he dead yet?"

Dorian glared. "Not yet, mighty warrior."

The imp transformed into a tiny chicken, then slid back under the parked car. "Lemme know when he's gone."

The enforcer jumped to the top of another car, then down. He ran toward the second floor of the garage. Dorian heard the gears of the Toyota truck grind, then the rig lurched and pulled free. Again, metal stretched and Al-Kanani revved the engine. The side of his skull still crawled together and repaired the damage from the .45. His eye sockets now glowed an unholy red—hot as hell with anger stared at him.

Dorian sprinted between the rows of vehicles and

again the agent stomped on the gas. Tires spun and gray smoke spewed as the rubber burnt against the concrete.

The enforcer stopped, drew his second pistol, and turned to face the oncoming truck. He lunged toward the vehicle. Three feet before the pickup's bumper would make contact with him, he leapt into the air and came down on the hood of the rig, then fired his HK's through the windshield into the face of Al-Kanani. The last thirteen rounds of ammunition he had were spent as the bullets punched through the safety glass of the pickup.

Brass shells clattered as the pistols spit out the empty shells. The agent's face exploded in blood and bone that showered the inside of the cab of the truck. The rounds punched into his face and eye sockets, and then blew out the back of his skull. The back window of the truck shattered into a thousand tiny shards.

The body of the jinn twitched and clawed as his head was ripped apart by the bullets. Dorian rolled over the top of the cab, then landed on all fours in the bed of the truck before he leapt out and rolled to a stop on the floor. The truck smashed a parked baby-blue Toyota Prius. Steam from the shattered pickup radiator spewed into the air.

Dorian stood and cautiously approached. As the steam swirled, he could see the back of the agent's demolished skull. The bone slowly regenerated, the skin and hair blindly groped for something to connect to. The enforcer peered through the shattered driver-side window.

Al-Kanani's head hung limply, but his feet and fingers twitched as the monster healed. Dorian watched dark muscle, slick and wet, slowly reform. He reached down, grabbed the giant scimitar by the pommel, and put the blade against the side of the agent's neck. With a powerful thrust, the razor-sharp cleaver sliced cleanly through the jinn's neck and his head toppled into his lap.

Dorian stared at the stump. Black blood spurted straight into the air from the arteries in the Al-Kanani's neck for several beats. The fluid splattered against the roof of the cab, then dripped down. It took his body a few beats to realize it had lost its head, and the heart became weaker and weaker as more blood fountained upwards. The wound didn't heal itself—the magic sword seemed to do the trick and the agent's heart stopped pumping. He was finally dead.

The Enforcer quickly ran back towards the Cayman. Keith changed back into his little piggy self and jumped up on Dorian's shoulder.

"We showed dat bastard a ding or two," the imp said. "Da bigger dey are, da harder dey fall."

"You better make sure no cameras caught any of that. We are in so much trouble already."

"Not really 'we', comrade. You're in trouble. I'm small enough ta sneak between prison bars," the demon said. "Besides, don't I always take care of ya, big guy?"

"Yeah. It resulted in the Seattle Police terrorizing innocent clowns everywhere. Who will pay for the chaos today?" Dorian said.

"Let's just say tomorrow will probably be a bad day

to be a mime in da Seattle area," Keith chuckled, and then climbed into his pocket.

The pair arrived at the car. There was no sign of Paige. Dorian snuck up to the Porsche and peered through the window. She was hunkered down in the passenger side of the car, in cover. He tapped on the window and she screamed.

"Unlock the door," Dorian said. Paige's hand shook violently as she reached over and hit the button. The door clicked and he pulled it open. He pulled off the ruined Louis Vuitton coat and stuffed it behind the seat, then climbed into the Porsche. She had been crying—her mascara was smeared and her eyes were puffy.

"What the hell is going on, Dorian?" Paige shouted. "God damn it, this is like a dream I can't wake up from. Why did that man have no eyes? How could he survive like that? You shot him dozens of times. No one could have survived that!"

"I told you what he was," he said quietly.

Dorian took the key from her hand and inserted it in

the ignition. He reached up to inspect the cut on her forehead from where she was knocked against the hospital door. Paige swatted his hand away. "Don't touch me! What happened in there?"

"He was a demon. I understand the denial. It is bound to happen. He is dead now—he cannot hurt us. I have to get us out of here."

Paige punched Dorian in the arm several times. "What have you done to me? Why do you have all those guns? Who are you really?" she shrieked hysterically. Tears rolled down her cheeks.

"I told you. My name is Dorian Christianson, which is probably more than I should have told you. You have seen a shadow of the world beyond what normal people see. Most never see or believe it. Spirits. Devils. Jinn. Angels. Demons."

"I don't believe in demons or jinn!" she shouted.

Keith leapt from Dorian's pocket and stood on the dash. He waved his porcine paw at Paige. "If dere ain't no such dings as demons, princess, how da hell do ya explain me?" the imp shouted.

Dorian sighed and shook his head. Paige let out a high-pitched wail and passed out.

"Well, that sure as shit did not help anything," the enforcer growled. "This ought to be hard to explain when she wakes up. Why did you do that?"

"I'm tired of listenin' to dat broad whine," the imp said. "Besides, I'm hungry."

Chapter Six
—Blood—

FBI Agent Ibrahim Al-Faqih casually scanned the sports section of the Seattle Times. His trip had been a colossal waste of time so far, and now he had a couple hours to kill before catching a return flight to Washington, D.C. Every time he glanced at his phone, it seemed to drag the wait out longer.

The Abraham Lincoln Building was a gray thirteen story highrise on 2nd Avenue, near the waterfront in Seattle. It was just a couple blocks away from the Bainbridge Island Ferry. He had considered catching a ride across and back just to kill time, but that would cut his visit close. Al-Faqih had no interest in extending this visit.

Absentmindedly he opened another package of Peanut M&M's. The one advantage that the material world had was chocolate. When this world is extinguished, it will be the one loss he would feel. Humans had taken a simple bean, processed it, then mixed it with ordinary ingredients like milk and sugar and made a little bit of heaven. As close to heaven as he ever wanted to be.

Al-Faqih stretched his long legs, and then shoved a handful of candy in his mouth as he turned the page. The door to the conference room opened quickly and one of the local FBI agents pushed his head in.

"Agent Al-Faqih. We are getting reports of a shooting at Seattle Harborview Medical Center. It's on the news. You might want to see this," the agent said. "We are monitoring radio traffic. SPD is enroute."

"Sounds like a local problem, unless they ask for our help," Al-Faqih said. He tipped the bag back and filled his mouth with M&M's. "They are already wasting our time with that shooting in Bellevue."

It took several more minutes to finish the sports section. Outside of the conference room, people rushed up and down the hallways. Petty mortals with petty mortal concerns. Al-Faqih opened another bag of M&M's—this time with peanut butter. Truly, the pinnacle of what humans have accomplished.

Suddenly his chest burned. He coughed, and half melted M&M's wet with spit scattered all over the sports section of the Seattle Times. Each candy left a colored slobbery skid mark across the page.

The pressure on his chest increased, like an elephant as it pressed a giant foot down on him. Black tears rolled from his eyes as the weight increased. Al-Faqih gasped for air like he really needed the stuff. He knew the agony of the pain of one of his kindred in the throes of death.

Then it was gone. The pain of one of his brothers, gone from this world. It was like a divine switch had been flipped, smashing him like a cry for help. Al-Faqih also knew who had departed the mortal realm—Al-Kanani.

He slammed his huge fist against the table, and then stormed out of the conference room. The FBI agent looked to the left, then right. Al-Faqih could see a crowd gathered down the hall. He stormed towards them. They had surrounded a flat-screen television in a hallway intersection. Currently, the scene showed video from a helicopter that circled Harborview Medical Center.

The crowd of secretaries and FBI agents watched quietly as the voices of a reporter echoed through the room. "...the number of gunmen or any casualties is as yet unknown. Seattle Police are converging on the area. All officers are ordered to report for duty, and SWAT teams are en-route. Witnesses have reported dozens of shots fired."

Al-Faqih put his hand on the shoulder of one of the secretaries. "I need my flight to Washington, D.C. cancelled, and a car. Now."

***

Tessa Paul took a break from the logarithms that had been kicking her ass all evening to watch the television with her mother, Serenity. The local station had interrupted reruns of The Big Bang Theory with coverage of the shooting at Harborview.

"Well. That means Dad will be home late again," Serenity said. "I hope there are no casualties."

"It's a shooting, Mom. There will be casualties," Tessa said. She looked at her phone on the table as it buzzed with an incoming call. "There are always casualties."

She picked up the phone. Tessa's smart phone showed a smiling picture of her friend, Angela Gentry. The photo had been taken after school, as she posed on the steps of the school. Her dyed black hair, black clothes, and nose ring set her apart from 'normal' students.

"Hey," Tessa said as she hit the button on the phone. "What's up?"

"Nothing!" Angela said excitedly. "Let's go cruising. My parents are going to let me use the car. Let's go downtown."

"Did you see that shooting at the hospital?" Tessa said.

"Yeah, but I got the car. We aren't going by the

hospital, anyway. Your dad won't be home to nag you about homework tonight," Angela said. "Some of the other kids at school are going cruising. C'mon. It will be fun."

"My life is logarithms now. I shouldn't go. I have homework," Tessa said.

"A couple hours would clear your head a bit. Give you a chance to regenerate all those worn-out brain cells. I'll help you in study hall. You'll think better, and thank me later." Angela giggled. "Walk over to the house and by then my folks will be home with the keys."

"Fine," Tessa said. "Talk to you in a bit."

Serenity was watching the television. It showed footage of Harborview in the lower corner as the helicopter circled the hospital.

The voice of a reporter droned. "...we are at the corner of Broadway and Boren Avenues. This intersection has just been cordoned off by SPD. They have not yet fully sealed the area as most of the police units are in traffic, snarled on the I-5-"

"Hey Mom," Tessa interrupted the voice on the television. "I'm walking over to Angela's. Be home in a couple hours."

"Be safe, honey," Serenity said. "Senseless, all this violence. Just senseless."

***

Nicholas Paul checked the safety on his .40 caliber Glock. He hated when he had to wear his bulletproof vest. Even with an undershirt, it was still scratchy. Now, every officer in Seattle was on their way to Harborview Medical Center.

The detective hitched a ride with a uniformed patrol. Now they were bogged down in traffic on the Interstate. It was stop and go, but mostly stop. Radio reports had panicked people in accidents around the hospital. Not only were they trying to leave the area, the sudden influx of emergency units had bogged things down.

"Traffic in this town is horrible," Nicholas grumbled. "Exit 165A is snarled. How far do we have to go?"

The uniformed officer who was driving looked to his left. "165A is under repair already. Reports have it bottlenecked from the roadwork, and now the panic of people fleeing the area. We are two miles out. Probably fifteen minutes at this speed. Other units have arrived and are deploying."

Nicholas hit the dash angrily. "I could move faster if I got out and walked."

***

Dorian had driven the Cayman out of the parking garage and parked two blocks away at the intersection of 9th Avenue and James Street.

"I dink we should just ditch da broad. Dump her out here, and den skedaddle," Keith said. He sat on the dash and swung his tiny cloven hooves over the edge. His tail twitched. "It's a shame, but dis relationship ended badly. Quickly. Probably easier dat way. Less attachment."

"Yeah, dump a witness to the whole event out of the car. Just open the door and give her a little shove, hope she does not tell anyone. Great plan, you idiot," Dorian snapped.

"It may not be a great plan, but it's a plan," the imp sulked.

Dorian opened a first aid kit, took a smelling salt and snapped in under her nose. The stench made her quiver, and then roll her head back against the seat. "Paige. It is Dorian. Open your eyes."

Paige shook her head as she tried to avoid the stink. "Where? How did I get here?"

"Just a little dust up. A few shots were fired. No big deal. Cops are going to have this place fully cordoned off in the next five, maybe ten minutes at the latest, so I have to get going," Dorian said.

She raised a shaky hand and pointed at Keith. "What is that thing? It's a puppet, right? I just can't see the strings?"

"Do you think it's a puppet?" Dorian inquired. "That would be the easiest explanation."

"I gots yer puppet right here," the tiny demon declared and grabbed his crotch.

"That... thing looks so real," Paige whispered. "But there is no way..."

"We do not have a ton of time. I told you, demons are real. There is a whole world that most people never see. Never experience. You have just put your toe in an ocean of supernatural, beyond anything you have ever believed in," Dorian said. "I know this falls on you like a ton of bricks. Sorry. This is Keith. He is a demon of lust and gluttony. He is all right."

"Bill Clinton is my hero," the imp announced. "His pecker has a distinguishable bend in da middle, or so I have read. I loved dat Starr report. It was like a letter to Penthouse Magazine."

"This can't be real," she sobbed. "There is no such thing."

"Oh, fuck me. Here come da water works," Keith grumbled. "Broads. Dis is why I'm single."

"Why doesn't it have any pants on?" Paige cried.

Dorian rolled his eyes. "You have just seen your first real demon and you are worried about where his pants are? Seriously?"

"Why doesn't it wear pants!" Paige screamed. "Where are its pants?"

"He's always Porky Piggin' it. It is his thing," Dorian said.

"I like da breeze, sister," the imp snorted. He changed himself to look like Bill Clinton. "I find pants so constricting. Perk of the office. Depends on what the meaning of the word '*is*', is."

"Porky Pigging it? What's that?" she asked. "That thing is repulsive."

"Repulsive?" Keith said.

"No pants. Porky Pig only wore a shirt, no pants. So going around without pants is Porky Piggin'it," Dorian said quietly. "He is a filthy little exhibitionist. Demons of lust and gluttony are not considered couth creatures, even by demon standards."

Keith was still in the form of a tiny Bill Clinton. He raised a cigar to his mouth. "I love it when a plan comes together. Or in her. Or on her blue dress."

"He can't be real, can he?" Paige said.

"He is real. Just like that jinn you saw back in the hospital. It was weird that jinn came after me like that—like he knew me. I cannot explain it," Dorian said. "I had experience with one of these entities in Iraq. They are powerful, temperamental, violent creatures. The dark side of Middle Eastern mythology."

"Are you a demon?" Paige asked. She squinted at the imp who took the cigar out of his mouth, then stuck his tongue out.

"No. Half angel on my father's side, actually. Well, fallen angel. A nephilim is what my kind is called. Half human, half angel," Dorian said. "I rescued Keith there from a Mullah in Afghanistan. They thought he was a genie. The idiots had bound him into a brass lamp. Kept trying to get him to grant wishes."

"We had no fucking cable in dat place. Had to watch videos of Jersey Shore over and over. The mullah loved dat show. It was my only entertainment in my formative years," the imp snarled. "It's where my accent comes from."

"Sorry if I find this all a bit hard to swallow," Paige said. "I can't believe any of this is real. This challenges everything I have ever believed. I don't even go to church."

"Dat's what she said," the demon laughed. "I can't help myself. I love swallow jokes."

"It doesn't matter if you go to church or not," Dorian said. "He's real."

"I love Unitarians," Keith giggled. "She said 'swallow'—it's funny when she says it. Can't get enough of it. Welcome ta da big leagues, princess."

"I understand this is tough. I realize it shakes your view of the whole world. If I had more time to work through it with you, I would. Right now I have to go. I do not know what comes next, but I am going to drop you off. You need to wander off and find some police. Tell them you hit your head and do not remember anything after that. Symptoms of a concussion are: light and sound sensitivity and memory loss. Stick with that, do not embellish the story beyond you do not remember anything and you should be fine. You hit your head and do not remember anything after that. It is plausible," Dorian said. "That bump on your head will make it believable."

"Why do you have so many guns and a car plated with Kevlar? What do you do? Really?" she said. "No bull this time. Be honest."

"I fix problems," he said. "Just stick to the story. I will be in touch in a few days, make sure you are all right. Sorry about today. This was not my plan."

Paige shook her head and climbed out of the car. "It was a pretty horrible first date, for sure. Even worse apology. I'm not sure I want you to get in touch."

"That is understandable. Stick to the story. Everything will be all right. Bump on the head, cannot remember anything after that. We get through this, and I will tell you more," Dorian said. "Trust me."

She took a few unsteady steps toward the hospital and the enforcer hit the gas pedal. People and cars were exiting the area and the flashing lights of law enforcement were all around him.

"We shoulda wiped her mind, boss," Keith said. "You will live ta regret dis. Thinkin' with yer dick, not yer head. I coulda done it and she never woulda been da wiser."

"It is still an option. Just be quiet—I have to think to navigate out of this. In fact, we need to split up. I need you to go find those nurses that saw me on the fifth floor. That woman at the help desk. They need to not remember seeing me. Got it?"

"Shit. Sounds like a lot of work. I can do it. You owe me," Keith said and sprouted wings.

"Not Paige. Just the others. Got it?" Dorian said seriously.

"I got it. Broads—nothin' but trouble," the imp sighed. "Can we get pizza when I'm done?"

***

Tessa knocked on the door to Angela's house and it took a few seconds for her younger sister, Marisol, to answer. The girl, a year behind the other two in high school, was dressed in her usual Goth get-up. Black skirt, black painted nails, and a spiked dog collar.

"'Sup, Tessa?" Marisol said.

"Nothing much. Gonna do a little cruising with your sister. Are you going to come along?" Tessa asked.

"Sure. Got nothing else goin' on tonight," the dark haired girl said. "Let me go get my purse. Come in."

The foyer of the Gentry household was clean and neat. A small table was by the door with a bouquet of black flowers in a vase. An unused coat rack was to the left of the table. The carpet was a crisp tan. Perfectly organized furniture was in the living room. Mrs. Gentry was an immaculate housekeeper.

Angela came into the foyer. "Heeyy, whassup?" she laughed

"You'd better be able to get me online with this logarithms thing or I will be in so much trouble with my parents," Tessa said.

"Sure 'nough," Angela said. "Let's get out of here."

Tessa peered into the living room. "Where are your

parents?"

"Who knows? Who cares? Probably getting ready to do it 'cause they know we are leaving."

Tessa puckered her face. "Ew, I don't need to know that!"

"Your parents probably do it, too."

"Double ew! I was adopted. I know they don't do it." Tessa snorted.

"Your dad isn't bad looking, for an old guy. I bet they do it a lot more than you know," Angela said.

"Triple ew!" Tessa yelped. "Let's get out of here. You're driving me nuts! What is it with you tonight?"

"Marisol! Meet us in the car!" Angela shouted.

***

The traffic on the I-5 southbound towards the 165A exit was now totally snarled and stopped. A car had tried to pass a semi-truck and ended up underneath the trailer. The injuries were minor, but the accident had shattered the front axle of the trailer and now it leaned precariously close to falling over. Detective Nicholas Paul cussed repeatedly about being stuck in traffic. He abandoned the patrol car and its driver and set out on foot. He grabbed a radio and unlatched the door. It was a dangerous move, but the traffic was so bottled that he felt confident he could get to Harborview.

He counted three helicopters overhead—two were television news choppers, one was a SPD helicopter. Nicholas jumped a concrete barrier. The traffic was so slow that he held up his badge and crossed into the oncoming traffic. Two cars honked at him as he moved across the concrete ribbon of I-5. He noticed the row of cars entering the freeway from the onramp. They crawled forward. They tried to merge with the frozen-molasses traffic that crawled north. They should have merged like the teeth on a zipper, but instead some woman driving a Honda Civic with Montana plates had a fender-bender and now tied up a lane.

Nicholas set out at a fast jog down the onramp against the traffic. He looked at the row of cars, bumper to bumper now as they tried to escape the area. The eyes of every driver and passenger stared at him as he ran contrary to the flow of the vehicles. He could see their eyes, wide with fear, as he moved.

The detective noticed one vehicle in particular. Something about it bothered him. The driver of a gray Porsche Cayman wore sunglasses and did not even look his direction. The man had an intense expression. He took a few steps past the sports car, then stopped and looked back. A weird feeling settled in the pit of his stomach. He could see a pink bobble-head of some kind through the window on the dash that wobbled back and forth.

The radio crackled and he turned back toward the hospital. The first SWAT team had arrived and was deployed by the East Hospital building. He refocused on his destination and ran toward Harborview.

***

Paige Gray was being treated by EMT's at the corner of 9th and Jefferson, in the shadow of Harborview. The place was surrounded by cops when she walked to the perimeter. They hustled her away to cover. The paramedics applied a blood pressure cuff and repeatedly asked her what happened. Against her better judgment, she said she hit her head and couldn't remember anything more. Besides, if she told the truth, who would believe her? That some heavily armed son of a fallen angel brought her chocolates and a gift card for the Kushibar, and then got in a running gunfight with an evil genie? That would be the end of her career for sure.

The EMT looked at her nametag. "Paige, it is not unusual for a concussion to result in memory loss. Do you remember seeing anyone with a gun? Or hearing the shots?"

"I... don't remember anything. My head hurts," she said. "I am an employee of the hospital."

"I see that. You have on an ID badge. Do you have any health problems that you know of?" the EMT asked.

"I think I might be having a psychotic break," Paige mumbled. "Does that count as a health problem?"

***

FBI Agent Ibrahim Al-Faqih arrived at Harborview Medical Center. The closer he got to the place, the more he could sense the untimely death of Nabil Al-Kanani. The anger in the jinn had built to a rage. How dare a mortal defy one of his kin? How dare some finite sack of meat and bones interfere with the course of events? Even more galling, how could some human kill a jinn?

Al-Faqih stalked past groups of policemen to the parking garage then stepped over the yellow police tape that had cordoned off the area. SWAT and SPD watched him as he moved—his anger was palpable, his rage barely concealed, as his long legs propelled his huge frame.

Officers were tagging shells and bullet holes and taking pictures of shattered windows in the garage. Al-Faqih was drawn to a damaged red Toyota pickup. The windows in the vehicle were shattered, the front end crumpled, and bullet holes pockmarked the bed. The smell of blood and the dark liquid puddles stoked the jinn's rage even further.

Al-Kanani's headless corpse was still sitting in the truck. His head was in his lap—dead eye sockets stared blankly at the roof of the cab. The skull was severely mangled—obviously the result of being shot multiple times in the face. The massive scimitar was on the floor of the truck, covered in black blood. The body concerned him little—in a couple hours it would return to its original components, and the mortals would have no evidence of it.

The agent could sense something otherworldly, something divine and something demonic beyond Al-Kanani. It was a little bit of both sides of the spiritual coin, but he was now sure it was separate entities. The divine was not as strong as it should have been—the spiritual energies left behind that permeated the place were not as strong as an angel. Maybe a half-angel?

The demonic energy that radiated was also not as strong—some minor imp or lesser minion of hell. Curious. The question was, was the pair together, or was he sensing old spiritual energies? Either way, the sword radiated the angelic presence. Whatever had killed Al-Kanani had used the sword to do it. Al-Faqih wondered if some agent of a higher power was on the terrestrial plane, trying to head off coming events. The world of man would end soon, and it would be like God to send in too little too late to try to plug the dike. No amount of pasty-skinned angelic fingers could plug the hole that was coming. The deluge of destruction would be delicious.

"Hey. You're contaminating the crime scene," a man in a suit said to the agent. He wore a lanyard with ID that identified him as a Seattle Police Department Detective. "Watch where you're stepping, please. Look for the tags."

Al-Faqih saw red and took three huge steps towards the man. He grabbed him by the throat, picked him up, and slammed him against a parked blue Chevrolet SUV.

"I might contaminate the crime scene with your intestines, little man," the agent hissed. "You need to keep your mouth shut. That was my friend in there. Just do your fucking job."

"My job... is to make sure... you don't contaminate the crime scene," the detective gagged. "Put me... down."

"Whoa. Just ease him down gently," Detective Nicholas Paul said calmly. "You must be FBI Agent Ibrahim Al-Faqih. I recognize your voice from the conference call. I'm really sorry about your friend. We are going to get the guy who did this. Your friend will have justice."

Al-Faqih released the detective pinned against the Chevy, who fell to the ground as he gasped for breath. The agent turned to Nicholas. "I am going to get this guy. I have a lot of questions before I kill him. I don't care about justice, just revenge."

***

"Holy shit, what a day," Keith giggled. He finished off his fifth McDonald's chocolate fudge sundae, and licked his lips. Inside a bag were a dozen apple pies from the restaurant. "Yum. Another dead soldier. Well, I'd better get after dose pies before dey get cold."

Dorian sat beside him in the Cayman. They were parked in the parking lot of the McDonald's on 4th Avenue South. It was across the street from a post office, and the enforcer watched people come and go. His mind was a fog from the day's events as he sipped on a Diet Coke. "Put your trash in the bag before you start on the pies."

His cell phone rang. Dorian looked at the number. Leo Giovanni.

"This is Dorian."

"Switch to a burner," Leo said. "Now."

Dorian hung up his phone and pulled an envelope from beneath the seat. He drew a cellphone and a battery from the package, inserted the battery, and dialed a number. The phone was answered halfway through the first ring.

"D, I'm watching this thing on the news. Are you involved with this?" Leo asked. They never used names when on the burner phones for fear of government computer software tagging the conversation. "This is a disaster. How many are down?"

"Only one by me. That one was not human."

"What do you mean?" Leo said. "Not human? You're not making sense."

"Mister G, the thing that attacked me, was not human. It is too much to explain right now. Worse, it was also a government agent," Dorian said. "There will be more heat than you can imagine."

"Can anyone identify you, D?" Leo asked quietly.

"I do not believe so. There were a lot of potential witnesses though, so I cannot be one hundred percent positive," the enforcer answered. "I was not looking for trouble. It found me. I have no excuse. There is still a tentative offer on the table from Ito for employment. I do not have to be your problem, anymore."

"D. Son. Lay low for a couple days. Make sure you are not tailed. Then come this way and let's formulate a plan. You have needed a vacation for a while. That will give me a chance to figure out if they know who you are," Leo said. "If they do, you may have to take the honorable Kumichō Ito up on his offer if this gets too hot. We can't risk the Family. Understand?"

"Of course. I wouldn't dream of it."

"D, was there any other way out of this situation other than what you did?" Leo asked. "Did you have any other choices?"

"Put a bullet in my head or let the thing take me alive. I did not see any other options," Dorian said.

"Glad you are ok, son."

"Yes, sir." Dorian took the battery out of the phone, broke it to pieces in his hands, and put the fragments in the McDonald's bag. He stared at demon that was lying on the floor while he finished his last apple pie. "You ate all those already?"

"I have an unusual skillset," the demon said. "I go through pies like Rush Limbaugh goes through wives."

***

Detective Nicholas Paul had calmed FBI Agent Ibrahim Al-Faqih enough that the two now stood in the security office of Harborview. Local FBI Agents, Church and Reed, also joined them. The office was a bank of monitors, twenty-four in total that were mounted over a desk workstation. On the desk were three more computer monitors, keyboards, and mice to control the security cameras in the hospital.

Just as every cop had been activated in the Seattle area, every security guard had been called in. The local news media had converged, so now chaos reigned. Hospital corridors were now crime scenes, a mangled elevator that defied understanding, a dead ATF agent who was decapitated by a gigantic sword. It was like a surreal nightmare for the detective.

"You are not going to like this. We might have a couple seconds of the shooter, but that's it," the security guard said. "We seem to have some type of cascading security camera failure. Maybe data corruption, but it happens in a chronological order. We could have been hacked, although IT says they see no evidence of it. They are going to call in the security software vendor to see if there are traces of a hack."

"Pull it up," Al-Faqih ordered.

"It started with the parking lot cameras," the guard said. He clicked several buttons and one of the screens showed the entrance to the parking garage. "Here. At seven-twelve. The first camera goes dark."

The screen slowly faded to static. "It stayed like that for almost four minutes. Then, the cameras that cover the parking lot."

The guard clicked a button and it showed two cameras that watched the lot. They suddenly faded to static. The third monitor that showed the inside of the garage started to clear.

"These cameras stay non-functional for almost three minutes. Then as the entrance camera goes out, these start to come back. They are timed at the speed it takes to walk through the lot. These strategic malfunctions happen all the way across the first floor, into the elevator, then onto the fifth. Then they reverse themselves and cascade backwards as the shootout happens," the guard said. "It's obvious it is used to conceal the video evidence."

"At walking speed. That would be when someone who walked was in front of the cameras. Either they made a homemade device that jams cameras, knocks them offline, or maybe some type of military grade device they have stolen is doing it. Some kind of DARPA technology that has fallen into the wrong hands," Nicholas said. "It would seem military grade, made for covert operations. Could an EMP do it?"

"Nothing like that exists, or we would be aware of it," Church said. "Especially if it was in civilian hands."

"That is impossible. If it were an EMP device, it would knock out every electronic device including cells and those curly-cue light bulbs. Anything with a chip. Cars with electronic starters would be unable to start. Something, somehow caused those cameras to go offline. I would think that is more the territory of a computer hacker," Reed said.

"Witnesses to this event have wildly different stories.

According to them, Agent Al-Kanani had the sword and was chasing a couple through the hospital," Webb said. "We found pieces of his gun up on the fifth floor. It had been hit with a bullet."

"Caliber of the primary shooter's guns is a .45. We cannot find any prints on them," Reed said.

"That sounds familiar," Detective Paul said. "Where and why the hell would the agent have a sword? Is that standard issue ATF equipment now?"

"That would be the sword that was used to decapitate him in the parking garage. How odd," Reed said. "Most of the time back-up weapons are pistols in ankle holsters.

Al-Faqih bristled. "He is dead. Show some respect."

"We do have witnesses that say ATF Agent Al-Kanani was in pursuit of a man in a coat. From there, we get stories that vary wildly. Unfortunately, it is not backed up by the few seconds of video we have," Paul said.

"This bit of video of the shooter is less than helpful," the guard said. "It happened between camera failures when the interference moved back into the garage. So far, it is the only piece we can find showing the suspect Agent Al-Kanani was pursuing. Here it is."

The static faded and showed a figure as it hopped up on a car in the parking garage. It lasted just a second before screen turned to static.

"That was quick. Let me rewind and freeze it." The guard clicked a button, and then froze the image.

"Can you enhance that?" Al-Faqih said. "Give us a better look at the man who murdered Nabil Al-Kanani."

The group stared at the monitor as buttons clicked and the image zoomed in. It was clear—a little black beret, a horizontally striped shirt, black pants, and white makeup on the face.

"It's a fucking mime!" Paul grumbled. "Jesus Christ. I can't believe this. This isn't happening."

"Is this some kind of joke?" Al-Faqih shouted. "An ATF agent is dead and this is what we have to work on? An APB on a mime? This continues with Seattle PD's theme of trying to find clowns, jokers, and jesters for every crime in this town. This takes the cake. This is why I hate working with small-town PD's."

"We're not small town," Paul spat. "It's the evidence we have. It's what the screen shows. You can see it with your own eyes. Until we can prove otherwise, it's what we have to go on."

"The Bureau has enhancement software. Our IT guys might be able to pull more data out of that," Church said.

"I wonder what politician we will find under that makeup," Reed said. "Sky's the limit."

"I can't wait to find out," Paul said.

***

The sun had gone down for the day. On the 405 South near the Seattle city limits, Angela Gentry was going just over the speed limit. The freeway was busy as usual. Puget Sound freeways were always busy.

"Woo hoo!" Marisol shouted over the wind and the blaring radio. She stuck her head out of the sunroof of the Honda Accord as the girls sped down the highway.

Tessa laughed, and looked up to see the girl's dyed black hair as it flowed uncontrollably in the wind.

"We'll catch the 516 at Kent and cut across to the I-5 and head north again. I told Morgan and Danielle that we would meet them downtown later," Angela said. The wind pushed against Marisol and swept through the car. "Homework can wait!"

"You'd better help me get through it," Tessa grumbled. "I don't want to take logarithms again."

Marisol sat back in the back seat and combed her hair with her fingers. "I love fresh air!" she shouted.

"God. We are right here," Angela said. "Inside voice."

"Sorry. The wind made it hard to hear," Marisol said.

Angela drove down the highway. This stretch of the road was not too congested, and she kept the speed to just over the limit. Tessa turned the stereo up as they drove and the girls sang along with the music.

"Do you ever think about your parents?" Angela asked.

"What?" Tessa questioned.

Angela turned down the stereo as she exited off of the 167 onto the 516. "I said, do you ever think about your parents?"

"As little as possible," Tessa laughed. "You're not going to tell me my dad is cute again, are you?

"Not those parents, but your real parents." Angela said. "The ones who gave you up for adoption."

Tessa shook her head. "Where the hell did that question come from?

"I was just curious. You're the only person I know who is adopted."

"I dunno. I've never really thought that much about it. I don't remember anyone other than my parents," Tessa said. "Y'know, my parent parents."

"You've never tried to find them? Or look at records for their names?" Angela said. "You're not a little bit curious?"

"Only a little bit," Tessa said. "I have great parents. Really."

"If you could meet them, would you?" Angela

continued. "Wouldn't you want to get to know them, ask questions about your family history and all that stuff?"

"I guess. Are you writing a book?" Tessa laughed. "Why do you want to know all this stuff all of a sudden?"

"Just wondered. So if you were to just run into them or if someone knew who they were, would you be ok with it? Like if you just bumped into them unexpectedly."

"How would they know who the hell I am? They haven't seen me since I was born. This whole conversation is ridiculous," Tessa said. She rummaged in her tiny purse and grabbed her E-Cigarette. She puffed on the vapors and savored the cinnamon oil that was mixed in the water. "They probably don't even know where I am."

"I bet they do," Angela said.

"You two are always so serious," Marisol said. She held out her hand to the E-Cig. "Lemme try that."

Angela passed it back to Marisol. "Your sister is asking all the crazy questions."

Marisol puffed on the cig and blew out vapors that immediately dispersed in the wind. "It's an interesting question."

"It's an irrelevant question," Tessa said. "I don't really care one way or the other, honestly. If they really loved me they wouldn't have dropped me off at the hospital in the arms of a nurse and left. That's how my dad and mom got me. My dad was just a patrolman and he responded to the call from the hospital. Then they adopted me, after a bunch of social services paperwork."

"But you wouldn't be mad if you met them?" Angela said and switched lanes. "Your biological parents."

"I'm past it. I really don't consider them my parents, anyway," Tessa said. "Why? Are you taking me to meet them?"

Angela turned and stared at Tessa. "Yeah. I am."

***

Dorian had found a quiet area behind a seedy K-Mart and parked the Cayman. He sat and blared *Theory of a Deadman* on the stereo. His fingers traced the cuts in his

Louis Vuitton jacket. The damage was not worth repairing—plus it would leave a trail if he tried to have it fixed. He pulled a lock blade knife from underneath the driver seat, and then cut the coat into long strips.

Once Dorian had finished his Diet Coke, he threw all of the McDonald's trash in a dumpster. The pieces of the burner phone he had used were safely tucked in a bag, and would never to be found. The shreds of his expensive coat followed. He cussed when he tossed them in.

"You always get moody listening to dose guys. Don't worry about material possessions, I say. Easy come, easy go, I always say," Keith said when Dorian climbed back into the Porsche. "You got another coat at home you can use."

"It could be worse. You know I am really pissed when I listen to *Glycerine* by *Bush* over and over again. Do you know how much those fucking coats cost?" Dorian growled. "It is cheaper to replace lust demons than Louis Vuitton jackets, I can tell you that. Just shut up."

"Jesus Christ, you on da rag or sumpthin'?" Keith mumbled. "Sound like a chick. Miss Dorina Christianson. Maybe you should take up knittin' and watchin' Oprah, you sound like such a chick. Join da National Association of Gals. Eat some coconut bon-bons. Get a manicure."

"I said shut up!" Dorian leaned over the passenger seat and roared. He looked up to see a blue-shirted K-Mart employee smoking a cigarette, hidden in the shadows. Sneaking a smoke on company time. The kid looked surprised. He dropped the smoke and disappeared back into the door of the loading dock.

"Nice job, dumbass. Dat kid can't see me. He thinks yer nutty as a fuckin' fruitcake, yelling 'shut up' ta yer car repeatedly. Dat's damn funny," Keith said.

***

FBI Agent Ibrahim Al-Faqih stood near the nurse's station on the fifth floor of Harborview and let his senses open up. He could feel the divine and demonic presence that saturated the very walls. A darker than usual thought crossed his mind—that the Heavenly powers had really sent an agent to thwart the coming end of times. It would be an unusual move. Usually they were content with endless self-reflection and narcissism, and let this mud ball mire in misery.

The end was coming. There was no doubt about that. The Al-Masih Ad-Dajjal's time was here. Whether the decadent westerners used the name they preferred, the antichrist, the Al-Masih Ad-Dajjal was here now. It did sadden the jinn that the conception had occurred in the United States. If he could sense the birth mother, get his hands on her, he might use her to take the child to where the jinn had entered the world—Yemen. It would just be more appropriate if the Ad-Dajjal had ripped itself from its mother and entered this festering mud ball in the Middle East. But, instead the entity could move.

The agent looked down to the floor. He reached down and picked up a box of chocolates with a flower tucked in pink ribbon. The sense of the divine entity was strong. The angelic entity had held this box.

Al-Faqih sniffed the box and read the gift card to the

Kushibar. He then pulled the iris out, sniffed it, then ate it. "Hm. Seems like my angel has a sweetie," he hissed.

***

"Nicholas, I have a problem," Forensic Specialist Trey Allen said. He pulled the detective away from the other officers who were dusting the elevator for prints.

"God, we need another problem," Detective Nicholas Paul said. "You geek squad guys are always having some kind of problem. Lay it on me."

"Something is wrong with this whole crime scene," Allen said, then held up a vial filled with a thick, black substance. "This is the blood from Agent Al-Kanani."

"Looks more like dirty motor oil than blood," Nicholas said. "Can you explain that?"

"I can't. Also, how the hell could anyone carry a five-foot sword the size of the one we found past a hospital full of people? And what kind of federal agent carries a five-foot sword as a backup weapon, anyway? This whole thing is just plain weird."

"I hear that," Nicholas said.

"That sword. It looks ancient. We bagged and tagged it and are sending it to forensics. I have a guy who is an expert on medieval weaponry from Eastern Washington University coming in to look at it. It looks like the agent tried to cut up the elevator with that thing. There were gashes in the ceiling of the elevator. Y'know something else? Witnesses say he kicked a security guard who was on the ground. Now they were running away at the time, so their impressions could be flawed. But why would he do that? Why wouldn't he call SPD? He attacked an elevator. SWAT should have been called in. The FBI has their own regional SWAT Team," Allen said. "If he was trying to apprehend a fugitive, why wouldn't he call in some kind of backup? At least inform the locals he is serving a warrant or following someone?"

Nicholas shrugged. "Those are all good questions. This whole situation is crazy. I get the feeling these feds have not told us the whole story. There is something more here than meets the eye."

"If this was a wanted fugitive, locals should have

been notified to at least back him up. He wasn't wearing a bulletproof vest. He was doing tactical operations without a vest? That makes no sense, either. He wasn't equipped for tactical operations, especially going at it alone. How many policies does that violate?"

His phone buzzed, and Nicholas looked at the screen. He sighed and shook his head. "In the middle all of this chaos, Jill Washington managed to rip a strip off of her gown and get it around her neck. She's dead. My one witness to the shooting in Bellevue. Dammit. This day is getting worse by the second."

"Detective Paul," FBI Agent Ibrahim Al-Faqih said loudly as he strode down the hallway. "I need a list of hospital employees who worked the fifth floor. You have that already, yes?"

"I have a list of everyone who worked that day, yes," Nicholas said. "I have lists of everyone on duty and off that day."

"I just need the ones from the fifth floor. Female names only will be fine," the agent said. "I want to question them personally. Every one."

"We have already started debriefing them. None of them saw anything that helps us. In fact, none of them even remember seeing Agent Al-Kanani, oddly enough. They remember evacuating. They remember shots, but did not see where they came from," Nicholas said.

"How is that even possible," Al-Faqih hissed. "No one remembers a shooting on their floor? You must not be asking the right questions."

"Don't tell me how to do my job," the detective shot back. "Maybe if your friend would have followed protocol before waving his giant sword around in a hospital, he would be alive right now. Seems like there is a whole lot going on here, and we don't seem to be in the loop. This started with the Sharks investigation. You feds seem to have surveillance up everyone's asses, but don't share anything substantial. Record every phone call in this country. Snoop through everyone's email. Read their text messages. If you want better help, we need to share information, Agent Al-Faqih."

The FBI Agent leaned close enough to Nicholas that he could smell his breath. It was an odd odor, like death. "Maybe if you spent more time doing your job and less time worrying about what the Federal Government does, more would get done. Just get me that fucking list, Detective. Do your fucking job."

***

"You're not very funny, Angela," Tessa said.

"I wasn't trying to be funny," Angela said. She switched lanes on the 516, also called South Kent des Moines Road, as she drove down an off ramp. Traffic was relatively light tonight. She took an off ramp at a cross street called Meeker, and then turned right to double-back under the 516 to a road called Reith.

"We are going to a warehouse on Military Road South. Not far from the National Guard Armory. Your folks are there."

"I don't know what type of trick you're up to, but it's kinda sick," Tessa mumbled. "If tonight is going to be bad jokes instead of cruising, then you'd better just take me home. I have a ton of homework."

"No joke Tessa. I met your real parents. They want to meet you."

"This is so exciting!" Marisol said in the back seat. "It's just like a movie."

"If you've met my parents, why didn't you tell me? I feel like this is some sick surprise. I'm serious, if this is some joke we won't be speaking when this is all done," Tessa said. "This is not something that is funny to make a joke about."

"I've actually known your parents for a while. This is not the first time I've met them. They've known my parents for years. Maybe since before you were born. Things are not always a coincidence. They will explain that to you. It's a way longer story than I can get into. I don't know all the details, anyway. I hope you are not mad—they are great people, really. They had to hide you from others, and the only way to do that was to put you somewhere that no one could ever make the connection. You were actually born in New York, not

Seattle."

"Oh my God," Tessa sighed. "New York. Ew."

Angela turned onto a side street, and then drove several blocks to an industrial part of Kent. Drearily painted buildings were tagged with graffiti. Occasional vagrants and assorted addicts wandered the streets as they passed. Several groups of thugs hung out on street corners. Dealers. Bangers. Worse, maybe. She would never have come here at night by herself. Why in the world her biological parents would want to meet her here was beyond crazy.

"This is so exciting!" Marisol said. "Maybe someday, they will make a movie about this. I hope that Scarlett Johansen plays me."

"I think she's a little old," Angela mumbled. "Maybe Emma Stone would play me."

"I think by the time they write and pitch it, Emma Stone will be a little old. Why would she play you, and not me?" Tessa said as she forced a laugh. "Besides, her ass isn't big enough to play you. I just want you to know if this is some trick, I will never forgive you."

"My ass isn't big! Hey, in the movie, I hope that Kevin Bacon plays your father, Tessa," Marisol said.

"Marisol. Drop the movie thing, ok? It's not happening," Angela said, then turned and stared. "I know you don't believe me. This is real. This is happening. I am taking you to meet your parents. In a few minutes, it will all be clearer."

"It had better be," Tessa mumbled.

***

"Miss Gray, these are standard questions. We are just trying to understand what happened. You do understand that an ATF Agent was found decapitated in the parking garage at the hospital. This is serious business," the policeman said.

Paige squinted at the officer's nametag. His last name was impossible to pronounce—Badertscher.

"Officer Baderchester... Badechestershire-"

"Officer Badertscher," he interrupted, and then repeated his last name phonetically. "Bod-ach-urr. I know it's hard to pronounce. It's easiest to call me by my first name, Jeremy. Officer or Jeremy is fine."

"Officer, I don't remember anything. I was working, and then I was wandering. Then I found a group of police officers who were escorting people from the hospital. The medics say I have a concussion. Memory loss," Paige said. She felt her lies were unconvincing.

"So you were on what floor that you last remember?" Badertscher said.

"I was assigned the fifth floor today. I am usually assigned the fifth floor. It my normal duty assignment," Paige said.

"I understand you went through a very traumatic experience, and I am glad that you are okay, Miss Gray. It's beyond me how you got hurt, and then made it five floors out of the building during a shooting to wander two blocks away and then wander back? It seems a little far-fetched," the cop said. He jotted some notes in a tiny, spiral notebook. "Are you sure that's all there is to the story? This might have been a terrorist attack that left a federal agent dead."

She could feel the room close in on her. Paige was not a good liar, and she could tell the cop didn't believe her story. "Look. I don't remember anything helpful. Don't remember anything at all other than what you know. I would be happy to take your card and call you if I remember anything. I just want to go home and get some sleep," she complained.

"You were seen running hand-in-hand with a man in a long coat. Witnesses say you were running towards the garage. Do you remember any of that?" the cop questioned.

"Maybe it was a good samaritan who realized I was hurt. I don't know. I don't remember anything. I don't even remember how I hit my head. Are we done?"

Officer Badertscher stared at her. "Yeah. Don't leave town without letting us know, Miss Gray. I will get you a ride home."

***

Nicholas Paul took a break and sipped lukewarm

hospital coffee. The sun was just barely visible as it set. Clouds reflected the orange and made for a fabulous sunset. Shades of red and gray highlighted the orange. He had been in Seattle most of his life. The banks of clouds were a harbinger of rain tomorrow—not that a prediction of rain in Seattle was a hard thing. Odds were, it would rain.

He took another drink. The cup was empty. Here he was, in the middle of Seattle, drinking horrible coffee. Nothing about today made sense to Nicholas.

"Well, this is what a working man looks like," Bellevue Detective Quinn Webb said as he walked towards Nicholas. "Drinking coffee, taking in the sunset. Things we Bellevue Detectives never have time for."

"Maybe if you spent less time at strip clubs and more time doing your job, you would have five minutes to watch the sunset," Nicholas said. "Besides, seems like the last few days my energy has been wasted on that apartment shooting in your town. What are you doing here?"

"Just came by after my day. I heard what happened. I would offer moral support if I had any. This hospital thing has made national news. Already the politicians are banging the gun-control drum. And yeah, sorry that other investigation seems like a total dead-end. I was talking with the other detectives about that case. I was informed late yesterday that Kerr Martinez's name had come up once as a possible suspect in an unsolved drive-by shooting against the South Side Locos over on Beacon Hill. The Sharks and the Locos have been going at it pretty heavy," Webb said. "But Kerr had an iron-clad alibi that checked out. Not that it matters now that he's dead."

Nicholas turned. "That shooting was not in my case file. Wasn't there a Loco killed in that drive by? Why don't people tell me this stuff? Who was that case assigned too?"

"Naw. Just some guy in the wrong place at the wrong time. Businessman got shot and died on the way to the hospital. I think the case was assigned to O'Connor,"

Webb said. "Stupid white guy out for a walk or something. After the investigation, no connection could be found to the Locos. I read the summery of the investigation this morning after hearing Kerr was mentioned and his alibi investigated."

"Now I find all this out. I doubt the people above me are going to give me any more time to work that case. This shooting will be top priority, especially since it is a national story. Who was the guy shot on Beacon Hill?"

"Some guy named Alesio Conti. Left behind a family. Sad," Webb said. "Wrong place, wrong time I guess. This gang crap sure racks up the innocent victims."

"Alesio Conti. Interesting name. Where's he from?"

"Italian immigrant," Webb said. "Legal, I checked with Immigration. Almost had his citizenship. Did everything the right way and ended up dead. Ironic, isn't it? All that work to end up in America, then he gets killed. Sad story."

"What did he do for a living?" Nicholas asked.

Webb shrugged. "I don't know. The summery never

said his occupation other than businessman. Your department, not mine. I figured you would have known all about that case. You should ask someone."

"I will."

***

Forensic Specialist Trey Allen tagged packed boxes of samples from the crime scene. At the rate he was going, he would be here all night trying to tag and bag everything. So far, hundreds of pieces of evidence had been collected and prepped for the lab. The elevator, by itself, represented a day's work in prints alone. In all of his years as a forensic specialist, this had been the largest and most complicated crime scene he had ever been part of.

Allen loaded several cases into the SUV. He had taken several from the scene of Al-Kanani's death in the parking garage. The sword had been a particularly interesting piece of evidence.

"Forensic Specialist Allen. Where will all of these items go for analysis?" Al-Faqih asked as he came up behind

"The state crime lab here in Seattle. We have so much evidence it will be overwhelming to them. It may take weeks for some of this stuff to even get analyzed. Hopefully, we will have caught our suspect before the stuff is even done, and we will be just using it at trial," Allen said. He went around to the driver's side of the van and unlocked the door. Al-Faqih followed him quietly.

"Are you transporting these items right now?" the agent questioned. "You have the sword, yes? In this van? Samples of blood?"

"Yeah. I need to take this load over. We will have more stuff later. We are trying to work around medical people, keep them out of our stuff and get the evidence tagged. It's going to be an all-nighter," Allen said as he sat behind the steering wheel.

Al-Faqih grabbed him, and then placed his meaty hand on the Forensic Specialist's forehead. "You little mortal maggot. You will forget this conversation. You will forget this evening. Sleep, until I allow you to wake.

If I allow you to live."

Allen exhaled, and then slumped over the steering wheel.

***

Tessa sat with her arms crossed and stared out the window of the Honda. "This is total bullshit. You know that? If we get kidnapped in Kent, I hold you personally responsible."

"No one ever gets kidnapped in Kent," Angela said.

Marisol leaned forward. "What about that college kid? Or those girl scouts? The missing homeless people? That social worker? Those Jehovah Witnesses-"

"All right," Angela snapped. "That's not going to happen to us. Those were freak incidents."

"Only a couple dozen of them," Tessa said. "Are we there yet?"

Angela pulled into a deserted parking lot. A few weeds stuck up through cracks in the cement. The lines that designated parking spaces were faded and chipped. Most of the streetlights that shined in the lot functioned marginally well. Ragged fences between buildings were topped with razor-wire to keep out unwelcome visitors.

A light gently wafted through a single window in a metal-sided warehouse. The three cautiously locked the car and walked to the door of the building. Tessa noted that another car was parked near the northwest corner of the lot. It had Nevada license plates.

"Are my parents from Nevada? I hope they're not Mormons," Tessa said. "Wouldn't that take the cake?"

"Maybe they're aliens," Marisol laughed. "Area 51 aliens, not the other kind. ¿Qué pasa?"

"Not funny. Not in the least," Tessa said. "Borderline racist."

"Oh. My. God," Marisol sighed. She clomped her feet. "So dramatic."

The trio stopped at the door of the warehouse. It was a glass door with bars. Angela pushed on it and it opened. Inside was a waiting room lit with one flickering fluorescent light overhead. Marisol fumbled for a light switch. She found one, flicked it, and the banks of lamps sputtered and lit.

Angela led the trio through the lobby, into a doorway, and down a long corridor. To the left a door opened into a brightly lit conference room. She pushed it open and the three cautiously entered.

The room was simple. The paint was institutional tan. In the corner of the room was a water cooler and a plastic trash can. A dispenser of paper cups hung on the side of the clear jug of water on the top of the cooler. A large wood table was surrounded by commercial-grade wood chairs with reddish brown upholstery. On the table were two cans of caffeine-free Diet Coke.

On two of the chairs sat a man and a woman. Both late thirties. His hair was brown, parted smartly on the left side. He was immaculately groomed with a black leather jacket over a cream-colored button down shirt. She had shoulder-length blonde hair that rested on a dark blue blouse, and light red lipstick. Their eyes followed Tessa as she entered the room.

The woman smiled. Perfect teeth were revealed

behind her pink lips. The pair stood and the man pressed his quivering lips together.

"Tessa," the woman said. "You look great. You've grown into a fine woman. How I have thought about you all these years."

Tessa could feel her body tense. Her eyes watered as she looked at the pair, then at the cans of soda. Sudden panic set in. "You're not Mormons, are you?"

***

Dorian Christenson stood at the water's edge of Dash Point State Park and looked across the bay at the lights of Maury Island. He cradled the two barrels he had taken from his Heckler and Koch HK 45 pistols and threw them. They spun as they sailed through the air, and then splashed far away from shore.

The ripples disappeared rapidly in the choppy waters. The enforcer contemplated how, if someone threw a stone into smooth pond, the undulations would work all the way across the water. Here in the chaos of the wind-blown chop, the splash vanished after a second as the churn erased the evidence. How appropriate he thought of it as evidence, because it was.

He watched the lights of Maury Island in the distance reflect on the water. It would have been a serene place, except the distant hum of engines from vehicles reminded him of the presence of other people. Dorian contemplated how to extract himself from the mess he currently found himself in. If he would have gone with the jinn, he might have been able to fight him later out of sight of the public. Or he would be dead.

As he watched the reflection of the lights, he realized he had become distracted. That distraction now created risk. The public shoot-out with a federal agent created insane risk. Witnesses created risk. He had fucked up.

He cautiously walked back to the Cayman. Keith was asleep in the passenger seat. He snored loudly as his little hoofy foot twitched. Dorian wondered what a demon would dream about.

"We have work to do," Dorian said. "I have made a decision."

The imp stretched and yawned, then scratched. He looked intently at the enforcer. "I recognize dat expression. Its da 'get ta work' expression dat precedes a job. What are we doin'?"

Dorian took the envelope out from under his seat, removed a burner phone, and put a battery in it. He dialed Leo's number. The phone rang and he heard the old man's voice.

"Mister G. I need information. I need the names and addresses of anyone who might be able to identify me from the incident we discussed earlier. Can you use your source in the SPD to get a list of anyone that seems to be a reliable witness to the incident today?" Dorian asked.

"The feds are involved now, so some of it is out of my hands. I will do my best to get what you need. Where should I start?" Leo said.

"Specifically, if there is anyone the investigators think will be a reliable witness to what happened. People were panicking and running," Dorian said. "I think, even as public as the incident was, there will not be that many. Names and addresses would be great. I am positive that the cameras were out. I am going to clean this up, Mister G."

"Let me get back to you. This will make for a sleepless night, D. I don't like sleepless nights."

"I know. This will be fixed. I need the address of one witness in particular, a nurse-practitioner named Paige Gray," Dorian said.

"Call me in a day or two. I will have what you need on her. Let my connection in the department earn the money I pay them," Leo said. "Good luck."

Dorian pulled the battery out of the phone. He looked at the demon. "You ready to work?"

"Yeah," Keith said. His tail twitched. "What are we gonna do?"

"I need you to wipe Paige Grey's memories. When the heat is off, we are going to do it."

The imp nodded. "Good call, boss."

***

Inside the SPD van, FBI Agent Ibrahim Al-Faqih took a

bag of blood he had stolen from the hospital and replaced the samples of ATF Agent Nabil Al-Kanani's blood with human blood. He pushed the vials of thick, black liquid into a trash bag, and then put the replacement vials and bottles in the plastic bags. After he was satisfied, he then replaced swabs and strips with ones that had touched human blood.

Forensic Specialist Trey Allen was in a stupor. He slumbered fitfully, magically induced by the power of the jinn. Al-Faqih took the scimitar from the van. It was wrapped in several layers of plastic, labeled, and taped. There were too many pictures of the crime scene for the FBI Agent to do anything about. However, by tampering with as much of the physical evidence as possible, then contaminating and replacing the rest, he could throw the investigation into chaos. He was saddened by the untimely death of Al-Kanani, but the silver lining was that he knew the mortals would be confused. They would chew up their increasingly fleeting lives in a vain attempt to understand what happened here.

They were just marking time until the awakening of the Al-Masih Ad-Dajjal, anyway. The birth had taken place, and now it was just a matter of time for the Al-Masih to take its rightful place. After that, this world would be blood and flames as it was reformed into something more brutal. He smirked as he took the sword and put it in his SUV.

His phone rang. "This is Al-Faqih," the FBI agent stated. "You have the list I asked for? Great. Send it to me."

He walked around to Allen and pulled him close. Al-Faqih pushed his meaty hand against the Forensic Specialist's forehead. "Wake and remember nothing, you son-of-a-whore."

Allen coughed and sat up. He stared at Al-Faqih blankly. "What... happened?"

"I think you were getting ready to take this evidence to wherever it is you people take it," the FBI Agent said.

"Uh, yeah," Allen said. "Thanks."

"Think nothing of it," Al-Faqih snorted.

***

The blonde woman took a step towards Tessa. The man smiled. "No. We're not Mormons."

"Oh, thank God," Tessa said. "I can only handle so much craziness in one night."

Marisol and Angela laughed. "Tessa, I want you to meet James and Brittaney Currin. Your biological parents."

Brittaney had tears rolling down her cheeks. "You are so beautiful. I'm not surprised—the women in our family have great features."

"Your mom is right. Great genetics," James said. "It is so good to see you."

Tessa stared at the pair. "This is all really weird," she said emotionlessly. "I have parents. They didn't leave me at that hospital."

Brittaney raised her hands to her face. "We are so sorry about that, Tessa. We had to protect you from those who would want to hurt you, and we were so young. If they knew who we were, and who you are, your life would have been in danger. The only choice we had was to create as much distance between us as possible. You are the future, in more ways than you know-"

"Your mom is laying it on pretty thick," James interrupted. "We just wanted to let you know we are here for you. That it was never about not wanting you, but protecting you from evil people. What a relief it was to know that Officer Paul and Serenity had adopted you. You can't believe how hard it was to watch from afar and not introduce ourselves."

"How long have you four known each other?" Tessa said. "Why didn't I know?"

"Most of our lives," Angela said.

"Christ. And you have managed to keep it a secret? You are the biggest blabbermouth ever, Marisol. I can't believe any of this," Tessa grumped. "This is all very overwhelming. I'm sorry if I don't seem to be jumping for joy. Things are moving very fast. No matter what, I will always consider my parents my parents. I mean Nick and

Serenity my parents. You know what I meant."

"Our parents were very tight-lipped and keep secrets pretty well," Marisol said demurly. "We didn't know what was up. Besides, they threatened to ground us for life once we knew."

"It's understandable. We just wanted you to know we are here. No pressure," Brittaney sniffled. "We would never try to replace your adopted parents. We've quietly been behind the scenes all these years. Been to a couple of your soccer and volleyball games. Saw one of your violin recitals. Never to close, but we've checked on you. Always maintained distance so as to not lead anyone to you. We're so proud of the young woman you have become. I hear you have great grades, too. I understand you want to be a nurse. Great career choice."

"You know so much about me. All these years, within arm's reach of me at times and I never even knew it. It's just so weird," Tessa said.

"You want to go get coffee or something?" James said. "Catch up a little bit?"

"No," Tessa said. "I kind of need to process all of this right now. One thing at a time. It's not that I don't want to get to know you. This is just really heavy and a lot to take in all at once. Twenty minutes ago I thought we were going cruising. Now, I have met my birth parents who I didn't even know were still alive. It's just a little much all at once."

***

Theresa O'Connor had been a Detective in the SPD for over five years. She had the day off, but the department had activated everyone once the shooting had been reported. She arrived at Harborview Medical Center and crossed the police line.

Detective Nicholas Paul had sent her a text that he needed to talk to her. She moved through the officers who supervised the parking lot and searched for evidence. O'Connor asked a patrol supervisor if he had seen Paul and he had directed her towards the entrance to the hospital.

She saw him and carefully walked toward him. He

was talking to two men she recognized—local FBI Agents Church and Reed. The three saw her and nodded.

"Detective O'Connor. Glad you could make it," Paul said. "Sorry you got activated."

"It's the job," she said. "Nicholas, good to see you. Agents Church and Reed—it's been a while."

"Detective O'Connor," the agents said together.

"I have a question about another case you have been working on," Paul said. "That drive-by on Beacon Hill. The one targeted at the Locos. You have any leads in that case?"

"You don't have your hands full with just one shooting, Detective?" O'Connor smiled. "Why are you worried about that case?"

"Just tell me what's up with it," he said. "I ask because one of your early suspects in that case was killed in that Bellevue apartment shooting."

"Yeah. I heard that. I checked out that Kerr Martinez guy. He is a banger, for sure. Had quite a rap sheet. Several stints in juvenile detention and one in the state pen over in Walla Walla. South Side Shark. But he had multiple witnesses that corroborated his story, all Sharks, however. No way it was him," she said.

"The guy who was killed, Alesio Conti, what do you know about him?"

"Just some business guy. Worked for an outfit named Asian Import and Work Specialists Corporation," she said.

"Does he have a record?" Paul asked.

"Nothing. I ran him, ran variations of his name. Just a guy in the wrong place at the wrong time," she said. "No big. A few parking tickets."

"Asian Import and Work Specialists Corporation cross pollinates with the Italian Mob," Agent Reed said. "Someone should have flagged that for you."

Paul and O'Connor looked at each other. "No one told us," she said.

"FBI offices don't always share everything with local law enforcement. We are concerned about information leaks," Reed said. "Honestly, Attorney General Holder doesn't much care for local cops. We are under orders."

"So the guy killed in the drive-by might be in the Mob and nobody saw it. Nice," Nicholas said. "And we have an apartment full of stiffs. All this time and no one put it together."

"You're not thinking-" Reed said.

"I think I just found my connection," Paul interrupted.

***

James and Brittaney walked the three girls through the lobby and out to the Honda in the parking lot. Brittaney choked back sniffles as James made small talk. Tessa was quiet, completely overwhelmed by the night's events.

"We sure hope you will see us again," James said.

"I would like that," Tessa said. She looked around the lot. "Is this your building?"

"Yeah," he smiled. "We do property management and buy foreclosures. Flip properties, like you see on TV. It's usually pretty lucrative work, if you can do it right.

The last couple years have been feast or famine, but if you're smart you can make it work out. I have a degree in accounting, so I plan for the down times and don't panic. Write off every nail and paintbrush. Part of the business."

"Wow," Tessa said, "sounds interesting."

"Probably not for a teenager, if you're honest," Brittaney sniffled and held out her hand. "Well. Until we see you again."

Tessa shook her hand, and then gave her birth mother an awkward hug. The woman burst out in tears. James gently put his arm around Brittaney and pulled her away. He held out his hand. slowly. Tentatively, she reached up and shook. Stiffly, she leaned into him, and then gave him a hug. Oddly, her birth father felt comfortable. She could feel the biological connection. A whole weird, strange, hidden world had just opened up to her. Right now she was in shock. Later, she would have a million questions.

"Sorry I'm so overwhelmed," Tessa said.

"It's overwhelming. Sorry to be so sneaky," James said. "Our love for you has never wavered. Please don't doubt that. We had to set you free from the family cage to keep you safe."

"Why would my life have been in danger?" Tessa asked. "That sounds ominous."

"Long story for another day. You have blood in you that is unique, carried down for centuries. Think of it like royalty." James laughed. "But you are already overwhelmed."

"That's so cool!" Marisol said, and curtseyed. "Queen Tessa Paul. M'lady."

"Hardly," Tessa said.

The three girls drove away in silence. Tessa looked in the rearview mirror as her birth parents disappeared. She turned, glared at Angela then slugged her in the arm.

"What the hell was that for?" Angela cried. "I thought you would be happy!"

"I'm not sure what I am, but I'm pissed you kept this

from me all these years. Take us home."

***

Brittaney sniffled as the girls drove away. James put his arm around his wife and watched the tail lights of the Honda Accord vanish into the darkness.

"Do you think she will tell her father and mother that we met?" she asked.

He shrugged. "It's an unknown variable, for sure. It's too far into the game now. She had to know sometime. Too much rides on her. We needed to move her into the big world. This is something she can't hide from, and we can't hide her much longer."

Brittaney started to bawl again.

"For god's sake, woman. Turn that valve off," James growled. "She's gone. We will see her again."

"Tears of joy," she sniffled. "A parent just hopes for the best for their kids. She has grown up so fast. She seems so mature and well adjusted. I just hope we did the right thing all of those years ago."

He shrugged. "Time will tell. She was raised as part of

a great family, and look how she handled tonight. She has strength of will, an iron psyche, determination. Exactly what we knew she would be. Family traits. Even without us, our daughter turned out perfect."

Chapter Seven
—Threads—

Two days after the shooting at Harborview, Detective Nicholas Paul looked at folders filled with contradictory interviews. He had read and reread every one of them. They were so confusing and worthless. The investigation was a mess unlike anything he had ever seen.

Worse, now the evidence collected at the crime scene was in total disarray. Samples were cross contaminated, improperly tagged, and missing. The body of ATF Agent Nabil Al-Kanani spontaneously combusted several hours after his death. The forensics teams had not even finished bagging samples. No one could explain the mysterious reaction that caused the flames that destroyed his corpse. The samples of the blood that were left over were of multiple types. The sword that had reportedly been carried by the agent had vanished into thin air. Multiple pictures of the weapon still existed, and the expert brought in to examine it said any origin or age would be impossible to establish. Based on the photos, he guessed ancient and Persian. It made this worse. A genuine artifact of that age would have been worth millions.

Forensic Specialist Trey Allen had been suspended pending an investigation by Internal Affairs. The FBI threatened a grand jury. He was missing large blocks of time, and had the symptoms of a concussion. However, he had no physical injury he could remember. The union became involved after a thorough battery of urine and blood tests had come back negative for drugs or alcohol.

The final straw was that people were changing their stories. Consistently, the witnesses who had seen little to begin with in their panicked evacuation of the hospital now remembered different details. The suspect involved had started as a white male, thirty years old, in a long coat. Now he had every description from tall African male to short Chinese. Beard, no beard, long hair, short hair. The consistent thread was that the story had changed. Something else was at play here that he did not understand. Nicholas had contemplated witness tampering of some sort, but even under intense questioning none of them cracked.

FBI Agent Reed was on his way and Paul began to straighten his desk. His stomach was tied in knots and his head hurt. There'd only been a few times in this job that he felt overwhelmed. He felt that way now as events seem to spin out of control.

Nicholas saw Reed stride into the room. The FBI Agent surveyed the area, and then spotted the Detective over the cubical walls as he waved. The two met halfway and shook hands before the agent handed over two folders.

"Agent Reed. So glad you could come by," Paul said.

"No problem, Detective. Here is the information you asked for. I would greatly appreciate you not sharing this information widely. Crime families have a way of hearing more than they should, and it just takes one person in a department this big to be on their payroll."

"Thanks. I owe you," the detective said. "I hate to run like this, but it's been assholes and elbows since Al-Kanani's death."

"Any forward movement from the federal level on the case?" Paul asked. "Between us?"

Reed shook his head. "If I had anything to tell you, I would. We are stumped. This fiasco with the evidence has us in a mess. Missing weapon, body combusting. We have samples, looking for residue of the chemical reaction that caused the fires, but nothing we can identify. NSA has been rooting through thousands of texts and phone calls. Nothing we can put our finger on there, either. The terrorist chatter in the Seattle area is no more than normal. I read a summery about your witnesses changing their stories, so we have subpoenaed their bank accounts. Not one has had a sudden influx of cash that might explain a change of story. We are stumped. The plan is to continue to look at electronics until we get a lead."

"What about the samples that the feds took? Any

luck?"

"It will take weeks to get anything back, and preliminaries are looking bad. I can't explain all the mistaken tags and contaminated samples we have. If I didn't know better, I would say someone tried to mess it all up. We are opening a federal probe into Trey Allen. We don't know what else to do," he said. "Problem is, he isn't the only one who handled samples. Usually this kind of stuff is cut and dried. To make matters worse, our IT guys at Langley worked over your mime image. It's less than impressive and in the folder."

Paul opened the folder and stared at the image. "You're kidding, right?"

"No, I'm not. When you recolor the photo with skin tones and eliminate the paint, that's what we get. Spitting image, right?"

The detective sighed as he read the name at the bottom of the security camera photo. The mime was Vladimir Vladimirovich Putin, Soviet Dictator. "You would think he is too busy invading small countries to come and shoot up a hospital in Seattle."

"Yeah. So chances of extradition on this one are pretty slim. Good luck, Detective." Reed patted him on the shoulder and strode away. "If you leave now, it should only take about twenty-four hours to fly to Moscow."

Paul shook his head. "I don't know who is doing this or even how, but I'm gonna find the bastard," he hissed under his breath. The detective took the folder back to his desk and opened the thicker one. It was the fed's file on Asian Import and Work Specialists Corporation.

He flipped through several sheets of financial information and assets. Then he found a picture of an older fellow, taken from a distance. The caption of the photo was *Leo Giovanni, CEO. Head of the Giovanni Crime Family, Italian Mafia.*

"A dead Italian shot in a drive by. Well, hello Leo Giovanni," Paul said. "We need to have a conversation."

* * *

Paige Gray paid the cab driver, and then slowly

walked up the sidewalk to her condo in Central Seattle. The yard was surrounded by shrubs and trees and the grass had recently cut by the lawn care company. A strip of sidewalk connected the street side sidewalk to a set of steps that led to the entrance of her unit. Her condo was on a quiet side street, and traffic was very light. Around the back was a carport where her car was parked: she would be glad when she would be cleared to drive again after her concussion. A light hummed on a pole near the house, casting artificial light across the yard.

The sun had fallen, and she was bored stiff from inactivity. Her supervisor had insisted that she take time off work due to her head injury. She had protested that she was able to work, but he repeatedly pointed to the fact her head injury was serious enough to cause memory loss. She was struggling to maintain the façade of ignorance.

She had been interviewed four times now by the SPD. Each time she said she remembered nothing about the incident. Each time they pushed harder to get answers. Paige maintained her ignorance, but the detectives sent to interview her were more persistent every time.

Paige wandered up the walkway. She stopped to survey the shrubs her gardener had trimmed earlier in the day. He had done a fine job. Movement caught her eye and she gasped as someone lurked in the shadows.

"I've got pepper spray and will use it if you come close to me," she growled. Paige's shaky hand shot into her purse and she produced a canister. "I know how to use it!"

"No need for that," Dorian said. "I was hoping we could have one conversation that didn't end poorly for once."

"Jesus Christ, I'd thought maybe you were a bad dream," Paige said. "At the very least I would never see you again. How did you find me?"

"That is not important," he said. "How are you doing?"

"Just fine. Lying to the cops every day, multiple times

a day. Pretending to be hurt worse than I actually am. Just peachy," she grumbled. "Not really the career path I had hoped to be on and at this late date."

"Well. Good to know," he said. "Sorry that things went sideways like that."

"Everywhere I go, I look for demons now. Spirits. I've read three books on witchcraft in the last two days. I'm still not even sure you and that little Bill Clinton puppet exist."

"Oh, I exist, princess!" Keith shouted from the pocket of the enforcer's coat.

"I came to talk to you about what happened," Dorian said.

"Talk to me about turning my world on its head?" Paige snapped. "What's next? Aliens? Bigfoot?"

"Could you put that pepper spray back in your purse?" Dorian said. "I really don't think you will need to use that on me."

"Are you sure?" she said.

"Pretty sure, I think."

"What really happened the other day? Are my memories accurate? That man was a monster. You said a jinn? And you have a demon you carry around in a little bag?" Paige questioned. "Dorian, I am struggling here. Before I met you, I had a normal life."

"The world is not the normal place you thought it was," he said. "It is far bigger and darker than most know. I am here to help you with it, however. I can give you that normal life back again."

"What do you mean?" Paige said.

"I can take your memories away. I can make it like it never happened. The knowledge you now have I can have removed. You can go back to your life before meeting me. I'll be just a figment of a man at your Aunt Pauline's funeral. I am here to help take your life back," he said. "I can make this go away. You do not have to live with the lies anymore."

"Is that part of your powers as an angel?" she said. "You can erase my memories?"

"Not my powers, but his," Dorian said quietly. "He

can do that."

Keith climbed up from the pocket of Dorian's new Lois Vuitton coat and perched on his shoulder. "Dem powers reserved for me, sister. Erasin' minds is more of a demon ding dan an angel ding."

"It's that demon thing again!" she said and pointed. "It is so creepy!"

"More than a little creepy, for sure," the enforcer said. "You should see him eat. It is disgusting beyond belief."

"Hey! I'm right here. Maybe you two shouldn't talk about me like I can't hear. I might erase both of yer memories back to fourth grade. You will be overwhelmed by da urge to dunk her pigtails in da inkwell. Wouldn't dat be a bitch," the imp said. "Fuckin' humans, anyway. I get tired of all of yer antics."

Dorian took several steps towards Paige and she met him. They stood on the grass, and she looked up into his eyes. "Maybe there are things I don't want to forget."

"Oh, my God," the demon squealed. "Really? We

come here ta wipe dis bimbo's mind and now we are havin' a moment? Dis is like da plot of da worst porno movie, ever. Now if we just had a pizza delivery guy show up we could get dis show on da fuckin' road. Lights. Camera. Action!"

Dorian brushed the imp off his shoulder. Keith tumbled into a bush with a squawk. "Ignore him. I usually do."

"Whatever you do—hit man.. assassin... CIA... is there a future with us?"

"There is no future with me. The best thing is to erase me from your mind. Let us do this. Just clear your thoughts. It will be over in a few seconds."

Dorian could see the reflection of the lamp light as the tears in her eyes started to pool.

"Dorian, will this hurt?"

"This will not hurt. I promise, Paige."

"How will I know? I won't remember what happens or what you said," she said. "I won't remember you, will I?"

"That is the best thing for you," Dorian said. "I will remember you, Paige Gray."

"Since I won't remember this anyway, what are you?" she said.

"Paige... I work as a mob enforcer. I'm a professional killer."

"Makes as much sense as anything else that has happened in the last couple days." Paige sighed and leaned against him. He could feel her warm breath against his throat. She gently placed her lips against his neck, then again on his cheek. Dorian turned his head and their lips touched. Her lips were soft and her tongue tasted like cinnamon gum.

They kissed, and he held her tight. Dorian's eyes opened. The demon had climbed up the back of his coat and gently slid onto her shoulder. Keith rubbed his little porcine paws together and reached for her temple.

"I am sorry, Paige," the enforcer said. "I'll see you around. Keith, do it."

The demon placed his hand against her head. His tail

twitched as he concentrated, then he stepped away. The imp turned to Dorian.

"You ain't gonna believe dis, boss. Somethin' has been in her mind," Keith said.

Dorian and Paige both turned to stare at the imp. "What do you mean?" the enforcer asked. "What is in her mind? Is she possessed?"

"No. Not possessed. Something has been in her mind before. Something old. Ancient. Powerful. It has not damaged her memories, just searched dem," the demon said. "Somethin' much more powerful dan I could ever hope to be."

"I'm sorry. I would know, wouldn't I?" Paige said.

"Not necessarily," Keith said. "It has masked its tracks. I can tell. It has snooped in yer brain, and den tried to conceal its intrusion. But I can tell."

"Why am I even talking to you?" she asked. "I'm not even sure I believe in you."

"Whatever, princess. Talk to da hand," the imp said as he stuck up his paw. "Dat's what I love about broads.

No matter what, you always know less dan dey do."

"Just finish this," Dorian said. "It will not matter when you're done."

"I dunno. Dis complicates dings. It might rebound back to me. I'm not willin' to take dat chance," Keith protested. "Find another sucker to do dis."

"Kseryth Nysreff. I order you to wipe her memories of me. Now," Dorian said.

"Fuck! Dirty pool, old man," the imp said. "Fine. I never should have told you my real name. Now da broad knows it, too."

"She will not once you erase it from her memory," Dorian said. "Finish this."

"I want to know what else has been in my head. Wait a minute," Paige said. "We aren't doing anything until I have more answers."

Keith exploded in a mist of blood and guts. His blood and entrails splattered as Dorian heard the crack of a gun. He pushed Paige backwards and spun in the direction of the shot. His hands went to the handles of his pistols.

"Don't do it," a voice boomed. A large man in a dark suit stepped out of the darkness. Heavily muscled, six and a half feet tall. The giant held a Sig P228 pistol. "You can't get to them before I can put a bullet through the nurse."

Dorian could see the empty eyes sockets, the tiny rough horns like a sacrilegious crown of thorns around the jinn's head, the rough-reptilian skin. The demon licked its lips with a forked tongue. Its ragged teeth glinted with moisture in the lamp light. Another jinn.

"Then what is the next move?" Dorian growled.

Paige stood up and took a deep breath.

"Don't scream you little bitch, or the next bullet will be in you," the jinn ordered. "The half breed and I have business."

"You seem to know who I am. Who are you?" Dorian said.

"FBI Agent Ibrahim Al-Faqih. You knew my brother ATF Agent Nabil Al-Kanani. You murdered him. Now it's time for a reckoning," Al-Faqih said. "This all makes sense, now. The lust demon. You being a half-breed angel. Son of a fallen angel, yes? I was worried that you might be the vanguard of God's holy army. Instead, you are the remnants of a night of forbidden passion. It must be a huge stone that hangs around your neck your whole life to know you are alive because some angel didn't pull out fast enough to spurt his seed on your mother's stomach. You're just an accident. A nephilim mistake."

"Do not talk about my mother. At least I have one. Is everyone who works for the Federal Government a demon?" Dorian said angrily. "I have often suspected as much. Why the hell would God send an army to Earth?"

"Are you counting congress, or just the possessed? Just slowly take your pistols out and throw them this way. One finger only. No sudden moves," the FBI Agent commanded. "I'm not afraid to kill her to make a point, you fool."

"You have made your point, already," Dorian said. "So let me guess. This is about revenge."

"Does it matter what it's about?" Al-Faqih said.

Dorian slowly lifted his .45s from their holsters and threw them to the jinn. They landed on the grass in front of him. He picked them up, pulled the magazines, and ejected the cartridge in the chamber with a pull of the slide.

"You had better take good care of those," the enforcer said. "I want those back when we are done with our father-son talk."

"The end is not what you want it to be," Al-Faqih said and held out his hand. Molten metal spurted from his hand and filled an invisible mold. Sparks flew and the smell of sulfur became overwhelming. The glowing steel flowed into the form of a giant scimitar. The giant cut the air as he swung the sword around his head several times.

"During the Middle Elamite period, southwest Iran was ruled by King Untash-Napirisha. He was the undisputed ruler of Elam. He founded and built Dur-Untash. I forged a blade similar to this one for him.

Folded the iron ten thousand times. One of his court sorcerers had summoned and bound me in what is now Yemen, and then travelled back to Elam. My final act for him before his death. I stayed bound, handed down from sorcerer to sorcerer until I was released when the city was destroyed by the Assyrian king Ashurbanipal in 640 BC. It was my first time in the physical realms, and I never returned to what you would refer to as Jahannam," the jinn said. "This realm is so violent. I saw the World Wars in person. I was there through the wars with Israel. This world is covered in blood. To call humans animals would be to denigrate beasts."

"Jahannam?" Paige murmered.

"Muslim version of hell," Dorian said. "Even hotter than Afghanistan."

"The next war will make all the ones before pale in comparison. The Al-Masih Ad-Dajjal is here. Now. On this world, waiting to be awakened to the power to create ultimate chaos," the jinn said. "I wonder how many billions will die? Exciting prospect. I love war."

"Every version of Armageddon ends up with the bad guys losing. I am not sure why you are so excited about it," Dorian said. "I would think you would do all you could to avoid it."

"Don't worry about it. Now, we need to talk about the death of Nabil. It's time for revenge," the demon said. "And once I've killed you, your woman is next."

"I'm not his. He has been very clear on that, if it makes a difference," Paige said. "He is a confirmed bachelor."

"Sure, play that card now," Dorian grumbled.

"We'll do this by hand," Al-Faqih said. He raised the scimitar, and then stabbed the sword two feet into the ground. "We don't need guns for this."

"Paige. Run!" Dorian said as he took off his new Louis Vuitton.

Al-Faqih charged forward. The enforcer threw the jacket to the ground and lunged. He took three steps. The demon's huge legs had already crossed the yard and the two met in the middle. Dorian leapt and caught the agent between his legs as he swung his meaty fist.

The enforcer scissored his legs together and made Al-Faqih sprawl forward onto his face. Dorian rolled quickly onto the jinn's back, hammered his fists against the back of the demon's head, then grabbed his long left arm and rolled backwards. The agent rolled over and was caught in an arm bar.

Dorian could feel the strength in his opponent's arm as he fought to pull it back. The two struggled as the agent rolled to his feet and the enforcer pushed forward with his hips. The elbow cracked as he pulled it backwards and Al-Faqih roared. He grabbed Dorian by the neck, lifted him up, and threw him. He tumbled and rolled to his feet.

Al-Faqih stood and grabbed his wrist. He jerked the arm back into the socket and roared again. Dorian advanced with his fist raised. The giant threw several punches and the enforcer bobbed and weaved to avoid the blows.

"You should have heard Al-Kanani squeal when I

lopped off his head."

The demon shook his head angrily. "You cannot beat me. You might hurt me, but you cannot win this. Eventually, you will tire. Your body will give out and then I will rip out your heart."

"It is going to be a long night, then," Dorian said. He threw a low kick. His shin drove into the side of Al-Faqih's left knee with a crack. The knee gave way as ligaments and tendons stressed and ripped. The knee started to bend inward and the enforcer spun backwards. The heel of his foot caught the agent's right knee on the outside, and the joint separated. The demon went down to the ground.

Dorian stepped back then aimed a kick at Al-Faqih's face. The bottom of his Brioni smashed against the demon's jaw. Bones shattered and teeth splintered. The jinn tried to roar, but it came out as a loud gurgle. Through the pain, the giant reached up and grabbed the enforcer's leg and pulled it out from under him. He fell backwards and landed on his back with his hands out to break the fall.

The jinn reached for him and Dorian hammered his face with the heel of his foot. Al-Faqih's nose fractured and was pushed back into his face. Several more kicks landed on target as the enforcer drove the heel of his right foot against the soft tissues and bones. One of the kicks pushed the fractured jaw out of socket and it hung loosely. The demon clawed at his face, trying to stop the blows and he let go of Dorian's slacks.

The enforcer rolled backwards away from the jinn and to his feet. Al-Faqih sat up and pushed his jaw back into place with a wet crunch. His nose pushed itself forward out of his skull and began to straighten itself. He worked his mandible back and forth as new teeth erupted through bloody gums to replace the ones that had been broken.

Dorian took a quick step forward, jumped up on his left foot to gain momentum, then kicked with his right. The ball of his foot caught the agent squarely on the forehead. The impact snapped his head back with enough force to break his neck. The bones grated together as the vertebrae splintered. A normal man would have been decapitated by the force of the elevated front kick, but the jinn fell backwards onto the grass and seized.

The enforcer began to repeatedly kick the demon in the ribs and chest while he was down.

"Dorian! For god's sake, he's dead!" Paige shouted.

"No, he is not!" Dorian shouted back. "He can rebuild his body in the material world. No matter what I do, eventually it heals. Besides, I thought I told you to run!"

"You cut the last one's head off. You need the sword," she said. She jumped forward and tugged at the massive blade. It was impaled too deep into the earth for her to pull out. She tried with all of her strength, but it was stuck. She worked it back and forth to try to loosen it.

Ribs cracked as Dorian continued to kick the giant. He brought all of his weight down on Al-Faqih's chest in a powerful stomp. The agent's sternum fragmented and the breastbone separated from his rib cage. His ragged gasps for breath became wheezes as broken ribs ground together. Another stomp to his throat crushed the demon's larynx.

Dorian could see Paige still trying to pull the sword out of the earth. He leapt over his antagonist and grabbed the handle of the blade. It took several tugs and the scimitar began to loosen. As the blade pulled free, Paige screamed as Al-Faqih pulled the enforcer down to the ground.

The demon was much stronger than Dorian. The pair rolled several times, and Al-Faqih ended up on top. He pulled back his fist, and threw several punches. The enforcer covered up and shifted position. Some of the blows missed and cratered the yard. Two struck squarely on the side of his head, and the bastard son of a fallen angel saw sparkles of light. He fought to maintain consciousness.

Dorian wrapped his legs around Al-Faqih's left leg and locked them down—the Brazilian Ju-Jitsu position of

Half Guard. He pulled the demon close, then reached down with his right hand and hooked it under the jinn's left leg. The agent's face was close, and the enforcer could see the damaged tissues of his opponent's face knitting back together after his kicks.

Al-Faqih's breath was hot against Dorian's cheek. He tried to bite, but the enforcer grabbed him by the throat and pushed him away.

"You cannot win this, half-breed. Just let me finish this quickly, or when I win I will rip your woman apart from the inside out. I will make sure there is enough of you left alive to watch me bend her over and take the spoils of my conquest. Human women never survive, however," Al-Faqih snorted. "Not strong enough. Internal injuries. Never goes quick."

Dorian was still locked on the demon's leg. He reached up with his left hand and ripped the demon's ear off. The giant howled.

"Eight pounds of pressure to remove an ear from a human head. Now that I know things can be removed, watch this," Dorian whispered. He reached, down and grabbed the demon's testicles and yanked. The pull ruptured and separated the agent's balls from his body. The scream that had followed the amputation of his ear was nothing like the animalistic scream that followed his neutering.

In intense pain, Al-Faqih tried to double over, but was pinned by Dorian who kept him locked down with his legs. Demons are not omniscient—they know what they have seen, know what they can learn. Jinn are highly intelligent and have keen memories, but sometimes the vagaries of the modern world have passed them by.

The agent had basic skills in ground fighting and Brazilian Jiu-Jitsu as part of his academy training. However, a couple days of basic moves does not begin to entail what the knowledge of someone who had trained for decades would possess. So when Al-Faqih brought his left knee forward towards Dorian to try to escape, he had no way of knowing what was about to follow.

The enforcer pulled the demon's left leg up with his under hooked hand and pushed his right leg down with his legs. Dorian rolled to the left. Al-Faqih was forced to do the splits much farther than his material body allowed—his hip cracked as the left leg was dislocated.

"That is the problem with taking a material form. With it comes vulnerabilities," Dorian hissed. He rolled the demon over onto his back and untangled his legs. Al-Faqih tried to grab, but doubled over in pain and clutched at his crotch. The enforcer wasn't sure if it was the pain from the dislocated hip or the neutering. He had a hunch, however. A quick glance at the sundered ear showed new cartilage and tissues grew to replace the lost extremity. The half-breed assumed the same was going on with the demon's nuts, but wasn't about to check to see if his theory was accurate.

Paige was trying to lift the scimitar, but it was too unwieldy to do more than drag. Dorian grabbed the handle, hefted the razor-sharp blade and turned back to Al-Faqih. The agent's eye sockets stared at him and his expression was one of unrequited rage.

"You fucking half-breed!" the demon spit. A mist of black blood sprayed. "I'm going to eat your flesh while you watch!"

Dorian raised the giant scimitar above his head. "Tell Al-Kanani when you see him in hell that Dorian Christianson says sorry about cutting off his head."

He brought the blade down on the jinn who raised his hand. The blade cut the first two fingers off that it made contact with, but then the demon gained mental control of the blade and it liquefied. Dorian pulled his hands away at the sudden heat. Still, it was not fast enough and it scorched the palms of his hands. The Al-Faqih roared as his severed fingers fell to the ground.

The enforcer screamed as the metal splattered onto the jinn. "Dammit!" the enforcer shouted as he pulled his hands back and shook them to try to cool the burns.

The molten metal splattered on Al-Faqih, who was unaffected by the heat. The metal ignited his suit. The cloth combusted spontaneously from the steel, and quickly engulfed the jinn in flames. The synthetic fibers burned and melted against his scaly hide.

Al-Faqih tried to stand. His knees were still broken, and he spit blood. His nose and ear continued to regrow themselves. Slowly, he rose up, an unholy demon engulfed in fire. It was not lost on Dorian that the jinn burned, ironically. It was immune to the flames, and held up its mangled hand. Bones slowly pushed their way through the agent's hand and reformed where his fingers belonged. Muscle and skin slowly crawled to knit over the bones.

Dorian realized it was not the sword that keeps him from regenerating, it was his head being attached to his body.

The demon lunged. It kicked low several times and the enforcer blocked with his shin. The burning demon stepped forward and threw several punches. He ducked, and countered with punches to the body. The giant's fists barely missed his face. Then the agent reached forward and grabbed Dorian. He bunched the material of his shirt and Brioni double-button jacket and picked him up off his feet.

Dorian kicked Al-Faqih in the chest, and then grabbed his hand. He placed his feet on the demon's face, pulled the arm close and popped it out of socket. Then he bent back the jinn's thumb and fingers and dislocated them for good measure. Dorian tumbled onto the sidewalk while the agent shook his thick arm several times.

His hands felt like a million bee stings where his palms and fingers had been scorched. Something on his leg felt hot. The enforcer looked down and realized the left leg of his slacks were on fire. Dorian rolled several times to put the flames out. He looked up and the demon had crossed the distance between the two and kicked him in the chest.

Dorian was lifted off of the ground and flew backwards. He landed with a hard thud against the yard and rolled to a stop. His head spun from the impact.

"Dorian. Pst," a familiar voice whispered. Dorian

looked down... it was Keith. He held one of the Heckler and Koch HK .45's. The pistol was bigger than the lust demon. He balanced it upright with both of his hoofy paws. "Magazine is in, chamber is hot, now go kill dat fucker!"

The enforcer snatched the pistol and aimed at Al-Faqih. From his prone position on the ground, the jinn seemed even larger. The pistol barked—the bang muffled through the silencer. Black blood erupted from the knees of the agent and he took a final wobbly step and fell face-first. Dorian stood and cautiously advanced forward. Al-Faqih's suit was in smoldering shreds, melted onto his body. His now visible blue-tinted scaled skin was scarred from untold battles.

"That hurts, but eventually, you will run out of bullets. Half-breed, do you realize how futile this fight is? Even if you could defeat me, which you can't, the Al-Masih Ad-Dajjal is here. On Earth, now. There will be special tortures for someone like you. Especially after you killed Nabil. It's not just the hosts of hell that are after you—it's the might of the United States Government," the jinn said. "Prepare for your death."

Dorian fired two more shots. Each one fractured one of the demon's clavicles and he moaned. His arms dropped uselessly to his sides.

"They are probably the same, the way this country is going. I do not think it is my time," the enforcer said. "Not tonight. Armageddon will be bad for business, and I am not going to let it happen. Mister Leo Giovanni relies on me to solve problems, and you and your minions are a problem. It has interfered with my job, and for that, you cannot be forgiven. My time is Mister Giovanni's time."

The bullet wounds in the demon began to knit. Dorian grabbed the head of the jinn and spun it hard. Al-Faqih's spine shattered and he fell to the ground and gasped. His hands and feet twitched involuntarily as the signals from his brain were scrambled and the nerves were severed by shards of vertebra.

"You're... a dead ...man," the jinn gurgled.

"Tell me about the Ad-Dajjal, the antichrist. Tell me where and when I can find him?"

The demon laughed as blood bubbled from its cracked blue lips. Its jagged teeth were stained with the jinn's own blood. "I won't... tell you... anything. You will have... to kill... me. Why would you... assume... it's a man?"

Dorian fired the remaining bullets into the neck of Al-Faqih. The enforcer gripped the sides of the agent's head and spun it repeatedly. Bones and ligaments gave way. The spine cracked and shattered repeatedly, cutting into the surrounding tissues with loud grinding noises.

"Oh God, Dorian, what are you doing?" Paige cried. "His head is going to come off!"

He glared at her as he spun the agent's skull. "Not yet. You had better not watch if you are squeamish."

Keith now held the grenade from the messenger bag in the Porsche. The demon raised it up over his head. The enforcer reached down and took it from him. The metal was cold as death. He pulled the pin and held the device in front of the demon's face. Al-Faqih's eyes widened as his neck tried to heal. Too much damage had been done to the jinn and his throat struggled to knit the splinters of bone together. Dorian could see the neck pulsate and wriggle as the demonic tissues moved the shards and tried to reconnect tendons under his scaly skin.

"Do it, boss," the imp implored. "Blow it off!"

The jinn's body continued to shake. His sharp teeth ground together and Dorian found a pressure point and forced his jaw open. The he shoved the grenade in Al-Faqih's mouth and jammed it in as far as it would go.

"Paige, run! Keith, I need you to conceal the sound," the enforcer ordered. "Deceive!"

"Got it!" the imp said. He raised his paws into the air and concentrated as Paige ran.

Dorian pulled the lever on the grenade and ducked behind a tree. He put his fingers in his ears and waited the last three seconds of Ibrahim Al-Faqih's time on Earth. The grenade exploded, vaporizing the head of the jinn. Shrapnel struck the tree and the night was lit by the flash of the explosion. Pieces of skull and flesh rained down across the yard, and splattered against the trees. The sound was no more than a muffled thud—Keith could not simply eliminate sound as a demonic power. He could conceal the noise if he thought of it as deception. The imp's goal was to deceive anyone who might hear the sound of the blast. It worked. Dorian waited, and then peeked around the oak he had taken cover behind. The mangled corpse of the Al-Faqih lay on the ground. A small crater in the ground was where his now vaporized head had rested.

"Hot damn. I love dis fuckin' job!" Keith shouted, then jumped up and tapped his heels together. "Picture perfect endin' ta dat creep. Home team two, jinn zero!"

Dorian stood over the remains of the jinn. His mangled stump of a neck did not regenerate. "So, if a demon in the physical world loses their head, they are dead? So that is why you did not die when he shot you?" he said.

"Yeah. It's a trade. By becomin' physical, a demon can manipulate physical objects and such. It also creates a lot of vulnerabilities, based on da form we choose. Dose jinn are not dead, dey return to Jahannam. Arabic Hell itself until summoned again. I doubt you will see him again in your lifetime," the imp explained. "Unless someone brings him back."

"One bright spot in this day, I guess," Dorian grumbled. He looked down at Keith. "I thought you were a goner when you took that bullet. Glad you pulled through."

"Hurt like hell, I can tell you dat," the imp said. "If I woulda caught dat bullet in da head, it would have been over for me. Back to Hell. I follow da same rules."

"So how come you did not wipe her memory, Kseryth Nysreff? I used your real name to order you to do it," Dorian said. "I would think you would be more compelled than you seem to be."

"Um, oh yea, where is dat broad? Let's suck da memories out of her like da frosting out of a Twinkie," the tiny demon said. "I forgot about it."

"You deceptive little fucker. That is not even your real name," Dorian grumbled. "I should have known."

"If that vermin touches me, I will bite his head off and smack you, Dorian," Paige said angrily. "Keep that filthy thing away from me. The last thing that little pervert is going to do is wipe my memories. Let me see your hands."

The enforcer held them up for her inspection.

"I'm a demon. Whaddya expect? Besides, I dink I've proven my loyalty several times over. We don't tell anyone our real names," the imp pouted.

"Second degree burns. I need some first aid stuff from my house," Paige said.

Dorian nodded. "Yes, you have proven your loyalty, Keith. We make a good team. What should we do with the body?"

"In a couple hours, it will evaporate. Without da will of da jinn ta hold it together, it falls apart. In da case of a jinn, dey are beings of smoke and fire so dey will combust and vanish," Keith said. "Dat means Al-Kanani's body is gone by now, also. Dis one will be gone by sunup. We drag it into da bushes and it will vanish by morning."

"If it combusts, won't it start a fire?" Paige asked.

"Probably. Maybe. I doubt it. Ya never know. Have da garden hose ready, just in case," Keith said. "But it will destroy da evidence."

"In my shrubs!" Paige said. "Dammit, Dorian Christianson. You came here to wipe out my brain, then fought a demon in my front yard, blew his head off with a grenade, and now you are going to leave his decapitated body in my shrubs until he combusts and possibly lights my hedge on fire?"

Dorian shrugged. "Yeah. Sounds about right. Keith muffled the sound of the blast. None of the neighbors should be pissed."

"Also muffled da gunshots. I'm a team player, dats for sure," the demon said.

"Ugh!" she shrieked. She stomped up the sidewalk away from the pair. "You two are insufferable! No wonder you make such a good pair."

Dorian and Keith watched her. "Can I call you?" Dorian said and forced a smile.

She turned and glared. Paige paused, deep in thought. "After all the shit you two have put me through? I suppose. All of this craziness had better be over. Demons, genies, grenades, and gunfire. I hope I wake up from this nightmare and realize it never happened. I will be back in a minute to treat your hands for those burns, though."

"I'm startin' ta like dat dame," the demon said. "She's a bit feistier dan I dought."

Dorian leaned over and searched the corpse's pockets. He pulled out a wallet, and a tiny, black-blood stained envelope. He pulled a gift card out that he immediately recognized as the one he gave to Paige for the Kushibar. "That was fucking sloppy of me," he muttered.

"What's our plan?" the demon asked.

"Wait until this body vanishes. We search the area,

and then make sure we have removed as much evidence as we can. Lay low and make our getaway like nothing happened," Dorian said. "You think Al-Faqih was just messing with me, talking about the antichrist being a woman?"

Keith shook his head. "Given da culture of da jinn, I doubt it. Women aren't always held in highest regard in some places in da Middle East," the demon said. "It was a weird ding to say. Out of character enough I don't dink he would say it, honestly. I just wonder if dis woman knows who she is?"

Dorian shrugged. "How could she not?"

***

Tessa Paul walked home from Angela's house, deep in thought. The events of the night had made her stomach ache like it was tied in knots. She thought of James and Brittaney Currin, and the sudden revelation that they were alive and in Seattle. Her brain was overloaded from the surprise meeting with her birth parents, and she did not know what to do.

She was afraid of telling the people who had been her parents for the last seventeen years of her life. On top of that, she felt betrayed by Angela and Marisol. They would be lucky if she ever talked to them again. As long as she had known them, they had harbored this secret. True friends do not do that to one another.

She angrily put one foot in front of the other. The more she stewed over the situation, the angrier she became. By the time she stomped up the stairs to her house, she was in a rage. With shaky hands she unlocked the door and entered.

The house was dark. No doubt at this late hour her parents were upstairs asleep. Tessa went to the kitchen, filled a glass with ice water from the fridge, and sat at the dining room table. In the dim light she could see her math book open on the table. Logarithms were stupid. Algebra was stupid. It was dumb she had to struggle with this crap, on top of everything else. Someday, somehow, she would have some power and make some changes to this world.

***

"This is a little fucking much at ten-thirty at night. Someone is going to get an earful tomorrow at city hall," Rocco Giovanni fumed. He stood in the foyer of Leo's house in a bathrobe. "My grandfather is elderly. Waking him up like this is harassment. You really need a warrant for this bullshit, detective. Whatever this is, it could have waited."

Detective Nicholas Paul continued to hold up his identification, and so did Theresa O'Connor.

"Mister Giovanni, this is more of an unofficial visit. I'm sorry to do this at this late hour, but I need to speak to Mister Leo Giovanni. On paper he is the CEO of Asian Import and Work Specialists Corporation. I just have a couple questions and want to show him a picture," the detective said. "Then I will be out of your hair."

"Follow me, Detectives," Rocco grumbled. He led the cops through the mansion to the office of Leo Giovanni. The old man sat behind his large desk and sipped at a cup. Paul could smell the strong coffee from across the room.

"Sorry to disturb you at this late hour, Mister Giovanni," the detective said. "I am Detective Nicholas Paul. This is Detective Theresa O'Connor. We are doing some work on the murder of Alesio Conti. He worked for you."

"It's a pleasure to meet you, detectives, even at this late hour," Leo said. "Yes, Alesio Conti worked for me. For almost ten years. His death was a horrible tragedy. Left behind a wife and young children. I had heard this case was at a dead end. I'm glad you two are following up. Coffee?"

"No, thank you," Paul said.

"Not for me," O'Connor said. "Do you know why he was in North Beacon Hill? That's South Side Loco's territory."

Leo took a sip. His eyes slowly went from the cup to the Detectives. "I don't know what Alesio was doing in North Beacon Hill. I don't keep track of my employees on their personal time."

Paul nodded. "I understand. I thought you might have some insight into where he went and who he associated with."

"We don't stalk our employees, Detective Paul," Rocco said. "He was a family man. That's probably where most of his time was spent."

Paul looked askance at Rocco. "I understand. We would sure like to bring his killer to justice."

"Well, we honestly do appreciate your efforts in this matter," Leo said. "Justice for Alesio."

"Yes. For Alesio," Paul said. He pulled a photo from his jacket pocket and unfolded it. "Does this man look familiar to you?"

Rocco took the photo and stared at it. His brow furrowed and he laid it on Leo's desk.

"Do you recognize the man in the photo?" Paul said.

"Never seen him before," Rocco murmured. "Can't make much out, anyway. His face is covered."

"You're sure?" Paul said, skeptically. "There was a moment there-"

"I said I don't recognize him," Rocco interrupted.

Leo studied the picture.

"This was taken outside of a gang-banger's apartment by a hidden FBI camera. His name was Kerr Martinez. You might have heard of the murders in Bellevue. We believe this picture is of the man who we suspect is responsible. Unfortunately, the long coat, the dark glasses and covered face has concealed him. Maybe there is a connection with Alesio Conti. We would sure like to find it, if there is," O'Connor said.

Leo looked away from the photo. "I don't know this man."

"Are you sure?" Paul questioned.

"One hundred percent positive," Leo said. "It's late. Do you have anything else for me?"

The detective shook his head and put his card on Leo's desk. He took the picture and folded it. "No. That's all. Here's my card. I appreciate your help, especially at this ungodly hour. If you think of anything, please let me know. I would like to catch Alesio's murderer."

Leo stood and smoothed his velvet bathrobe. He took a final sip of his coffee and set the cup in its saucer. "Thank you for your diligence in this matter. I wish I could help you. Good luck, detective. We look forward to you finding Alesio's killer," the old man said. "Goodnight, detectives. Thank you for your service to our fine city."

"Thanks again, Mister Giovanni," O'Connor said. "Sorry to visit at this hour. We were hoping for a break in the case."

"Thank you, detective," Leo said.

Rocco escorted the Detectives to the front door of the mansion. "I'm not as polite as Mister Giovanni. Come back during business hours next time. Good night, detectives."

Paul and O'Connor walked out the front door and down the sidewalk in front of the mansion. "Well. What do you think?" she asked.

"I think they know more than they are telling us," he said. "Gut instinct."

"Mine, too," O'Connor replied.

***

"Police these days," Leo said as he walked towards his bedroom. "Courtesy thrown right out the window, to wake us at this ungodly hour. What is happening to this younger generation?"

"They'll pay for this disrespect," Rocco hissed. "Stupid cops. They're on to Dorian. They have a photo of him. Time to cut our losses."

Leo stopped. "We will do nothing. They know nothing. Just play our cards close and don't panic. They are grasping at straws and got lucky. This will blow over."

"They've connected him to the shooting. Then that crap at the hospital. We are in trouble. We need to get out in front of this before it gets uglier than detectives showing up in the middle of the night to ask questions. Courtesy call, my ass," Rocco grumbled. "Dorian is not a made man. We can't risk the family business for him."

"I'm going to bed. This will all work out. I will make some calls tomorrow, spread a little cash around, no one will be the wiser," Leo said. "Now I'm going to bed."

"Grandfather, this is serious!" Rocco shouted.

Leo stopped and glared. "I know it's serious. It's my call. Now, remember your place. You've been forgetting it lately. Besides, you want to get into a war with Dorian?"

"I have people, who from a distance could solve this," Rocco said. "Our hands would be clean."

"It makes me wonder, what schemes you have in place to remove me," Leo said emotionlessly. "Go to bed before you really piss me off. You're not the head of this family, and probably never will be!"

Rocco walked away as Leo slammed his bedroom door. His body was tense as he tightened his fists. He walked through the huge house. The stomp of his feet echoed on the marble tiles. In his apartment on the east end of the house he stood for a long time. Something had to be done about the old man for the sake of the family. This obsession he had with the family enforcer had to come to an end.

In the bathroom he lit a cigarette. The cherry glowed a hellish red and he slowly breathed in the hot vapors. He blew the smoke out, and then put his fist through the wall. Dust and pieces of sheetrock scattered over the ceramic tile floor of the bathroom. Rocco pulled his fist back. The skin was torn on his knuckles, and blood began to run over the fragments of sheetrock on his skin.

He screamed in rage and pain, and then punched another hole in the wall. Then he proceeded to demolish the bathroom with his bare hands. Rocco broke tiles and smashed glass before he pulled the vanity from the wall and kicked it to pieces.

After he turned toward the shattered mirror, he stood and stared at his face. The shards of glass made his reflection a fun-house kaleidoscope of shapes. Like his life, the mirror was shattered pieces and incoherent reflections. He punched the broken mirror again. After doing everything he could to make the old man happy, it wasn't enough. Rocco slowly turned on the cold water and put his hand under the faucet to dull the pain. His bathrobe had come untied while he washed away the blood from his hands.

The grandson of Leo Giovanni knew pain. The emotional pain of taking a backseat to someone who was not family. The physical pain of his bloody hands. The social pain of not being in charge when he should be. Rocco knew that as long as Dorian lived, the pain would not stop and the family would be in danger.

The enforcer was a dangerous enemy. So like a snake that waited unseen, concealed, biding its time, Rocco would wait to strike. He could see his path so clearly laid out before him. Clearer than ever.

What Rocco could not see was the creature that was living in his chest. Its mouth opened in his chest like a lamprey, circular and pulsating with jagged teeth. Red reptilian eyes were fused above the sucker-mouth, bloodshot and yellowed. Corpulent tentacles reached from the creature, through his ribcage and around his back where they merged with his flesh. The demon was concealed from its host and from prying eyes. A demon of rage, a parasite from hell that had resided in him for years. It did not control him, but delicately influenced him, pushed his anger until it was ready to explode. He was now ready.

"The Giovanni Crime Family needed a new leader," the demon whispered subtly, but the words came out of his mouth. Both Rocco and the inhuman parasite smiled at their reflections in the shards of glass. "Grandfather, you're risking what we've built. You'll move over or I will move you. Dorian Christianson, you're a dead man," the pair mouthed in unison. The puppet and the concealed inhuman puppeteer.

Look for the second book in The Chronicles of Dorian Christianson series coming soon!

About the Author

When most everyone fawned over prancing, sparkling vampires, Al toiled away writing about zombies. Fantasy zombies, western zombies, zombies and more zombies. To say that zombies are an obsession of his is an understatement. Very few zombie movies have escaped his cadaverous eye. A little known secret: when he was 12, he thought he was HP Lovecraft reincarnated.

A lifelong resident of Lewiston, Idaho, Al graduated from Lewiston High School and Lewis-Clark State College in his hometown. He spent the last twenty seven years working with children with emotional and behavioral problems and training other professionals to do the same. Recently, his career path switched from non-profit residential treatment to a State juvenile correction facility.

In his free time Al trains in martial arts, plays paintball, tells his rescued cats to get off of the counter, is a wargame/roleplay nerd, consumes large quantities of Thai food unapologetically, and is a connoisseur of fine dining: Arby's. He loves music and regularly attends concerts. Favorites include Tantric, Theory of a Deadman, Rob Zombie, Nickelback, and the Offspring. Montana and the Oregon coast are frequent destinations.

His biggest accomplishment is his 18 year old son.

Considered by some to be the neighborhood curmudgeon, he wears this title as a badge of honor. He hates writing autobiographies.

Al is the author of the Permuted Press paranormal thrillers Hellgate, Montana and Retributor: Hellgate, Montana Book 2. He also penned Mists of the Miskatonic, and coauthored Kinemortophobia: Zombie Dreams for Sleepless Nights with John Reed. Published short stories include Fire Team by Knightwatch Press, Goddess by Gorillas with Scissors Press, and Keeping

Score by Indigo Mosaic. His novel The Chronicles of Dorian Christianson: Nephilim will soon be released by Gorillas with Scissors Press and Al's first fantasy novel Empires of the Dead: Son of the Sea will be released independently.

My first fantasy book "Empires of the Dead: Son of the Sea" will be out soon?

Facebook:
https://www.facebook.com/pages/Al-Halsey-Author-Page/140691575976282

Twitter
https://twitter.com/AlHalsey1

Amazon Author Page
http://www.amazon.com/Al-Halsey/e/B00OWM1RAE/ref=ntt_athr_dp_pel_1

Other Works From Al Halsey

- **Nightmares and Echoes 2: The Return**
- **Mists of the Miskatonic: Tales Inspired by the works of H.P Lovecraft (Mist of the Miskatonic) (Volume 1)**
- **Kinemortophobia - Zombie Dreams for Sleepless Nights**
- **Grave Conversations**
- **Zombies Galore**
- **The Dark Bard**
- **Hellgate, Montana (Hellgate, Montana Book 1)**
- **Retributor (Hellgate, Montana Book 2)**

Made in the USA
Columbia, SC
21 September 2018